I0674367

~

Phoenix Rising

The First Novel in the Probed Saga

Written by: Skye Falcon™

Copyright 2013 GoodTimes
Publications

All Rights Reserved

ISBN 978-0-9893071-0-9

Without limiting the rights under copyright reserved
above, no part of this publication may be reproduced,
stored in or introduced into a retrieval system, or
transmitted, in any form, or any means (electronic,
recording, photocopying, or otherwise), without the
prior written permission of both the copyright owner,
and the above publisher of this book.

I hope you enjoy our first major work of fiction. Please
know that the names, characters, places, or situations
within this book are fictitious, or a product of the
Author's imagination. Any resemblance found to any
current situations, or person's living is entirely in the
reader's mind. The publisher of this book does not
control what other's post, or what is on third party web
sites regarding this book.

The scanning, distribution, and uploading of this book via the Internet or any other means without permission of the publisher is illegal and punishable by law. Please purchase only authorized electronic editions, and do not participate in or encourage electronic piracy of copyrighted materials. Your support of the author's rights is appreciated.

All my love & lustful thoughts to you, my main squeeze. This one's for you.

Acknowledgments.

-

BIG thanks to my KIDS...for allowing me the bits of peace I needed to get this done!! I love you three!! Noodle, thanks for easing up on the drama long enough to always get my sentences finished. Hopers, your lovey's always helped the long days. Nickel, I can't wait until you find your creativity outlet... because whatever you finally settle on, you're going to ROCK at. Now, SHHHH!!!!! ☺

Many HUGS and THANKS to my group of pre-readers.... Without your texts of excitement for more, some nights would've sucked. THANK YOU for the encouragement, and THANKS for letting me be me. ☺ Special thanks to Mom & Dad, and all my nearest & dearest for helping me with this!!

(Grandma, if you're reading this.... sorry about all the bad words and sex scenes...)

1

"I love you," were the last words that I forced out as I climbed out of the big truck, and went into work this Tuesday night. The past few hours of my day I had spent with him, doing exactly what he wanted to do. He rarely ever asked what I wanted to do anymore, not like it was when we first got together. No, these days it seemed to be his way, or the highway. I looked back at him as I climbed out of the truck, and his expression was vacant.

Eight months ago he would've fumbled out of the truck, around the whole damn thing, and opened my door for me. Seven months ago he would've leaned and kissed me goodbye. Six months ago he would, at least, hug me when I left. Five months ago he started to demand that I lean over, and kiss him "goodbye" when I got out of the truck. Four months ago, when I started college, he got so angry that I was excluding him from my life, that I dropped out. *Not that you were really having a great time going, Janie.* Three months ago, he became enraged that I took a management position, and started working more at the Phoenix. And that is precisely when things went to shit...

Two months ago, our sex life became very rough, and very physical. But if I went with it, his mood always improved, so I didn't question it. *Yet.*

"Please listen! Sean and I were just sitting and talking! Waiting for you!! He's your friend, for crying out loud!" Nothing I had said all day had gotten through. Now I was angry from trying so hard.

"Just don't Janie," he sighed. "Just get out of here. I can't believe you. You're disgusting." he looked at me one last time, as I shut the truck door. No sooner did the door close, and he slammed on the gas and sped away. I took my time collecting myself enough to walk across the parking lot, which seemed to go on forever at this point. *One foot in front of the other, honey. This is going to get worked out. Just don't give up...*

I was so upset that he had called me 'disgusting,' yet again. Just one of the many new words in his vocabulary for me. It was so hard to hear these things from him. Often so believable. One month ago, he first forced himself on me for the first time, and since then I've been desperately searching for... something. He would always get these random things stuck in his head, dwell on them, and then annihilate anyone who came near. This time, he was angry that I was waiting for him at the restaurant this morning with his best friend, Sean. I have been paying for this mistake all day.

I had only worked at the Phoenix a short time, and had found my place with some people that I really was beginning to trust. Before I went into the doors, I had to turn and make sure that he was gone. I brushed my long blonde hair out of my face, and adjusted my clothing to ensure I was covered, and that there were no visible signs showing. The handprint bruises on my upper arms were dead giveaways, and I wasn't ready to confront this head on. *Yet.* I felt a shudder run through me, I exhaled, and went through the door.

*   *   *   *   *

Walking through the doors of worked allowed me to breathe, and return to the normal almost twenty-one-year-old girl that I was. One that was carefree, and loved wholly. One who won races, had the fastest times, and ribbons lining the walls. One that knew right from wrong, and love from hate. One who could do things without being under his thumb. He was so suffocating. He was Michael Comaro. My oldest childhood friend, turned boyfriend, turned lover. For a little while, he was everything. A tall, muscular, wild eyed, blonde haired musician. For the first few months, it was all flowers, and everything he did was for me. Reminders daily, all around us, of our fun times growing up. And then it all changed. It was about the three-month mark where things started to turn dark, and that was five months ago. My escapes were now work, friends, and swimming. I headed straight for the bathroom to breathe for a minute before facing the customers.

Once I heard the click of the lock, I sighed loudly. Looking in the mirror, all I saw was a pale, tormented face. My green eyes had black circles, and I was so exhausted. I pulled out the makeup I kept in my purse to hide the black bags, and applied it quickly. There was a small smile creeping on to my face, and I knew exactly why. I adjusted my tank top, and put on my polo.

While heading out to check the schedule, I turned the corner, and ran smack into him. Gabriel's expression told me that this run in was not necessarily a chance encounter. Looking in his eyes gave me so much possibility, that I almost had to will myself to look away. I fell into the depths of his blue eyes regularly, and relished each chance I had to trip and fall into them at any time. During work, we would talk for hours, sometimes getting nothing done. There was some chatter at work about our status, if there really was one, between me and Gabriel, but no one could seem to confirm their suspicions. As I backed up from Gabriel, I smiled, he squeezed my hand, and we both went back to work. As I walked to the front to check the planner, the only thought running through my head was the one problem that could prevent Gabriel from being mine, age and our situations. He was almost twenty-five, rumored to have a girlfriend, and I was weeks away from twenty-one. My thoughts were then interrupted by my manager, Bill.

"Hey Janie! How're you doing today? How was your last meet?" Bill asked, while he rifled through the office paperwork.

"I'm doing pretty well, and the last meet was great! I swam the 400 in one minute under my fastest time! Won the heat, and got the trophy!" I smiled as big as ever. Swimming was something that I loved, and had for a long time. It was therapy to me, as many of my genius ideas and schemes come to me while I was going back and forth in the swimming pool.

"That's great Janie!" he noticed I was looking through the planner, and added, "you're out with Gabriel in the yard today. We just got a huge shipment of one and two gallons in. Hope that's ok with you!" He smiled very big. Bill was one who knew that something was going on, and I knew it.

"Oh Bill, you're so very sly. And that's why I love you." I smiled sweetly, and headed for the outdoor delivery bay. When I made it to the doors and they opened, I was hit in the face with the cool, fall air. And simultaneously saw Gabriel staring at me enjoying the breeze. I happily walked over to him, and we started working together, prepping the outdoors for the upcoming display. At 8 o'clock, Bill came out to check progress.

"Gabriel, do you think you can finish this in the next few hours?" Bill asked, hopeful.

"Yeah, that should be no problem. There's only two isles left to do, then the cleanup. I'll just have Janie stay, and we'll knock it out in no time." Gabriel said, and smirked at me. This comment, and the look on his face made my heart beat faster.

"That's fine," and Bill added, "just make sure to set the codes when you leave. They really want this project done, so this will make the big-wigs very pleased. Thanks, guys." Bill grabbed his briefcase, and headed out the door. The instant that the doors were locked, I ran and cranked the radio up. Gabriel turned off all of the lights for the store, leaving only some on for where we were working. I headed back out to the wet house to wait for Gabriel.

Out of nowhere, Gabriel's big body came from the right and embraced me in a full frontal hug. I loved feeling him on my body. He leaned forward so his breath ended in my ear, and he began to whisper. "Janie, so many months of this idle chit chat, and these brief and simple touches...I want more." His lips brushed by my neck, "and I know you want more, too."

His lips on my neck were making more of the sparks that I had missed. It had been a few weeks since we had exchanged touches, and I had dreamt of this moment. "You are right, and I do want you..." I trailed off, and hesitated. "I'm just afraid I want..." He cut me off, and hugged me hard.

"Don't worry about all that. It will all work out if it's supposed to. Let's just have fun now." He smiled, and swatted my butt. Off to work we went, peacefully, for the next few hours. The wet room was finished, and decorated for the displays right on time. As we were leaving work that night, we held each other's fingers out to our cars. I blew him a kiss, and promised to see him tomorrow. My drive home was too fast, because I couldn't wait until my head hit the pillow tonight. So many thoughts, and tomorrow morning I would have to face Michael early...

2

At the local breakfast hang out, Michael waited for me with Sean. Michael was becoming very upset. He hadn't heard from me the night before, and he was becoming increasingly agitated towards my work. He couldn't understand how the Phoenix was the greatest job ever, like I had made it sound. "There's just something I don't like about that place, Sean. She acts so distant, and hates when I stop in and see her." He looks down, and bangs his fist on the table. "She's mine, Sean. And I have a feeling that she thinks otherwise."

"Come on, Mike. I just don't see what you see. Janie's such a sweet heart, She'd never do anything like you're thinking." Sean was reasonably confident with his statement, but did agree with Michael that something was different about me these days.

As they sat, Michael paged me again. In the eleven months that we had been dating, he was sure that I was it for him. We had been friends since we were little, so twelve years later when we finally got together, everyone thought it was a great thing. As he was picking up the phone to re-page me again, I was walking up to the table, smiling.

"FINALLY! What, are you on some kind of "late" time frame?!!?" Michael wasn't quieting down, and wasn't even giving a hello. "Janie, this is ridiculous! When I page, you answer! There's no excuse!" The veins in his neck were standing out.

I sighed loudly before I began to try to talk. I was happy that I was at a restaurant, and knew no damage could be done here. "Michael," I said softly, hoping that would work. "I woke up late today, took a shower to get ready for work, and came straight here. I'm sorry if you worried." I braced herself for the rest, and idly glances over at Sean. Sean winced a little, and waved quickly from across the table. "Michael?" I asked.

"Janie, just get out of my face." He looked blankly at the table. I couldn't believe him. Always over reacting, lashing out at the wrong things. But today that was fine. I didn't really want to be around him anyway. He brought me no comfort these days. As quickly as I came in, I turned on my heels, and left to work.

The voices in my head were getting louder and louder with each passing day. *Janie, what are you doing? You wanted a way out, a way to get away from the bad. This is your chance. So why are you still waiting around to see what happens next? Things are progressing very nicely with Gabriel. Why not take things a little farther? No sense in missing out on happiness. And what Michael doesn't know, won't hurt him. Just be careful, and keep your eyes open.*

When I pulled into the parking lot, I parked next to Gabe. I had a huge headache because I couldn't stop thinking about Michael at the restaurant this morning. This had been such a careful dance for the last few months, but now I was losing the urge to try to protect one from the other. Or protect myself from what I hated any longer. The few hours of work that evening flew by, as the store was packed due to a sale. Gabriel hadn't gotten a moment to himself all day, let alone to go touch me, his secret love. In between jobs, I started to think about Gabe, and about us.

Gabriel was almost 23, and a real loner in the flesh. He'd had a few girlfriends, but none of them had given him any reason to stick around. I couldn't figure out what they were seeing, that I didn't. I can't imagine running, and he isn't even mine yet. I giggled. He was in college, but becoming increasingly bored with his classes. Dropping out seemed logical, but he told me he didn't want to fall into a "partying" only routine. He had a friend on the side that he needed to make some decisions about, and I had wondered about her. Things seemed to be getting more screwed up by the hour for him. And then, a few months back, he met me. I was a huge breath of fresh air, and not the typical girl he had fallen for. He told me I was blonde, and beautiful, but I was only twenty. That was a big BUT in our situation, too. He knew I was in some kind of rough situation. I know he could feel my longing, and my comfort whenever we touched. He had started dreaming of me he said, day dreaming of me even, and wanting to be with me more and more. Just then, he was next to me at my desk, rifling through his own stack of paperwork, out of breath.

Briefly glancing up, my eyes met his. For that second, we started at each other. There was an unspoken trust, and depth that we had together, and exploded every time we were close. *That you've always had towards Gabriel.* I shook my head, and broke our stare. Although, looking back down to my paperwork didn't distract my thoughts as I had hoped. *Feel the heat he's radiating towards you, Janie? He feels it from you, too.* My inner monologue was right....it had always been like this between us. Our conversations these past months have deepened, and we've gotten to know more about each other, and certain parts of our lives. It's been wonderful. *And you'd wish for more of him if you could. Maybe you should anyway?*

His head was spinning with the same thoughts that were going through my own. He hadn't filled me in on any of his feelings yet, but could feel that the day was coming very soon. He shook his head, as if trying to shake these thoughts out. He just wanted to be around me. He only had ten minutes until both of our shifts were over. He was still trying to catch his breath five minutes after standing next to me.

"Gabriel! What's wrong?" I asked, as he caught his breath.

"Ohh, sweet cheeks. Nothing's wrong, just wanted to say hello before it was closing time. I missed you today. Sort of a lot." His cheeks turned a little pinkish at his own honesty.

"Well, you must've read my mind, because I was thinking exactly the same thing that you were. You always make my day brighter." I said with a huge smile. He couldn't help but think how carefree, and beautiful I looked when I smiled, and thought that I should be smiling like that more often.

"Well Janie, come over here a minute." He motioned me into his arms, and held them wide open for me. I hesitantly walked over, and climbed inside the embrace. "I just wanted to feel you like this, just once, before the weekend." He sighed heavily.

I breathed in his scent as long as I could. I brushed his hair back from his eyes, and looked in them briefly. I longed for his arms to be the ones I ran to every day. But again, it was time for the weekend. The weekends were hard on both of us. When we were together, it was peaceful for us both. Our worlds away from each other were hectic, rough, and sometimes just terrible. He lowered his hands to my waist, and pulled me into his body.

"Someday..." he smiled. "Someday very soon." He smacked my behind, and we walked together to the door. Again we walked out with our fingers intertwined, all the way to our cars. It was becoming a ritual, that I really liked. The drive home for me, was lonely. I blared Jann Arden's Insensitive, and thought about the myriad of ways I could end things with Michael.

3

Saturday morning came, and I woke up late. I was going to be late to practice too, and would surely pay for that with laps. I didn't really mind though, as the water brought a calm to my very busy brain. Working through swim was not going to be the problem. The problem would come later, when the group was together for the band practice. While I lapped away doing my medley routine, I thought of Gabriel. I couldn't shake the feeling of him on my body, and I badly needed to see him. Or talk to him. God, I'd give anything at this point. I could feel myself becoming flushed. Just as I was reaching for the wall touch, I could hear my coach yelling.

"Janie! Don't stop there! You've got a few more laps to do for being late to my warm ups!" *Whatever*, I thought. Hopefully a bathroom break was not out of the question.

"That's fine, Matt. Just let me run to pee." I smiled, hesitantly at him. Coach was not one to mess with, as he could make each practice that much more miserable for me. And thanks to my current mindset, no further torture was really needed. When I hit the locker room, I felt better after peeing. I decided to briefly check my pager, and noticed I had 6 missed pages. All from Michael... *because who else couldn't give me a few hours for swim practice?* Only him. I shook my head, and ran out and jumped back in the pool. The anger started to burn into me, and so did my own internal questions. My body was raging, and I was speeding angrily through my last laps. With each stroke, and each tear, my head hurt more and more.

Does this mean you're going to allow Michael to start stalking you? Completely run your life? He's taken away so much of you from you already. No, don't think that. It is not just that he cares, and you know that damn well. He frustrates you daily, puts his hands on you whenever he thinks he should... WHAT are you waiting for Janie? Stop worrying about everyone else, and do what you need to do! As I climbed out of the pool, I tried to shake the thoughts out of my head. I headed for the showers to get cleaned up and ready for the rest of the day.

*   *   *   *   *

By that afternoon, the group had gotten together at the barn for their band practice. I loved going to listen, and help out where needed. The guys- Sean, Walter, and Preston had been my friends since they moved in when I was eight. If I was really lucky, I'd get to sing. One of my other favorite past times. Singing was a rarity though, as it was another thing that Michael did not approve of. My role to Michael in this band was to be cute, quiet, and obedient. I had recently figured this out, and by doing so had quieted some of our constant bickering. I wanted to step outside to smoke, and just be alone. Of course that never works when Michael was anywhere around me. I heard his footsteps moments behind my own as I went to walk down the long country drive way.

"Aw, Michael...I just wanted to be alone. Just go back in with the guys, please." My voice was cracking. Too much emotion, too much confusion. It was all finally starting to settle, and was making me feel sick. Or so I thought, until Michael started in.

"Janie...we need to talk." He came close enough to see my face in the dark, but stayed far enough that he couldn't touch me. He stayed at a slight distance, because he knew his closeness intimidated me, and scared me. "You're different now. I want to know what's going on."

After making dirt circles with my toes, evading his eye contact at all costs, I finally got up a little nerve. "I'm just having a rough time right now. I'm really stressed out with life, work, and swimming. It's hard to find a balance to everything." I hesitated, but let it all flow out. "And when you're in your moods, and screaming, yelling, pushing, and shoving me around...I just want to disappear. This isn't what I want anymore." Just saying the words lifted some invisible rock off of my back, regardless of the consequences, I inhaled deeply. It sort of felt good, and then I sort of felt bad. I reluctantly glanced up at Michael, and saw the anger and rage on his face. I braced myself for what was to come.

"You're such a whore." Mike gritted his teeth, and stepped towards me. "You think that just because you're having 'issues' that you can ignore my needs? MY wants?!" He was becoming frazzled, and I began to panic. "You won't even let me touch you anymore, and YOU. ARE. MINE. I'll touch you when I want."

Without another word, he was all over me. He fisted my hair, pulling it back so far that my eyes began to tear. He kept pulling my hair down, until we both sank into the wet grass of the field. Everything was dewy, and I was slipping and things were scratching my skin. His brother's house was so far out in the country, that there were minimal lights, and no one could see anything in this dark.

Once I was on the ground, he back handed me across my cheek, and my hand instantly went to protect the stinging area. It burned like no other. I hated open handed slaps, they seemed to hurt more than anything else. I tried to hold in my gasp when he struck, as that only seemed to make it worse in the past. He immediately started unbuttoning his pants, and pulling my Adidas warm up pants down. I went limp, and my brain instantly did what it had done for the past five months, every time this happened. It took me to happy places, with happy people. He became frustrated when my pants and underwear got tangled, *because his yank down job was piss poor...* I could feel the hot tears coursing down my cheeks, and the pressure and burning from between my legs. I started to black out, the voices came back again.

How many times will you allow this? This is not the girl I know you are. You are stronger than this. Don't believe that this is what you have to settle for! Fight, girl! FIGHT! But I couldn't. Fighting him only ended up with bigger bruises that were harder to explain. I knew that this was not my forever, but somehow being at his mercy was cathartic on some deep level inside me. Suddenly, thoughts from work were creeping into my head. Gabriel's eyes were in front of me drawing me in, and I moaned. My seriously misunderstood moan set Michael over the edge, and it was over. For now, I laid on the ground until he was back in the barn, and the drums were beating hard again. I sighed, and slowly carried my battered body back to my car, picking sticks, twigs, and grass clippings off the whole way. I wrote a note to Michael, that said simply: "I'm tired of that. I'm tired of this. You have a problem. I'm DONE."

Once I was home, my Dad was still awake. "Hey Jane, how was your night?" He smiled a little, hoping that I would open up to him. Since my parents' troubles, I had problems trusting that people would be there to help me when I needed. So I didn't go into any great detail with him. It seemed easier not to.

"Hey Dad. Night was okay. Just another night listening to the boys practice." I shrugged, and forced a half smile.

"Oh yeah? Was Michael playing well? He said a few days ago that he was sore and..." I cut him off mid-sentence.

"Yeah- he was great. Same ole Michael!" I turned and went upstairs. As I went up, Dad called out one last time.

"Hey Jane, someone called for you a bit ago. A guy, but didn't leave a message. See you in the morning honey!" He scooted back downstairs. I was secretly hoping that it had been Gabriel, but I was too tired, and too emotional after that encounter to call him. I didn't want to risk losing Gabriel if he found out what I was really dealing with. I showered in scalding hot water, and wondered what to do. I felt more alone than I ever had before. All I needed was a way out. My last thoughts before I fell asleep were of Gabriel, and his warm, secure embrace.

4

Although I wasn't scheduled to work the Sunday shift, I went in and worked anyway. I was in at opening, and surprised most of my coworkers. "Janie!" Bill was surprised, and ecstatic. "I'm so glad to see you! We've had a few call ins. Do you mind staying today?" I shook my head no, and smiled. "Mind staying... all day?" Bill asked me with a seriously worried expression.

"No, I don't mind at all Bill. In fact, will do me some good." I couldn't hide the sad expression on my own face from Bill, as he was really good at reading people. "Where do you want me today?"

"I'm sorry, Janie." he paused, and stepped closer to me. "You need to drop that fool. You know there is one person I have in mind who would surely treat you much better than that fool. But you know what I say about that one...and dating in the workplace!!" For a split second, I had to remind myself that he had met his wife at work, too. I smiled at him. He started laughing so hard that he had to grab the desk in order to keep himself standing. "You'll be outside in the wet house. Thanks again, Jane." I smiled again, and headed outside.

The cool, crisp fall air was relaxing my mind, and settling my electric nerves. I was quietly marking out much of the dead or dying product, when there was a rustling from behind the building. I cautiously went around the back of the building, where they kept the extra pallets, and shelving units. There was someone back there, digging through the markdowns. I bravely asked, "Who's back there??"

"Oh, Janie..." the rustling stopped, and a head popped out. "It's just me!!" It was Simon. Quite possible one of my best friends, at the moment. He was the same age as myself, but went to a different school. I had met him when I started at the Phoenix last year. "How have you been? I missed you when I was on vacation the last few weeks!"

He came over to me, and hugged me.

"I've missed you so much!! It's been hard not having anyone to talk to." I released him, and smiled.

"I can sort of tell, since you're working on a Sunday, and all." He patted my shoulder, and we both walked out into the nursery yard. "Need any help out here until Gabriel gets here?" He gave me a look, and smiled coyly.

I shrugged. "If you'd like to help, feel free. I'm just marking things out for now. Figured Gabriel would tell me what he wanted when he gets here." And back to work we went. A few hours later, around lunch, I felt eyes on my body. I began glancing around the yard, trying to find where the feeling was coming from. Then I saw him. It was Gabriel, and he was leaning up against the door frame, and his eyes were glued to me. At first I wasn't sure of what to do, until he smiled at me. He turned to put his drink down, and headed to the back corner of the yard where I was. My heart was beating out of my chest, and I was sure there was a giant butterfly in my stomach.

"Hey Sweet cheeks! I didn't expect to see you here today!!" His happy tone, and body language told me he was very serious. He was shocked, and happy that I was there. True emotion had been eluding me for the past year or so, and this was very refreshing to see.   "You look sad. What's going on?" His face turned to perplexed. He could tell by my body language, and how I talked about this guy in my life, that he must have been a real piece of work. He wondered, and maybe had secretly hoped, that I would open up to him, and let him help me. And maybe let him love me.

"I've just had a really bad few days." My eyes welled up, and I looked at the sky, and hoped my sunglasses did their job, and hid the tears. I wasn't ready to cry in front of Gabriel, not yet. I still feared that he would leave, or drop me, if he knew about all of this drama. "I'm just really confused about a lot of things." I cautiously looked up, and leaned into him and held on.

He held me back, and I could feel his breathing change. "Hey, I've got an idea. How about we go for a drive after work? We don't have to go anywhere. We could just drive around and talk." He smiled, "but only if you want to."

I thought about it hard. My heart, my head, and my body all screamed "yes!" But the voices in my head reminded me of the consequences if a certain someone ever found out. "I think that would be really nice. Are you sure?" I asked. *Are you asking if he's sure because you know that if Michael ever finds out he's a dead man? Or are you asking so that he can second guess himself, and change his mind and run? You're really being a dumbass right now, Janie. This happiness is going to cost you.*

"Of course I'm sure! I'll come find you when it's closing time! In the meantime, we'd better get this job taken care of and checked off of the list." He hugged me once more, and I could swear that I heard him inhale me, like he was smelling me or something. Whatever it was, it tugged at my heart, as I was always inhaling his scent every chance I had, too.

I spent the rest of my workday planning what I was going to tell everyone regarding my lateness for that night. I called my parents, and spoke with my dad. "Hey Dad, I just wanted to let you know that we're going to stay late tonight and get the wet house projects done. So, I'll just be a few hours late at the most." He didn't mind, as long as I was safe. Next was the hardest. Michael always seemed to know what I was doing, possibly because he was following me. I didn't have proof of that yet, but always felt his presence. But that could have also been my fear of his presence, I just wasn't sure. Then I got it. I picked up the phone, and dialed. And waited.

"Hello?" the angry sounding voice answered the phone.

"Hey Mike. It's me. How's your day?" trying to sound caring, and cheerful as always.

"Eh, the day is fine. What do you need? Is everything ok?" his voice was changing from angry, to inquisitive.

"Oh, I'm fine. My plans have just changed for the evening, and I wanted to let you know so you wouldn't worry if I didn't call your pages back." I braced, waiting for the blow.

"Oh, I see. What are you doing?" he asked.

"I'm going to meet Heather after work for dinner. Then I'll be home after that, and can call if you want me to." This was going much better than anticipated. The fact that it was going this well suddenly made me terrified. But I kept going with it, because what I was going to get out of this was so worth anything that could happen.

"Ok, well, call me when you're home then. Maybe I could come over then. Janie, I.." there was an inhale, and a sigh. "I'm sorry about the other night. You know, my temper, just really...gets out of control." Then he chuckled. My skin prickled with the sound of his laugh, and I got goose bumps. "Guess I just can't quite control myself sometimes. Or you make me crazy. Or maybe both?" Then silence. Had he just laughed that he'd hurt me? Again? I was speechless, but knew deep down that speechless wouldn't work either.

"I didn't do anything to make you crazy, that's the problem. Always the problem..." I trailed off. I saw Gabriel walk by the front, and I refocused quickly. "So, I'll call you when I'm home. No problem. I'll talk to you later, ok?"

"Ok, love you Janie. Bye."

"Bye!" I couldn't have been happier to get off of the phone with him. His sudden ease with the situation made me crazy nervous, but the mere thought of being alone with Gabriel calmed me right back down. I checked the clock. We were down to fifteen minutes until closing time. I decided to finish what I was doing, and head to the bathroom. On my way to the back, I passed Gabriel and he quickly smacked my behind and winked at me. I was beaming.

Climbing into Gabriel's blue Jeep was really exhilarating. Like my one wish was coming true. The whole car smelled like him. I wanted to remember this smell forever. He turned the radio on, and Faith Hill's Breathe was on. Certain words he began

singing out loud, and I couldn't help but wonder if they were to me. We had left my car in the parking lot at a local restaurant for cover, but still I was a little concerned for both of us. I tried hard not to let those feelings start to stamp out the current feelings of electricity, hot passion, and lust that were starting to roll through the car.

He was singing again. "I can feel the magic floating in the air...being with you gets me that way... Do you like this radio station? Want to put something else on?" he looked at me, and grasped my hand. I inhaled sharply, and my heart beat out of my chest. Even though he had touched me before, hugged me even, this was so much more intimate than ever before. His hands were so warm. Internally my fire burned hot, and there was no denying what I wanted.

"This station is fine." I looked at him right in his eyes, and tried to will him to touch me more, or pull over. My heart was crying out for him, and I tried to silence the calls as to not be needy. Soon after, my willing and wanting worked- he pulled over. We were in the middle of the country, on a dark road. I briefly had to stop and internally chuckle, because the other would always take me to places like this to deal with his temper... This time, in this moment, I knew I was more than safe. I adjusted in my seat so that my knees were angled towards Gabriel, and I leaned towards the middle. "So, what do you want to talk about?" I asked, with a sly smile.

"I may have changed my mind about the talking thing. So if you'd rather do something else... that's fine with me." And he leaned into the middle and met me face to face. Within seconds, our lips met, and were hot and wet all over each other. I yearned for his touch. Ached to feel him all over me. His hands held my face as we kissed. My fire was burning so hot, and so bright, I was sure I would explode at any moment. His hands moved from my face, gently down my neck and onto my chest. They started on the outside of my shirt, and slowly worked their way down, and back up under my shirt. Quickly pushing my bra out of the way, he held each breast in his hands. He licked each nipple carefully, as if I was the most delicate thing in the world. I arched my back into him, and moaned. His hands trailed down farther, to the waistband of my shorts. And then he was back at my mouth, kissing me deeply. These weren't the kisses that I was used to. *I was used to forceful, uncaring, cold kisses, and touches. I was used to being forced into doing lots of things....and now... this...* And he was taking such time with me. Being so gracious and careful. I grabbed Gabriel's face, and kissed him back, harder and more passionately than ever. One hand slipped behind his head, and fisted his hair.

Then I felt his fingers feeling their way up my thighs. I inhaled, and held my breath. He felt my reaction, and hesitated. "Are you okay?" His eyes were dead set on mine. I knew at that moment that I was more than safe with Gabriel, and that he could be the one to save me from this hell. I hoped that he was strong enough to handle my baggage, even if just long enough to get me out of this madness.

"I'm more than okay," I hesitated, and pulled his lips to mine again. "Please..." And I sealed my mouth to his. His fingers went straight to my hot core, and began rubbing outside of my underwear. He was making me so wet, and I was so ready for him. I spread my legs wider, and he got the message right away. He slid his fingers inside my panties, and began fingering me on that cool, fall night. He would alter his speed, change the pressure, all while nibbling and tasting me all over. I was in heaven. *There's nothing better than this heady feeling...* I could feel myself starting to clench, and his fingers sped up with my body. I came all over his hands, all while his hot breath ended in my ear. We laid with each other, and caught our breath for a little while. Then he kissed me, and climbed back to his seat. I couldn't stop smiling. This is how it was supposed to feel.

"Thank you for the car ride, sweet cheeks." He held my hand, and kissed it. "I'm glad we seem to be on the same page." And winked at me. But I didn't want it to end. I looked at my pager, and saw the five missed pages. *Did you think he'd just disappear? You're going to have to face him when you're home, and you know it. You just put yourself in more danger than you care to admit, and it's disgusting. Gabriel, too. Why risk both of you?* I knew the answer to that now. I'd risk it because I felt something very strong with Gabriel. Something hopefully strong enough to save me.

"Thank you for the car ride, Gabriel. You have no idea how much I needed that." I leaned over and kissed him, long and hard. I climbed into my own car, and headed towards home. This drive home was the hardest yet. My head had taken me somewhere else tonight, and I never, ever wanted to leave.

5

When I rounded into the cul-de-sac where I lived, I could see the Confederate flag, and Michael. Both of them were staring me down. The car behind Michael's looked to have Preston and Sean inside. I was hopeful that Sean was here, because Michael seemed to be easier on me when he was around. And I really liked Sean, even if he did pretend to be Michael's right hand man. I pulled in the driveway, and braced myself for hell. I cautiously opened my car door, ready to take it all. Luckily, at the same time my Dad came to the front door.

"Hey sweets," he looked puzzled why there was a crowd around. "Did you have a good day at work?" he always did somehow manage to not acknowledge the riff-raff when it was happening, even under his own nose.

"Yeah, Dad. It was a great day. Glad to be home, I'm exhausted. I won't be too long." I gave a small wave, and he went back into the house. Once the door was closed, it began.

"Janie. We need to talk. Let's go for a walk down to the school. The guys can stay here." His tone was ragged, and I knew better than to leave a safe place if I could help it. My eyes darted around, my insides began to shake. I was twisted in more knots than ever, and had officially lost my high from being with Gabriel. "Now, Janie. I'm tired of waiting." He grabbed my arm, and started down the sidewalk.

"No, I really want to stay here with the guys. We can just hang out for a bit, maybe a bonfire?" I was grasping at straws. My eyes began to tear.

"Hey Mike," Sean spoke up. I glanced in his direction, and his dark eyes met mine. Sean stood agitated, hands on his hips, reading the situation as I was. "She looks pretty tired man. Why don't we just hang out here like I said? A few beers and a fire sounds nice and relaxing." I could tell that Sean was doing anything in his power to help, but it didn't seem to be working. He stepped to reach for me, and Michael stepped into his path. "Come on, Mike, you're being ridiculous." Michael was still dragging me down the side walk.

"No, Sean. We'll be back in a few. Just hang out. Tell Paul we went for a walk real quick." His grip tightened on my arm. "I hate it when you lie to me Janie. You know how I can't control my temper when you're always doing stupid shit!" We were out of sight, and now by the school and forest.

"Michael," I tried to keep my composure, and keep calm. "I'm not sure what's gotten you all fired up. Can you please explain?" If there were any chance to talk him down, I'd have to know exactly what set him off. It could be so many things, I couldn't even wrap my brain around one idea. He was still walking. Now past the playgrounds, and towards the edge of the tree line. Tears were flowing down my cheeks; my legs began to tingle.

"I drove by your work tonight, and what do you think I saw?" He released my arm, and spun me around to face him. He was gritting his teeth, and his fists were clenched tightly closed. "Answer me." He demanded.

I tried to speak, but nothing came out. "I... I don't know what you mean. I worked, and then I went out with Heather, just like I said. And then I was coming home to call you, just like I said I would, but you were already waiting for me! I only do the work at work that they tell me to do! Yes, today, I worked outside with him!" I looked up at him, panicked and puzzled. "I don't know what else you want me to say!!!" I screamed.

"I saw the way you were looking at each other!!!" His voice grew louder, and more enraged. "You're always looking at him, and smiling like you're in love." He grabs my shoulders, and knocked me to the ground. His knee pushed sharply into the middle of my back, pinning me down to the ground. "You cannot be looking at another man the way you look at him! I'm going to remind you of this now." His eyes began to squint, and he started pulling my shorts off. Down to my ankles they went. He didn't even bother taking off my panties, just worked around them. Going in dry was often a punishment, and one of my least favorites, as it left me broken and in pain for days.

"Please Michael..." I cried. "Why are you doing this? Don't do it like this! Please!" My face was laying on the grassy field, next to the line of trees. No movement in anyone's yards. Yards that we had played in together as we grew up. We'd played house, and had pretend babies together. Gone hunting, fishing, and boating. And now he was filling me up with his hate, over and over again. I sobbed quietly, and hoped it would end soon. His hands swarmed my body, grabbing onto me forcefully. *Oh dear God...* I turned my focus back to Gabriel, and the warmth I felt with him. Suddenly he was off of me, someone had come out of their house with their puppy. With their porch light on, I could clearly see the man's face. He was still oblivious to what was going on a few yards behind his house, but just that he had come out, stopped Michael in his tracks.

"Get up, Janie. Now." He grabbed my arm, and quickly shifted me up, and hiked my shorts back up over my hips. "Let's get you back home." He says, suddenly caring and calm. I crossed my arms over my chest, and didn't say a word. My clothes had wet spots, mud, and grass all over them. *I think there's grass in your hair, too.* Neither of us spoke on the way back home. When we got back to my driveway, Michael lit a smoke, and began to chat with the guys. I stared blankly at my feet, sitting quietly, with my arms tightly crossed across my chest. *JANIE! Why are you letting this happen? Please! Please leave this man! Why do you keep letting him do this to you? This is not who you are! You are stronger than this! Reach out if you can't do it alone, but please don't give up!*

"Sean, can I bum a smoke? Please?" I turned and asked him. My eyes were blood shot, and I hoped that he would not mention it. His eyes tracked up and down my body quickly, and his forehead wrinkled.

"Yeah, of course." He opened his pack, and pulled out his upside down lucky, and gave it to me. "Looks like this one would be good for you right about now." If only he knew. I took his lighter, lit up, and inhaled long and hard. I was starting to smoke more, which was not good for swimming. It did seem to calm my nerves for a few moments at a time, so I thought it was worth it for now. We were just out of ear shot of Michael, so I stepped towards Sean, clearly handing back his lighter.

"Thanks for trying to keep me here," our hands brushed in the lighter hand off, and the feeling exchanged was undeniable. He smiled at me, and caught my eye. I shook my head no, and backed away from him.

"Thanks again," I smiled. "Well boys, I'm going in to bed. I've got to get some sleep before work tomorrow." I turned to Michael, "I'll see you later." He reached for me, but I was already spun around walking into the house, and locking the door. I leaned against the front door and sighed. I hustled upstairs and hit the shower. The hot water burned my sore spots, and after that night, there were many. I crawled into bed, and dreamed about my car ride with Gabriel from start to finish. Thinking about him made it so easy to block out the bad.

6

It took a few days to recover from the weekend, and I missed a few days of work. I missed a few days of swimming, too, which really bothered me. When I returned, I was pleasantly surprised that many of my coworkers were taking the time to ask how I was. When I clocked in, Simon greeted me, although his face was pained.

"Hey Janie," he said quietly. "Are you doing okay?" Simon knew what my weekends were like, he even knew some of the details. But I had asked him to keep quiet for now, and he said he would respect my wishes, as long as he could.

"I'm alright." I smiled, and patted his shoulder. "Thanks for asking, Simon. It took me a few days to bounce back this time. I'm doing much better today though. I'm so happy to be back at work again." I dove into a pile of paperwork on my desk, and began verifying deliveries.

"I'm glad you're here, too. Hasn't been the same without you the past few days. There were new hires, and everything!" Simon was always excited to meet and train the new workers. "Well, I'll leave you alone now Janie. Maybe we can chat later?" He smiled as he walked away. Such an awkward, but sweet boy, I thought.

I worked away, not really paying attention to anything around me. The landscaping business had really taken off for the Phoenix, and the recent influx of jobs and deliveries were keeping me on my toes. I was very pleased that I was almost through my entire pile of invoices, and it was only five o'clock. Two hours to go, and I could head back to bed. While I worked, Gabriel kept coming into my mind. I worried that if he knew about my weekend, he would be disgusted with me. Most likely because I was always disgusted with myself. I knew he was at work, but I was at a loss for words, and didn't know what to say to him. *You knew this was going to happen, Janie. Be honest with yourself. Who would want to end up with someone stuck in this situation? Covered in bruises, bumps, and scratches. Violated physically and mentally... just so much baggage for a 21-year-old.* Suddenly, I heard his voice coming towards the back offices. My heart started to beat out of my chest, and I welcomed the feeling.

"Ok, no problem man! We'll get it all taken care of before the weekend, hopefully before Friday night, too." I wondered what his Friday nights plans were, or wondered if he had moved on in those few days without me. "Sounds good, Bill.

I'll call you tomorrow." And then he turned the corner into my office. His smile was huge, like he had waited so long to lay his eyes on me. "Hey you," he said calmly. "I've missed you!" He stepped toward me, and put his arms around my waist.

"Gabriel, I..." he cut me off. He spun my chair around so we were face to face. I smiled at him, and blushed. "I missed you, too."

"Are we going to get any time alone? Soon, I hope?" He looked at her face, and he could see the torment. I wasn't as smiley as normal, and seemed to be a little held back. There was always talk whenever I missed work for days at a time, especially when I'd miss my swim meets, too. He rubbed my shoulders gently, while we stared into each other's eyes. I looked like I had lost weight, too. "Janie? You in there?" He rubbed his thumb gently down my cheek.

"I'm sorry Gabriel," I began. I didn't know what else to say, so I let my body take over. I reached for him, and pulled him into an embrace. Never before had our intimacy been so public, or loud. "Yes, I would love to spend more time with you. Alone." I didn't want to let him go, but heard people's voices getting closer, and he pulled away. This made me frown.

Gabriel sat down next to me, and rifled through some of the paperwork I had done. "You're doing a killer job on this, Janie. Thank you for helping me out on this." His hand was on my back again, carefully stroking me up and down. His fingers were getting braver, dipping farther down into my waistband each time he stroked. "Oh, Janie...I really want you right now." I could feel the heat radiating off of him, and knew he was serious. I wanted him badly, and I could feel myself heating up for him.

"Gabriel, let's go drive after work. I have somewhere I'd like to take you." I was careful to look around first, and just as I leaned in to kiss him, the office phone rang in. "PHONE CALL FOR Gabriel, LINE 2. Gabriel, LINE 2." He put his finger in the air, and answered.

"Good afternoon, Phoenix. This is Gabriel." and he listened. And I listened. "Oh, well, sure. We could do that." There were long pauses, and almost hushed words. My gut was twisting listening to only half of the conversation. "Ok, sure. That sounds great. Can't wait to see you, either. Bye." He hung up, and momentarily looked at the far wall, away from me. Then he looked, and saw my worried face. "Hey, what's wrong?"

"I... uhm..." I didn't know what to say. I was jealous. Jealous that he was making plans with someone else. Angry that what I really wanted, I feared I'd never get. Sad that stuck was how I felt again. "I just wondered if you were still going to be able to go out or not?" I fumbled with my fingers.

"I wouldn't miss hanging out with you for the world!" he glanced over to see if his comment had brought the beautiful smile back to my face. I was smirking, but I still looked so distant. "Don't have too much time left to work. In fact, let me see if I can get my stuff done early, and we could head out. Sound ok?"

"Yes, that would be fine." I was very happy that he'd still wanted to spend time with me, even after the past weekend's, the past few months, events. "Let me just let my parents, and Michael...know what's going on." I hesitated and looked at Gabriel's reaction to my mention of Michael. He didn't seem to have one, and I wondered just how much he did know about my situation. I picked up the phone, and checked in with my parents. I called and left a message with Michael's mom, figuring that this would be easier for now. "I'm set whenever you're ready to go." I smiled, a little bigger this time.

7

Gabriel spent the next half an hour cleaning up the outdoor plants, and I finished the paperwork for the week. I planned to leave my car at work until the next day, and catch a ride to work. If I was lucky, someone may steal it, and I'd be forced into getting a different car. Gabriel met me in the back room, and we both clocked out. Since it was still sort of light outside, I opted to not walk too close to him, or hold his fingers, as we'd done so many nights in the past. I couldn't be too sure where Michael was, or if any of his minions were watching. I climbed into his car quickly, and we were off. "So, Janie, you said you had somewhere you'd like to go?"

"Yes," I shifted in my seat, and my shirt slid down my chest, revealing the top of my breasts to him. I noticed that my clothes had shifted, and that Gabriel's focus was now shifting between the road, my face, and my chest. I loved the want that was written all over his face. I felt just as twisted inside, and wished I had the guts to tell him everything, and ask for his help. Fear stopped me again. "Let's go to the airport, and watch the planes land." I smiled at him, and went back to looking out the window.

"Ok, that actually sounds great. I think I know where you mean, too." he reached out, and put his hand on my thigh. His hands were so warm, I wrapped my hand back around his. The ride to their spot was quiet, but we never let go of each other. The constant contact relaxed me, and I became more present, more alive, to the moment. Gabriel pulled to the end of the field, and found a dark spot in between two trees to park. Gabriel wasn't a smoker, but he never protested when I'd light up.

"Sorry about this," I said as I held up my freshly lit cigarette. "Seems like I can't let go of this habit." I wrinkled my forehead. I made sure to hot box the smoke, because I didn't want to be wasting time on anything but Gabriel. I popped some gum in my mouth, and turned towards Gabriel. I very purposely put my hand onto Gabriel's thigh, and gently stroked back and forth.

"Janie," he sighed, and I melted. Within seconds, he had locked his lips with mine. I loved the feeling of his tongue probing into my mouth, and I wished to feel it all over my body. His kiss was just as always, full of passion, and want. I loved feeling wanted in this way. I touched him everywhere I could, without breaking the seal of our lips. His arms, his chest, his face, and his back. I loved his back. I'd dream the day away dreaming of laying on top of his back, feeling him on all of me. Just then, he shifted. "Come over here, baby." and he pulled me onto his lap.

"MMmm..." was all that would come out of my mouth. Sitting on his lap, leaning on his chest, face to face, tongue to tongue, I could taste his desire. I showed his hands the way under my shirt, and to my supple breasts. He held each breast in his hand, and sucked each nipple. My nipples were hard, and so sensitive to his touch. His touch was neither too hard, or too soft. It was perfect. I couldn't hold in the moans. I could feel his erection pushing against his pants, and into mine. I wanted him inside me, without question, but I didn't want to push my luck. I broke our kiss to lean to his ear, and I started to whisper. "More...Gabe...please." but it came out more of a plea.

"Ok, baby. More..." He positioned himself so that his legs were between mine, opening me up to him. He slowly caressed my face, down my neck, and stopped to squeeze my ample breasts. He pulled me towards him, as to not strain to suck on my nipples. He continued down my chest to my belly, and into my shorts. I was so ready for him, and he could tell. He didn't want to rush things though. He wanted to see where this was going to go, and do it normally with me. He rubbed my panties back and forth, and finally out of the way. My skin was so soft, and hairless. As he touched my core, he couldn't help but moan. "Oh, Janie..." He slid his fingers in and out, over and over again. He loved the way I kissed him when I was turned on. He could feel my need, and taste my passion. I was so tight to him. He wanted to take me, badly. His fingers were soaked, and his stick was throbbing. His pants were becoming uncomfortable, and he lifted me a bit to adjust. He looked at my face, and saw me smile. He thought that I looked absolutely adorable when I was this happy, and he felt great knowing he had something to do with it.

"Are you okay? Am I hurting you?" I asked. I lifted myself up a little more, and saw the bulge in his pants. I wanted to ease his discomfort, and started to back off his lap. I noticed the shocked look on his face. "It's ok...wait and see." I smiled very widely at him. I leaned over the seat, and center console, and put myself eye level with his lap. I slowly began stroking his cock through his pants, and each time, he twitched and moaned. I was so hot for him, which made every move I made just like normal part of life, or love. I unzipped his pants while I kissed his stomach, all the while staring into his blue eyes. I opened his pants, and began to kiss all around his most sensitive areas, and across his waist line. I could feel him throbbing under my neck, and on my breasts. I looked him very deliberately in the eyes, and lowered myself farther on to his lap. I slowly pulled his hot throbbing member out, and slowly began to stroke it. The head was hitting my chin, and I couldn't resist temptation any longer. I had been dying to know how he tasted, and now I was going to find out. I eased him slowly into my warm, wet mouth, and pulled him out again. I slowly lowered my mouth over him again, this time flicking him gently with my tongue ring.

"Ohh..." he moaned louder. He fisted my hair, and stroked my back with the other hand. He loved me like this. I was so confidant in my actions, and that turned him on more than anything. He wanted to feel more of my mouth on him, so he gently urged me to head back towards him. I was eager, and he couldn't contain his smile. I loved pleasing him, and he could feel it. And see it. He was very close to coming, but didn't want to in this situation. Slowly he started to ease away from me, and he could sense my confusion. "It's ok, baby. It's just getting late. I don't want you to get into trouble." He leaned over and kissed my mouth.

"Ok, you're right," I said, breathless from our kiss. "We'd better go. I'm sure I'll be in all sorts of trouble for this..." I mumbled and I dug through my purse to find my pager. I hit the recall button, to find no missed pages. I couldn't contain the smile, or the burst of excitement that made me lean over for the deepest, most passionate kiss yet. When I opened my eyes, he was still deep in my mouth, but his eyes were locked on mine. Now I felt him, tasted him, and could see what was happening between us. And I was scared.

8

He drove me back to my parents' house, and saw that I was inside alright. His head was full of so many new thoughts and ideas, that he needed to go to bed and process everything that had just happened. His head was telling him to stay with me, and protect me, but he wasn't sure that he was really ready for all of that yet. He had been single for a little while, but had maintained a fuck buddy for the past few months. He could feel that this chick was getting a little too hot and heavy, for their strictly sex-only relationship, but he wasn't sure how to break it off with her. And now me. He rubbed his head with both hands as he climbed out of his car once he was home. He was happy to find that his roommate was not home, so he could just be alone for a while.

Once I got inside, I went up to my room. My pager started to vibrate, and it was Michael's number. I went limp on the bed, and stared blankly at the ceiling. So much had happened today, that I didn't even know where to begin to process. I learned today that my body was somehow connected to Gabriel, because with the simple touch of his hand, it went weak. I yearned for him, and I didn't get enough of him today. I wasn't use to feeling such strong emotion so easily for another. I was use to forcing smiles, wincing through hugs, and becoming numb to anything intimate. I reached for the phone, as to not prolong the inevitable.

It rang twice before he answered. "Hello?" he sounded relieved to hear from me.

"Hey Michael, it's me." I was exasperated just pushing that out. I was ready to hang up.

"Hey honey. Would you like some company? You're home earlier than you said you'd be." he sounded like he was sitting on pins and needles waiting for my answer.

"Actually, I.." he cut me off mid-sentence.

"We'll come over for a little bit to say hello. Nothing crazy, promise. Won't even stay long. Preston has to be home soon anyway." He mumbled something to Preston, and I heard him answer in the background.

"Uhm, yeah... I've got an hour." Michael came back on the phone to add, "See you soon!" When the phone clicked, I sighed and slumped in the bed. There wasn't even time to cry, or to figure out a plan. Not even to shower. I quickly put on new underwear, sweats, and a sweat shirt. I paused momentarily as I took my shirt off.

MMmm…it smells like Gabe… I couldn't help take a few extra seconds to breathe him in some more. And then I headed downstairs, and out to the patio, where they would meet me. My parents' house was nice. The backyard was fenced in, and there was an enclosed patio off the side of the garage. The guys weren't inside yet, so I got comfortable, and lit a smoke. I could hear the truck's engine, and stereo system coming from somewhere through the quiet addition. Time seemed to stand still. I could hear the crickets chirping cease suddenly, and second by second my pulse sped up. It didn't help that each second drug on forever. I swore that the truck took hours to pull up, rather than just two minutes. I could see Preston and Michael heading up the sidewalk.

"Hey Janie, it's just us." Preston said as they approached. Preston was normally the quieter of the bunch. The withdrawn bassist, who bowed down to Michael just like the rest of the pack did. I felt that he was in a similar situation as I was, trapped. And even though he annoyed me, I felt for him, too.

"It's ok Pres, I see you." I tried to be cheery whenever his friends were around. I was instructed to do this many times, and also that these were "his friends," not mine. Michael would often get infuriated when I would talk to closely with one of his friends, or look at them inappropriately. Or blink. My thoughts ran wild. *Exactly. You get your ass beat for blinking, and you know that's true. We've already gone over, and over this. We know Michael's problems. You know you're not going to change him, and that he doesn't want to change this for you. You're shaking in your skin sitting there, watching him approach. You know what you need to do, and I can't imagine it's going to be easy. But it is a must. Stop procrastinating. You've got every reason you needed to go, plus Gabriel. I know you felt it tonight, the click. It's deep with you two. Physical. Emotional. Go with what works. Stop trying to force this...it's only going to make him mad.* Ugh. I felt like throwing up. The voice in my head was right, and I knew this. I was terrified of him. "Come on in, boys." Oh, was I trying hard. Michael walked up to me, and leaned in for a kiss. The numbness was already there. My walls were up the moment I saw him. When his lips touched mine, I was choked by the taste of cigarettes and coffee. I could feel the vomit rising in my chest. *This is disgusting. It feels so wrong... Hold those tears in Janie...* Thankfully, he released quickly, and sat down.

"So, how was your day?" he was smiling at me now, with the joker grin, and playing with his moustache. I knew how to play along.

"It was alright. Just another day at the landscaping company, you know. Invoices and delivery orders. Great fun." I smiled, and decided to try for the best. "How about your day?" I noticed he wasn't drumming on the table, or his leg, or me, like normal. He was calm, and it was eerie.

"Well, wouldn't you know my surprise when I went to see you at work this evening, to suggest some evening plans, and the store was closed, and..." he paused to ash the cigarette, and look me closely in the eye. "YOU...weren't there. So now I'm wondering...where you were. And I'm guessing I already know." His eyebrows went up, and he smiled even bigger. *I want to tell you to run...does he already know?!*

"Well, what time did you go? Guess we all left a little early, but I just came back here. Simon brought me, in fact. I was too tired to drive." I was playing the game as best I could, trying to keep stories straight, and decided to go a little farther. "Sat with my Dad for a little bit when I got home, then was laying down when you paged." I motioned to my clothing choices, which were that of my normal pajama wear.

"Janie, you know I'm not okay with other people taking you home. I've told you before that if you don't want to drive, you are to call me and I will come get you. If I can't, you can call one of the guys." His smile was fading, and the little "v" in between his eyes was wrinkled. That meant his temper was turning. He turned abruptly to Preston. "Hey buddy, why don't we get you home." I was confused. Was this going to be an easy escape tonight? "Go out to the truck, I'll be right there."

He turned back towards me, and closed the space between us. He stepped up to my face, and sternly grabbed my head in his hand. He was so much bigger than I was, it didn't take much for him to push me around easily. He started to stroke my face with his other hand, still clasping the back of my head. He smiled at me, and leaned in like he was going to kiss me. By mistake, I turned away.

In an instant, he had rammed me into the back wall, and was now holding me to it by my throat. He glared into my eyes, and had a tight hold on my neck. He didn't cut off my oxygen, thankfully, but it hurt enough to bring tears to my eyes. He gritted his teeth in my face, and then in my ear and said, "You just confirmed exactly what I knew was going on. And let me tell you, it's not happening, baby. You. ARE. MINE." With each word spoken, his squeezes got harder around my neck. Then he abruptly dropped me to my feet. He started to walk away, and turned around and added, "THIS isn't over." And continued out to the truck, and peeled away like an insane immature asshole that he was.

I waited until I could no longer hear the blaring music playing out of the truck. I believed it was Pantera, and that was my least favorite band on the planet. I trailed up to bed, and cried myself to sleep.

I spent the next two days at swim meets. Since I was turning 21 in less than two weeks, I was doing the last of my meets in this age group. If I chose to stay in, the next level started a more independent practice and routine, and I wasn't sure I liked that idea. With all of the drama, and stress, I could feel it pulling on me at swimming, and it kept me from doing my absolute best. Which was very frustrating for me.

9

It was Monday before I was back to work, and I had missed it, and Gabriel, more than anything. Since I had seen Michael last Thursday night, he had been very distant. I didn't mind the sudden space, but I knew he had something up his sleeve, because Michael never made idle threats, he always followed through. I couldn't help but smile a little at the space though, as it was just what I needed to free up some time with Gabriel. However, just as it had been a few days without Michael's suffocating personality, it had been the same amount of time since I had seen Gabriel. I was nervous to see him, because of all that had happened last week. When I arrived at work, and went to my office, I found a line of Hershey kisses across my desk. I blushed, and wondered if this was Gabriel.

"Janie!!" there was immense excitement behind her, and it was Simon. "Guess what?! We're having a cookout out back of the store today! One of the guys is bringing his grill, and Gabe said we can buy some meat from the Mexi-mart!" He chuckled to himself, and did an air high five.

"Oh, that sounds like a good time. I'm sure all the new landscapers will appreciate that!" I smiled, and was glad that this day was turning out to be normal, and on track. "Do you know if Gabe's here?" I glanced at him out of the corner of her eye.

"Yes, he was in a meeting with the owners..." he trailed off, and walked closer to me. "Uhh, we didn't use to keep secrets from each other, but I know a lots happened in your life. I, uhm, just wanted to say that these past few months you've seemed happier, and I know why." He smiled at me, and continued. "You deserve someone who will treat you right, and I can see it in Gabe's eyes. I'm happy for you Janes, and I'll do anything I can to keep you smiling." He put his hand on my shoulder, and I put mine on top of his.

"Aw, Simon..." I hugged him. "Thank you for being such a good friend." I backed up, and smiled awkwardly at him. "Things are very tense right now. I think that Michael knows something, and I'm a little nervous about that. I'm just waiting for the right time to set all of this straight..." I sighed. "That time just hasn't presented itself yet." I put my head down, and shut my eyes.

"It'll be okay, Janes. Just remember, I'm always here if you need me. I'll help you with this however I can." He patted my shoulder again. "But for now, I've got to get back to loading for the deliveries!" He nodded, and left the office. I organized my desk, and began working through the piles that piled up since Thursday. While I typed, I wondered if Gabe had noticed that I was here. It was hard for me to get through an hour without my thoughts turning to Gabe, and his body, and his hands...and his heart. I shook my head, trying to focus on work. My pager went off, and it was my mom's number. I picked up the phone, and called back immediately.

"Hey Mom," I said. "I got your page. What's up?" It had been a few days since I had talked to my mother. Our schedules were so different, and my mom had been going to bed early. I missed her, but at the same time knew that she would never understand this situation, and probably wouldn't believe me if I tried to tell her.

"I just wanted to say hi to you! It's been days!" She said jokingly to herself. "Your birthday is only days away! Excited to be turning 21?"

"I guess so, but it sort of feels just like any other day!" We both giggled with each other.

"I also wanted to let you know that we'll be going out tonight, so Dad and I will be home late. I left some cash on the counter this morning, if you wanted to go out for dinner, or something." I could hear the smile in her voice. She loved doing nice things for me, and I loved her for it.

"Oh, thanks mom! I'm not sure what I'll end up doing, maybe just hanging out with friends." My head started turning out the scenarios. This could be a perfect thing.

"Or maybe you could have the guys over, and grill. Oh, your options are limitless." She giggled again. "Well, I'll leave you to your work. Love you honey!"

"Love you too, Mom." I hung up, and really wanted to run and find Gabe. But I was reluctant to, as he hadn't come back to say hello, or even seen me yet. It was lunch time, so I decided to go eat. As I approached the break room, I could hear his voice. I stopped momentarily to just listen, not to what he was saying at first, just to the sound of him. My heart thumped hard in my chest. *What the hell is going on here?!* But suddenly, every word was clear, and he sounded frustrated, and angry. I stayed out of sight, and listened. Trying to keep my breath under control, and attempting to not panic.

"No! This is not what THIS was supposed to be!" I heard him banging around, and sighing in between sentences. "I don't understand why you feel like you can change the rules, and just expect me to go with them. It's time for me to move on, and I have someone to do that with." There was a pause, and I could hear another voice. A woman's voice.

"But she's nothing compared to me. Look at her! Look at me!" I wrinkled my face in disgust. *Bitch, you knew about me?? I wonder if I've seen you??* I scowled into the shadows, and listened harder. "We're so good together, Gabriel. Come on," she pressed.

"No, you're just not getting it. Look, maybe in time we can still be friends, but now, it's got to stop. I'm not fucking with you anymore." He closed his locker, and I looked around the wall just in time to see the woman backing up out of the break room. She was petite with blonde hair, and just as I looked around the corner, she looked at me, and glared.

She snapped back to Gabe, "you know this isn't over. You can't stay away, and you know it." She reached for him, and grasped her hand around his head, pulling him to her. Her lips briefly touched his before he was able to pull away. He made a noise of disgust. and she stormed out of the store.

My heart sank. He hadn't wanted to see me, because he was seeing someone else. I felt the biggest pain of jealousy blow through my body, and it made my face hot. *OH, isn't this ironic? You're jealous now because he's got a girlfriend? That's pretty off, don't you think? Personally, I think this is perfect. You're both obviously with the wrong people, and this is just fate's way of putting you together. It's obvious what you need, now you find out what he needs to complete this puzzle.* I tried to focus my thoughts, but all I could picture was him...with that woman. *Don't panic, don't panic...*

she was better than me?? I felt sick, and needed the bathroom. I bolted for it, and as I did, Gabe was leaving the break room. He saw the distressed look on my face, and the paleness that was ensuing, and grabbed me by both arms.

10

"What's wrong, Jane?" his face was genuinely concerned, and it made it hard for me to focus. "You look like you've seen a ghost, or you're very sick." One of his hands went up to my forehead, as if feeling for a temperature. Suddenly, I thought of the woman, and tears came to my eyes. I tried to push him off, but he wouldn't move.

"Please just let me go." I paused. "It's obvious you have other people to worry about." I looked up at him, tentatively. His face changed, as if he understood what all of this was about.

"Oh, Janie..." he looked down. "I'm sorry you had to see that. Look, She's not what you think. And as you probably heard, I was trying to make her go away." His fingers traced my cheek, and he still had that genuine care expression on his face. His honesty was always appreciated, and his eyes always expressed his emotion. He could tell that I was wound tightly about this, and couldn't lose me like this. "Hey, come out back with me for a bit? I can't let you think what you're thinking about all of this. Please?" He held my hand so gently, and slowly directed both of us out the back door, and on to some pallets left behind the building. He noticed that I was staring at the ground, and wouldn't make eye contact with him. "Janie?"

"I.." was all that I could get to come out. My head was spinning, and I was devastated by what I had heard, and seen. But not for the sole reason of jealousy. How was I ever going to explain this to him? "You don't owe me anything, Gabe." I slowly looked up at him. He hadn't taken his eyes off of me once. I continued, "I mean, what are we anyway?" I pointed with my hands between the both of us, "This is so much fun, more fun than I've had in a long time. I feel safe with you, and that's why I haven't minded any of this..." Gabe's warm hand cut me off. He put it directly over my mouth.

"No, don't finish. Please." He put his head down, and hands on his forehead. He didn't have conversations like this with people. Ever. Something about me though, made him want to divulge his deepest, darkest, most dangerous secrets. without any hesitation at all. He took a deep breath, and dove in. "I'm going to be really honest with you now. I hope that you can hear me out, and that you can be understanding. I hope for this because I feel..." his eyes trailed from his hands, to my chest, to my eyes. "I feel different when I'm with you, and I don't want to lose that feeling right now. The girl you saw was a friend of mine, well, shit. Actually, I don't know what we are.

Or were." He shook his head, as if there were a shrieking siren going off in his ears. "I guess you could say that we were 'friends with benefits,' and that wasn't working for me anymore. So, you heard me ending that. She was no girlfriend; I can promise you that." He paused again and asked, "still with me?"

I cleared my throat, and nodded. *It's time to get a little more honest Janie. Show him you can do this, too. Just breathe, baby.* "Gabe, I understand what you've said, and I'm fine with it. There's really not much I can say about your situation, when you know I have my own..." my words were becoming hard to force out, and my voice was shrinking. I sighed. "Michael and I have been dating for 8 months. He would be the truck you always see outside. The pages I'm always getting." I paused. *The marks on your body. Say it, Janie. Please.* "He's a very difficult entity in my life right now. *And I'd do anything to get away from him. Safely.* I don't want to bog you down with drama, so I won't. *I need you to help me get out of this.* I'm waiting for the right time to end things, but that's tricky. So, just know that I get it, and it is what it is, right?" I smiled at him, and reached for his hand. "But, I do feel different with you, too. And I don't want that to change right now..." I kissed his hand.

He just wanted to wrap his arms around me, and hold me. I tried to tell him what he already knew, but couldn't. He could see the pain in my eyes, and feel the hesitation in my words. He was relieved by my response, but now he wanted me more. "Janie, I..." he couldn't resist any longer. He engulfed me with himself, and buried me deep in his kiss. His hands grasped the back of my head, holding me to his soft, passionate kiss. His tongue probed around deeply into my mouth, invoking uncontrollable moans. My hands clung to his back, digging into him at times, trying to pull him into me. He wanted me more than ever. There was no denying it at this point. Suddenly, there was a muffled coughing behind us. We broke our deep kiss very quickly, and turned to see Simon. We both internally sighed with relief.

"Uhm, sorry guys! Wow, what a trip!" Simon shook his head in disbelief of what he had just seen. Now looking in both of our faces, he too saw what was happening between us. "You know I love you both. I think I love you both more, together." He shot both of us his biggest grin.

"Simon, I uhh..." I paused, and looked at Gabe. I smiled and shook my head. "Simon, please don't say anything about this right now. Gabe and I are...just working through some things." I felt myself blush, because in reality, I wanted to get worked over by Gabe from head to toe, and back again.

"Don't worry Janes, you're secrets safe with me." He turned to Gabe and added, "yours too, buddy. I just wondered when we were going to start cooking lunch!" He pointed to the grill, and held up the bag of food.

Gabe walked towards me, and pulled me behind a wall. "I'm so glad we talked for a little bit, sweet cheeks. I don't want anything to change either. Unless it's that I'm spending more time with you." He kissed me quickly, and on the hand...and disappeared back to work.

I went back to my office, and finished the few invoices. I skipped sitting in on the cookout that the delivery boys were all having, but could hear their loud laughter roaring through the building. I wish there were more laughter in my life, but I could feel something turning, something changing deep inside of myself. I wasn't sure what it was yet, but it did make me hopeful.

11

Seven o'clock rolled up on me quickly, and as I walked to the time clock, I saw a note marked, "Janie." Hesitantly I opened it, and it wasn't until then, did I know who it was from. It read, "cum to gas station." Instantly, I was wet, and wanted him worse than ever. I couldn't get out to my car fast enough. As I drove down the road, I reapplied my make-up, and lip gloss. I could see his car parked at the station, and I pulled into a spot, and locked the car up tight. As I walked to his car, I could see him looking me up and down, and he had a smirk on his face. He leaned over the passenger seat, and opened my door for me.

"Hey Gabe," I said as I climbed in. "I got your note." I was blushing. He cupped my face in his hands, and kissed me on the lips.

"I just couldn't be away from you after today. I needed some alone time with you." He kissed me deeply again. "Let's go for a drive, and see where we end up." He smiled, and his whole face lit up. That was exactly how I felt inside.

"Ok, yes. Let's...I'm good as long as I'm with you..." I couldn't believe such heartfelt words had slipped through my lips. That kind of emotion only got me hurt, and I knew this. He started to drive towards the country, and I flipped through radio stations. I stopped idly on Ricky Martin's *Livin' La Vida Loca*, and wiggled in my seat through it.

"I love seeing you like this Janie...especially the smiling." He looked back at the road, and shifted his pants while he was sitting. He needed to pull over somewhere, because his thoughts were not focused on the road. In his head, all he saw was me, on top of him. Under him. Next to him. Touching him. Holding him. Kissing him, and loving him. He pulled into the 24 local supermarket and parked in a secluded spot. That was all he could take, and he had his seatbelt off, and was kneeling on the floor boards in front of me before he exhaled. Now on his knees, he grasped my face and kissed me so hungrily, so desperately, that we both came up gasping for air.

I looked into his eyes, and saw everything I needed. I wrapped my arms around him and pulled him into me. While we were kissing, his hands traveled the lengths of my legs, and back up to my breasts. His hands even felt hungry for me, and I loved it. I felt safe enough in this area with no lights, and under the heavy window tint to let loose. I pushed Gabe back towards the dash, leaned the seat back, and shimmied out of my pants. When I looked up, his cheeks were red, and he was breathing so heavy. It was in instant turn on. I re-lifted my ass in the air, in hopes that he would get the message. He indeed got the message.

He couldn't believe what he was seeing...I was arched, half naked, sprawled out before him. It was all he could do to not become a true cannibal and eat me completely. He slid my panties off, and exposed the treasure he'd been waiting for. He settled my delectable ass back into the seat, and lowered himself towards me. His fingers caressed, and rubbed all of my most secret areas, all that were now throbbing for him. He slid his fingers in, and pushed on the walls of my core. He had to give into temptation, and bent down and locked his mouth over my pussy. *Oh sweet Jesus...*

Instant electricity ran through my body when his mouth hit me. I could barely hold in the convulsions. Every time I looked down, he was looking right at me, lapping up my lust, and my need for him. His tongue was magnificent. *Now you know it's true...some guys have it, and some guys just don't.* Back and forth, top to bottom, inside and out. I was closer to the brink than ever, and I knew that he could tell. He grasped my breast with his free hand, and rolled my nipple back and forth. That was all it took, and I started falling from the cloud I was on. The electricity, and the adrenaline rushing through my body made my body tremble, and my legs shake.

His fingers were still deep inside of me, and he could feel me clenching on him. His dick throbbed for me, and he could feel that his boxers were getting sticky from his own juices. He wanted to take me here, so badly, but didn't want our first time together to be anywhere but a bed. He watched me after I came. My breathing slowly returned to normal, and he watched my half naked chest rise and fall with each breath. He slowly pulled his fingers out of me, and helped me back into my panties and pants. He climbed his way back up to my face, and pulled the lever to adjust my seat back up to normal. Now my face was directly in front of his. He couldn't find the right words, but could only smile at me, wide eyed.

I knew what he was thinking, because I was pretty sure I was thinking the same thing, too. Words were scarce, but these feelings were thick in the air. "Yeah, it was good for me too," I said jokingly, and still out of breath. I couldn't wait to have him, and inside, I knew why we hadn't screwed yet. It needed to be in the perfect place, not a car. But this was really great. My adrenaline was on high, and I was on cloud nine. Gabe leaned over and kissed me deeply.

"You're perfect. In case you were wondering." He hugged me, and got back into his seat. "I'd better get you back to your car, and home." After we both put ourselves back together, he drove me back to my car. As I was getting out, he couldn't stop himself. "Janie, wait…" he reached for me, and pulled me back for one last kiss.

My heart melted. An encore kiss? Oh, I'd need more than one of those. "Gabe…thank you so much for this." I blew him a kiss and closed my door. With the window down as I pulled away, I said, "I can't wait for MORE!!!" And headed home. Feeling the familiar vibration in my pocket, I checked the number on my pager when I came to a light. It was Michael. Of course. *Go home and go to bed. The clearer your mind, your fate you will find.*

Once I got home, I went straight to the three season porch, turned on the radio, and lit up some weed. This was not something that I did with other people at this point, but it really helped chill me out, and quiet the voices in my head. Each inhale I took calmed me more, and more. I had smoked on and off for years, picked it up as an early recreation with friends. The radio was on, and I was living in lyrics like I normally did. *Our time is running out, I won't let you push it underground. I can't stop it screaming out…* Then the pager went off again, and that was all I could take. Time to get this over with. Two rings later, and there he was.

"Janie. Jesus, I thought you'd never call! I was worried sick!" his voice was hesitant, like he was even unsure of where he was going with this. Over the phone, I had no problem of giving it to him more than I would if her were standing in front of me, for obvious reasons. *Yeah, real obvious. Look at your upper arms...* I chuckled. "Why the fuck are you laughing?" now angered.

"Because I don't know why you're worried sick. I went to work, and came home from work. What the hell is worrisome about that?" I couldn't help it. These days the sound of his voice made me want to throw up.

"Where are you now? I want to come and see you." I didn't know what was worse, his tone, or that he wanted to see me.

"I'm home Michael, getting ready for bed. I don't need visitors right now. We can plan something...later in the week." I was not changing my mind on this. I did not want him here, and tonight, I feel like fighting him. I don't know why, but I want to punch him in the throat. "Seriously." I waited.

"I can't believe you don't want to see me. I always want to see you. I guess I'll wait until a later time then." he said slowly.

"Thanks," I really couldn't believe that he agreed that easily. "I'll call soon."

"Yeah, you better." and he hung up. I knew that this would happen. He's like a loose cannon, and he's aimed directly at me. Suddenly, I don't feel as safe in the screened patio. Time to lock up

and head to bed, where I can dream away of my
one true love...

12

There were noises coming from somewhere, and they woke me up at one in the morning. I cautiously got up, and went to my window to check it out. It took me a minute to realize what was happening, but the sunken feeling in my gut gave me the answer I needed. Michael was on the sidewalk, with Walter, throwing rocks at my window. Oh, God. Logic hit me, and I opened the window. "Guys, what are you doing?!" I asked.

"Come down here Janie, I want to talk to you…" Michael said to me, stumbling over himself. "You know you want to see me too!" Oh, lovely. And he was lisping and slurring his words.

"I don't really want to see you when I'm sleeping, because I'M SLEEPING. Come on Mike, go home! I'm not coming down." I was stern, and I wasn't budging.

"Quit being a bitch, and come down here! We just want to say hi!" His voice was growing angrier by the second, and his facial expression was changing, too. He must think I'm fucking crazy to walk down there now.

"I said not right now. I'm going back to bed guys. Good night." I started to close the window, but it was open long enough to catch Michael's last words.

"I'll get you out here one way or another. You can count on that!" I was carefully peeking out of the window, watching their interaction. After he yelled his words, he turned and pointed his finger at my bedroom window for five minutes, and stared at it the entire time. What the hell did that mean? I was so confused. I carefully went downstairs, and verified all of the locks, on all of the doors were securely fastened. I went to the kitchen, and quietly opened the knife drawer, and got the biggest I could find. I watched a little television, and feel back asleep.

13

When I woke up, it was 9:36am. I had to be into work at 11:00, so I went to hit the shower. On my there, I yelled a good morning to my parents, only to find that they were already gone. There was a note, it read: "Have a great day, daughter! Heart, M & D"

I hoped it would be a good day. Time with Gabe would make it a great day. But suddenly reality hit me, and I remembered the threats and what had happened earlier this morning. My head fell into my hands. Back to the shower I went, shaking my head the entire way. I couldn't help but listen to the voices as I let the hot water run down my stressed out body. *So, is he going to be waiting outside? Waiting at work? Will he follow you? What does this all mean? You did a good job not going downstairs last night. Considering his last words to you, you know exactly how that would've ended.* I wasn't sure that talking to myself really gave me any extra answers, but it made me feel better in the moment.

After my shower, I was getting dressed when I heard the first of the noises. There were footsteps from what sounded like the basement, coming upstairs. I was pretty sure I was losing my mind, so went about drying my hair. It was now 10:06am. I was almost done drying my hair, when I heard a noise again. This time I swore I heard voices, too. Enough, it was time to go figure this out. I decided to put my shoes on too, so I wouldn't have to come back upstairs in case my parents were home. As I rounded the top of the stairs to head down, I thought I saw someone quickly walk through the kitchen. When I walked in the kitchen, there was no one. Not a noise, nothing out of place. *Maybe it's just your paranoia starting to come out in different ways? I think it's time to start checking in when you're going from place to place... just a thought.* I shook my head as if to declare that idea dead, when all of the sudden, I got knocked into the cabinets in front of me. There was no time to determine what had happened, but that someone or something had just cracked my head open on the wooden cabinets, and blood was running down my temple. I put my hand to my head, before I turned around to see what was happening. The hair on my neck raised, as I could feel the presence come closer.

"I warned you, bitch." He grabbed my hair, and forced my face down onto the kitchen tile. "I told you I'd come back to get what you owed me, so here I am. Time to collect." He pushed his thumb into the gash on the side of the head. It felt like a knife reshaping me through my skull. My head was throbbing, and the room was spinning. I didn't know what to do. He held my hands behind my back, and lifted my shirt over my head. He unbuttoned my jeans, and pulled them off, and threw them across the room. Next I felt burning, but I couldn't place where until I smelled the skin burning, and felt the pain. He was using my leg an as ashtray to snuff out his cigarette. "I'm so fucking tired of this, Janie! This is the only way you'll pay attention to me! It's not fair! I'm tired of being last on your list!" He spun me around so I could see his face. "I shouldn't have to tell you that you're mine, and I'm not sharing. Ever. If anyone tries, I'll take you away from them for good." His smile went crooked, into the infamous joker smile. I wanted to throw up.

I tried to stand up, but he only pushed me back down. I wished that if he was going to do this, he would just get it the fuck over with already. "I want you out of here, NOW, Michael." I said firmly. I could tell almost instantly that my one comment had pushed him over his tiny cliff, and I was in for it now. *Ok, or maybe you should've kept your mouth shut? Where are the neighbors when you need them?*

He smacked me across the face, and flipped me back over. He ripped my underwear off, and it hurt so bad. The snapping fabric split right by my most sensitive parts, and I could no longer hold back the tears. He was still holding my head into the tile, with his thumb digging into my shoulder blade. He had trouble getting into me, and this time the pressure from the forceful pushing was killing me. The hurt was indescribable, like nothing before. My body was rejecting him in every possible way, and it disgusted me that he was getting off on all of this. Every thrust made me cry louder, and every time I cried louder, his hand pushed my head into the ground harder. I could see the puddle of blood from my forehead on the ground, and felt it all over my cheek. My crotch was hot with hate, and I wished that he would continue to be the two-minute man. Just as I was giving up the hope of being saved by the light, he pulled out, and got up. He left me lay there as he walked away.

I didn't know what to do, or if I could or should move. I could hear that he had gone upstairs, to the bathroom. *Do something! Run! Call the police! Anything! GET OFF THE GODDAMN GROUND!* Yes, I must get up. Slowly I struggle to put my pants back on to cover myself. Once I was up, my head really started to spin. I tried to keep myself composed so that he wouldn't know the affect he was having, but I doubted that the blood on my face would cover that. I was facing the kitchen window, looking out to my old swing set. Wishing that life didn't include stupid shit like this, when I heard him exhale, and chuckle.

"You're such a stupid slut!" He shook his head, and crossed his arms over his chest. "You'll always give me what's mine. End of story." He looked me up and down, and added, "you look horrible. Fix your shit before you leave. And same as always, you tell, you suffer." He turned, unlocked the front door, opened it, and left. I was frozen in place, too afraid to move.

Ten minutes later, sense rejoined me, and I looked at the clock. It was only 10:38am. I slowly walked over to the small mirror, and saw the gash. It wasn't huge, and easily hid in my hairline. I cleaned up, and reapplied my makeup. I had the world's biggest headache, and I knew this day was going to suck. I grabbed my wallet, and my keys, and numbly walked out to my car. I was overwhelmed with so many emotions while I drove, and I did my best to keep them all safely locked up inside. I needed to talk to someone. I needed out of this situation, sooner rather than later. I knew all of this, but still something prevented me from taking the actions I needed to. *What's holding you back now is only fear. And I get it, completely. His temper has been worse these past few months, and you've ended up more battered than this ever started out to be. Add breaking and entering into his check list, too. Be brave, speak up. Someone will hopefully listen...*

14

I drove into the parking lot, and pulled into the closest space I could find. I had to close tonight, and I wanted to get out of there as fast as I could. The next few days I had swim meets, so I would have some much needed alone time. Just thinking about that was very refreshing, and I smiled a little. The first person I saw when I walked in was Heather. My best friend of ten years, she knew me better than I knew myself. She saw the look on my face, and instantly frowned and headed in my direction. I could see that she was looking me up and down, checking me over for new marks and bruises. When she was close enough to hug, I burst out crying.

"Oh Janie!!! No!!!" Her hug was tight, and she wouldn't let go. It was just what I needed then. "Honey, you have got to get out of this situation!" She urged quietly. I could feel her hands inspecting my neck, and she sighed heavily.

"What is it?" I managed out through the tears.

"You've got… Finger prints on your neck…" Her eyes filled with tears, and I could no longer look her in the eye. Not thinking, I tipped my head down to look away from her. "OH MY GOD JANIE!" she spontaneously yelled. "What the FUCK did HE do to YOU!?!" I could feel her fingers ever so gently trace over the gash in my hairline., and I sighed. And cried more. The commotion from Heather yelling drew attention to us, and Simon and Gabe came running over.

"Hey Janes," Simon paused. "What's wrong Heather? Everything ok?" he hesitantly asked. Simon and Heather had been my only supports since things had gone bad between Michael and I. They both understood the whole situation, and that leaving wasn't as easy when all of our ties were connected, so to speak. "Another bad night?" Simon's face changed, as he was realizing what had happened.

"Look at what he did to her! Look at her head!" Heather pointed out the gash in my hairline to both of them. I couldn't hold in my sobs, and so unexpectedly within seconds, Gabe wrapped me up in his arms. They thought I had cried before that, no, I was really crying now. Slowly he picked me up, and carried me to the back room. Heather and Simon followed closely behind.

"Janie," Gabe started. "I'm worried about you. I want to help." he paused, and rubbed his hands together. "However I can. I'm here for you…I hope you know that." He lifted my chin with his finger, and made me look at him in the eyes.

"Same goes for Simon, and I, sister." Heather said with a big smile. "I want my old Janie back. Not this pitiful, crying excuse of a woman." She gently punched me in the shoulder.

"Owww." I said, with little humor. Then I mustered a wink, so she would know I was kidding. I tried to collect myself, and I sighed hard. "Even though I feel really shitty right now, I'm really lucky that my three favorite people are here." I looked at the floor, not believing what was going to come out next. "It's time for me to make my move. I want to be away from him." I looked back up at my closest friends, and my secret love. I saw strength, hope, devotion, love, and trust in their eyes. I went on, "this is not going to be easy. He's been giving me small samples of how un-easy this is going to be. I've thought about this more than you all can even imagine, and I feel safe enough with you guys, that..." I stopped and got teary.

"Hey baby, it's alright. Take your time." Gabe was there, stroking my back and neck. He always knew just what to do to ease my pain, and it was working. I wondered if he had seen the marks on my neck, and I instinctively tried to pull away from him. "No, that won't work. I saw them already. Those marks aren't you though. You have to know that." He put his forehead to mine. "I mean it. Please don't doubt me."

I understood his gesture, but in my present state, those marks were me. All of me that I could see, and those marks were taking over my life. I shook the thoughts out of my head. "I want the three of you to know that I appreciate that you're always there for me. I'm going to be working on ending it with him over the next few weeks, and..." Simon cut me off.

"Why weeks? Janie? Weeks? How about a day?" He looked pained, and I understood why. God, I must've sounded like a lunatic right now, and this was almost impossible to understand.

"It's weeks because that's how Michael works. It's going to take me weeks to wean myself away from him, or him away from me, rather. I know this is hard to understand, and yes I know the risk." I exhaled. I tried to straighten my back, to seem confident about this. "Please just trust me on this. I just need you to be here, just as you are. That's all I ask." I was met by three sets of eyes, and three nodding heads. They all agreed. *Oh, thank GOD you've got better choices in your friends, (and true lovers) than you do boyfriends!* "Oh, guys... thank you." I reached for Simon, and hugged him first. "You've been like a brother, thank you for sticking by me." I turned to Heather, and put my hands on her face, and looked her in the eye. "I love you," I said, and leaned in to hug her. Lastly, I turned to Gabe, and he instantly swept me into his arms.

"I'm here. Always." he kissed the side of my neck, and buried his face into my shoulder. I could've stayed in that hug forever, for days, weeks even. But work had to be done, and we had all sat around enough.

"Ok! This therapy session is closed. Back to work!" I giggled, as everyone dissipated. I went into my office, and closed the door. I turned on the radio, turned on my computer, and began the invoices. Fiona Apple was blaring Never is a Promise, and I couldn't help live the lyrics for a few minutes. So far, this was working out exactly like I needed it to. I just hoped that the upcoming separation wouldn't kill me, so to speak. The work day flew by, and ended without a hitch. I was so glad for this, for once. I had swim meets the next few days, and wouldn't be at work. Gabe had already left for the day, but I wanted to slip him a note so he would get it in the morning. I sat at my desk thinking of just how to say what I needed. "Gabe, I won't be at work for the next few days. Only due to a few meets, and apartment hunting. I'll be back on Sunday. I'd like to do something with you then, or maybe Monday. Whatever's best for you. Maybe at your place? Here's my pager number- 555-9856 use it whenever. ☺" I didn't want to seem too... Needy? Pushy? Desperate? Oh, but for him, I was. "I'm looking very much forward to seeing you, and I miss you already. Xo, J" and I folded it up, and slipped it inside his locker. And out the doors I went. I needed to get lots of sleep to prepare for my busy days that were coming up.

15

It was Friday, and the biggest day of the series of swim meets yet. I had qualified the past two days to swim today, and I was so excited. Not only that, but it was my birthday, too. I was finally twenty-one. Legal for all intents and purposes. In the locker room, I slid my suits on. My team suit was so tight to cut the water drag, but I was pretty sure it was also cutting off my circulation. Of course very worth it, as I was sure that the suit alone was cutting my times down each time.

I put on my swim cap, and it snapped right over my cabinet injury. "Fuck!" I muttered to myself. The wound had closed decently, and there was a scab on it now. Luckily it was covered by hair, so still reasonably unnoticeable. Especially now that it wasn't swollen. *It's been so peaceful these last few days. Work, swimming, and best of all, no Michael! Your future is starting to open up a little, isn't it?* I couldn't help smile a little. It had been days since I had seen Michael, and each day without him around, I found myself breathing a little easier. I checked the mirror before I left the locker room, mainly to make sure all my important parts were covered. I looked at my face, and my eyes looked a little brighter. I checked the time, and turned toward the natatorium.

I found my mom and dad in the crowd quickly, and waved at them. I checked the clock, I had seven minutes until my heat was up. My biggest and best event, the 200 freestyle. I went to sit on the warm up bench to wait my turn, and I couldn't stop the thoughts about Gabe. It had been days, and I missed him like no other. *Your dreams are about him. You can't go an hour without his beautiful face popping in your head. Your heart aches for him...* Oh my, yes it did. Right now, in fact. I shook the thought off. Time to swim, and my first adult swim. I sighed loudly as they called my heat. I glanced at my parents, and saw Simon sitting with them. I smiled huge, and waved! *How sweet!!! I can't believe a friend came to see you!!* I smiled to myself.

I took my block, and started to lengthen my breathing. I loved the power that being on the block brought. It was up to me to prove myself. A race against myself, and I couldn't help but compare it to my current situations. My toes curled perfectly around the rough edges of the block, and I put my feet in place. *Tides are turning...* I bent over, and grasped the block with my hands, and toes now. *Things are going to get better...* "Swimmers take your mark..." *Time to be true to yourself, and no one else...* The gun shot, and I was in the water faster than a bullet's shot from a gun. My focus was swimming away from the pain. From the hate. From the disrespect. Swimming away from him, and back towards myself, and living my life. Most importantly, how I wanted to, with my own choices. *100 to go!!! You're in the lead!!!* My flip turn was perfect, flawless and fast. I came off of that spin remembering I was now twenty-one, an adult. That meant Gabe, and suddenly, I was going even faster.

I could hear my dad's voice, cheering in the crowd. I could hear my coach's voice, screaming his goofy chants to keep my speed. But the loudest voice was now my own, screaming at me to live my life how I wanted to, which at this moment, was so clear that it was no longer with Michael. *You've done it, Janie!!* I slammed my fingertips into the wall, and spun quickly to see my time. First place, and it meant so much, on so many levels. I caught my breath, before walking into my family and friends waiting congratulations and arms.

After I had changed, and emerged from the locker room, I was rejoined by my parents, and Simon. "Hey honey," my mom yelled. "We've got a small surprise for your birthday. Just a little birthday dinner with some family and friends." she smiled a little, and we all started walking out to the car. I was surprised to see that Simon was all smiles, and coming right along with us. My mom must have noticed my surprise, and she squeezed my shoulder. "Of course Simon is coming! So are a few of your other friends, too!" She hugged me with one arm, "I'm so proud of you. First place, again..." she sighed.

"Thanks for arranging this mom. I know it's going to be a great time." I couldn't help but wonder, in the very back of my mind, just who all was coming to this little celebration. I was almost to the car, and Simon tapped my shoulder. I could tell he needed to talk for a second, so I broke the hold of my mom, and said "Hey mom, give me just a second!" I turned to Simon, and he was all smiles.

"Janie! That was the best meet ever! I'm so glad your parents invited me!!" He paused, and punched my shoulder. "Why is it that your PARENTS had to invite me?! All this time, I would've been a GREAT cheering team!!" He was laughing hard.

"Oh Simon, thanks for being there today. It was really nice to have you guys up there. Even better that I could hear you while I was swimming!" I said, and added, "I don't normally invite anyone to my meets, but my parents. It's always just been "my" thing, and no one but them have ever showed any interest." I shrugged. And then I couldn't hold back the smile. "But you can come whenever you want! How's that? A permanent invitation." I was elated when he smiled back.

"That's perfect, Janie." He gave me a high five, and said "I'm going to meet you at the restaurant. After, you want to go shoot some pool or something?" Simon knew that this was a long shot, but after my admissions at work, he was determined within himself to be there whenever I needed anything. I was more appreciate of this than he would ever understand.

"Yes! I'd love to! Now, let's go. I worked up an appetite." I winked, and climbed into my mom's BMW. The ride to dinner was filled with chatter of my perfect swim meet, work, friends, and future plans. My parents were okay with the fact that I wasn't sure which direction that I was going yet, but that I was indeed working towards moving out.

"We'll always support your decisions, honey. You know that, and we're always here whenever you need us. Now, let's go have some fun!" She said with a giggle.

16

Once I climbed out of the car, I fully understood what was happening with this dinner situation. A crowd of people were suddenly singing "Happy Birthday," but all I could focus on was the mix of friends in front of me. Their eyes were all locked on to me, but the pair I could feel the most were his. Michael stood with Sean, Preston, and Walter. With Walter, was his girlfriend. Next to them was Heather, and her boyfriend. And Simon. And my oldest friend, Nichole, who I rarely got to see anymore, and missed terribly. This was going to be interesting, to say the least. But I couldn't help smile that they had all come to my birthday dinner, just for me. Secretly I swallowed the fact that the person I missed most wasn't here...

My parents had reserved the back room for the group, and we fit in nicely. I sat next to Simon and Nichole. Across from me sat Michael, and his followers all sat around him. I could feel him keep looking at me, trying to catch my gaze. And I knew why, too. I was not going to let him ruin this day for me, not if I could help it anyway.

"So Janie! It's been forever!!" Nichole said, as she leaned in for a hug. "I was so glad when your mom called and invited me!! She told me about your meet today, too!! I always knew you'd kill it in the pool, girl." She winked at me.

"I'm so glad to see you, too!! We need to catch up sometime. I've got about a year's worth of stuff to update you on!" I smiled, and it was so true. We'd been friends our whole lives, but these past few years had been tough, as we both went to different high schools. Even though our lives were taking us in very different directions, I knew she'd always be one of my closest, most dependable friends. I watched the conversation around the table, and for the most part, everyone was getting along. I felt Simon kick me under the table, and I looked up to meet his gaze.

"So, Janes... Wow, the swimming today. Whew. FAST. I had no idea..." he chuckled, and nodded in Michael's direction. *I really enjoyed his emphasis on 'F'...this one's a keeper.* "Good to finally meet you in person. Michael, right?" He extended his hand to Michael, and I held my breath for what would come next.

"Yes. I'm Michael, her boyfriend. You must be..." he said, asking quizzically.

"Simon. I work with Janie at Phoenix." Simon nudged my arm with his elbow, and added, "she's great. We all love her there!!" I knew exactly what he was up to, and I almost wanted to punch him for it.

"Oh? I'm sure you all do love her. Or, at least one of you, specifically..." as his voice trailed off, and his eyes darted around the table, I could tell it was going to start happening. The knot in my stomach was growing, and I hoped that no one would utter a word about Gabe. "Speaking of your coworkers, aren't we missing one very important one?" He smiled his joker smile, and looked directly at me. I swallowed hard.

"Oh, yeah..." Simon answered quickly. "There's a few of us missing from this dinner that love her like our own family." *Good answer,* my conscious sighed. Thank God for friends. Simon raised his eyebrow, and held his firm stare at Michael. I could tell that Michael was getting uneasy, and so could his followers.

I could tell that dinner was wrapping up, as conversation was growing thin with many. I couldn't help speed things along. "Well, I just want to say thanks to everyone for coming out and enjoying my birthday with me. I don't feel much different being a year old, and now legal." I held up my drink, a cosmopolitan, smiling. Here was where I again held my breath. "Tonight I'm going to spend my evening with friends, and then head home. I'm exhausted after the meet!" I started going from person to person, giving hugs, thanks, and sharing brief memories. Simon moved with me, and met each person that I said goodbye to. We finally got around the table, to my parents, and Michael.

"Oh honey, what a wonderful day for you! I'm just so proud of the woman you've become!!" My mom hugged me like she hadn't seen me in years.

"Same goes for me, Janes!" yelled my dad, as he got a running start and almost tackled me in the restaurant.

"Thanks guys. It was a great day today, with the meet, and then dinner. I'm going to head out with Simon for a while, and then I'll be home." I smiled, and turned to see Michael's face beet red. He had indeed heard what I said, but being that my parents and friends were close by, he hands and lips were sealed for now. Thank my lucky stars.

"Janie," Michael started. He looked up as he heard the anger in his own words. I noticed then that Nichole, Heather, and Simon were all at my side, and they had heard it, too. I looked back at Michael, with a slight smirk, and then it was on. His smile turned to a thin, stern line. He meant business. "I'd like to give the birthday girl her spankings before she goes out with her friends." I'd never heard so much emphasis put on the 'f' in friends before. "Come on over here, Janie." He pulled me into his arms, and started to slowly walk away from the group. Into my ear this time, as to not repeat his mistake, "now you're going out with that sorry excuse for a boy?! I have to sit through dinner looking at him?? Let me guess, he's friends with your work lover, too?!" His grip was excruciatingly tight, and tears were starting to prick my eyes.

"Yes, Michael." I quickly yanked my arm free, and took two quick steps backward. My voice raised, to draw atterftion to us. "I am going out with my FRIENDS now. If I'm not out too late, I'll call." I made sure to emphasis the 'f' just as he had, tit for tat. "See you later." I winked, and almost sprinted to Simon's car. I heard him take a few quick, hard steps, but then they stopped. Once I was safely in, I melted into the seat, and turned to peer out the window. Sean was holding Michael's shoulders in the parking lot, and I could see from there how hard Michael was breathing. *Nice one, Janes. Get him all riled up, then leave!* I was scoping out my new finger marks on my arm when Simon got in.

17

"Did he get you bad?" he asked without any hesitation. His face looked pained, but pleased. I imagined that my own faced matched his.

"Just got a few death grips in before I could get away. He was soo mad, Si." I shook the thoughts out of my head. "Thanks for agreeing to movie night at your place. I just really need some relaxing time. No pressure, you know?" I smiled, and felt my pager go off. The number I didn't recognize, but saved it to call back once I got to Simon's.

"I could tell he was mad. He really doesn't hide it well." He sighed loudly, and shook his head. "It was hard to watch. And I could tell he hated me, and Janie," he turned and looked at me directly in my eyes. "If it ever comes up, you tell him the feelings are mutual." He smiled huge.

Once we were at Simon's, I went for the phone. It rang twice before there was an answer.

"Hello?" an unrecognizable voice said on the line.

"Uhh, hi. Someone paged me with this number?" I was hoping that I wasn't crazy. I hated phones, and hated asking for people.

"Oh, yeah. Hang on, please." I could hear the commotion in the background, and whispered voices. I could've sworn I heard the voices say "it's your girl" to someone, and I could feel my face go from calm, to confused. Then the phone was moving.

"Hello? Janie?" My mouth fell open. "Happy birthday, baby." I could hear him smiling.

"Gabe?!" I couldn't contain my excitement. It was lucky for him this was over the phone, because I would've been all over him if he were in front of me.

"Yes, that was our house number. Thought I'd make you wonder who it was, until you called it back." He chuckled. "So, tell me about your day. I hope it was wonderful." I was back on cloud nine, just as Simon brought me a water bottle, and turned on some music.

"My day was great, and this phone call is like the cherry on top." I giggled. "I'm at Simon's now, just breathing for a little bit. My meet went very well... first place." I paused, I wasn't good at talking about myself like this. Gabe made me feel so...appreciated.

"First place?!" His voice was cracking at the seams. "I wish I could've been there to see you kick all their asses! That's so awesome, sweet cheeks." I loved the jittery sound of his voice. "And you're 21 now, huh? What did you have to drink" I heard the chuckle.

"Thanks, and yep. Perfectly legal, and I think it was a cosmopolitan." I paused, and noticed I was breathing slightly heavier than normal. "There's only one thing missing from today. One thing that it's getting pretty hard to be away from..." Did I really just say that? *Yeah, that was you.*

"Really? Well..." he tried to sound convincing. "I'd like to reserve your Monday night, if you're still open. I've got a few ideas I'd like to go over, like Cosmo's maybe, on Sunday, at work." he waited for the answer. I was busting at my own seams at this point.

"Monday is on, for sure. In fact, I wish it were Sunday now. Listen, I'd better go for now. Don't want to be mean to Simon. What're you doing this weekend?" I'd never asked him that before, and I was sort of in shock that I had just asked that now.

"I can't wait to spend more time with you on Monday. You're right, it does seem pretty far away." he paused. "Not too much going on this weekend. Family stuff tomorrow for a bit, then I may go out tomorrow night. I'm very glad I got to

talk to you today, and wish you a happy birthday."
He was doing that cute voice-smile thing again.

"I'm really glad you paged. Thanks for thinking of me today." *You should probably know I dream about you constantly, and now that I'm 21... Well, what's holding me back?* "I can't wait to see you..." I said. I didn't want to get off the phone with him.

"Right back at ya, baby. I'm going to dream of you now. Sleep tight."

"Good night, Gabe." My cheeks flushed, and I sighed loudly. My body sank into the chair, as Simon and I both relaxed to the Led Zeppelin on the radio.

"That made your night, didn't it?" Simon giggled, and threw a pillow at my head. He was so right; it had made my night. As I drove home that night, I couldn't erase the smile. It wasn't very late, but I was exhausted. Once home, I went out to the patio to have a quick smoke and to call Michael. He answered the phone so fast, I didn't even hear it ring.

"Hello?" he answered with a slur.

"Hey, Mike." I didn't really have more than that. The awkward silence went on forever.

"So, how were your friends?" his voice told me that he was angry, and I could hear his restraint. Or, attempted restraint, so far.

"They were good. Just hung out really. I'm home now, and going to head to bed." I said as firmly as I could. I hoped that he would stay away. I was tired from the swim, and the birthday festivities. All I really wanted to do was dream about Gabe.

"Listen, Janie." Oh good Lord. What on earth...I couldn't wait to hear where this was going to go. "I really need to talk to you. It's important to me." His voice was anxious, and that made me nervous...and weak.

"What do we need to talk about exactly?" I wondered if I should even ask.

"Us, Janie." He sighed loudly into the phone, and I couldn't gage his mood. "How about tomorrow? We've got practice...the guys would love it if you came out and listened to us. It's been awhile since you've done that, you know." *Right, it's been a few weeks. Since the last time you wanted me to watch band practice. I remember how THAT ended.* "And I really miss you. I think I'm having withdraw symptoms.." He waited for my response. But nothing was coming out. Every thought I had was whirring through my head. *You miss me now? Why now? Is he on to the plan? Is he just trying to drag this out and make the inevitable take forever...oh god, I hope not. What if this is your chance to end it all?* I sighed heavily.

"I suppose we could meet up for a little bit. I'll come out to band practice for a while. But," it was out before I could stop it. "If you start in with your...behavior, I'm out. End of story." I waited, and hoped the response would be okay.

"Fine, that's fair. Thanks, Janie. I'll see you tomorrow then." His voice was calm, and for once, I didn't feel the awkwardness.

"Alright, good night." I was quick to hang up the phone, as these kind of mellow conversation endings were so rare. I finished my smoke, and headed up to bed. My eyes were closed within seconds, and I was back with Gabe, in my own personal, safe dream land.

18

I woke up Saturday morning to a note from my parents reminding me of their mini vacation. Their jobs had always taken them on out of state business trips, far away meetings, and just terrible schedules all through my growing up. I was pretty use to it now, and didn't mind spending time alone. I took the opportunity of the quiet to search the internet for apartments, or other living arrangements. The radio was blaring, the windows were open, and I couldn't help belt out the song Tangled while I typed away. The words of the song really hit me this time around, and I started thinking about my upcoming meeting with Michael. *...I never thought I'd feel this doubting. Oh, baby I'm so tangled... it was never ever meant to be... riptides of emotion are drowning me...*

It was time to get ready, so I headed up to shower. I couldn't place the feelings I was having, and it was all starting to make me rethink my decisions. I just wanted to be done dealing with his psychotic self, and I just needed to keep reminding myself of that. I zipped up my jeans, and buttoned up my sweater. I grabbed a small bag of stuff, as sometimes practice got a little boring. My book, water, purse, and mace all went into the bag. *Mace? Look at you, finally looking out for you.* I smiled at myself without hesitation. I threw it in the car, and headed out to the barn.

When I pulled on to the drive, I could see more cars than normal parked by the boys' vehicles. I was perplexed, but figured that they had just invited more friends to check them out. As I continued down the drive, as if it were a sign from the radio gods, one of my all-time favorite bands came on, playing 'Don't Speak." *Stop with the confusing thoughts! He's not your best friend! He hurts you, you're terrified of him! You don't need more reason than that...* "Our memories, they could be inviting, but somewhere all together mighty frightening." I put my head against the head rest as the words whispered out of my mouth. I parked, and turned the car off. I decided to have a quick smoke, before anyone figured out I was there. I quietly got out, and sat on my trunk. The band was loudly playing, and the drums were beating away. I could tell by the double bass thumping away, that he was doing what he loved. They loved redoing oldies, Guns and Roses, and a mish mash of everything else. Although, loud, obnoxious rock was by far their favorite. This time it was 'Faith," and again, I was singing along with them playing. "...from that emotion, time to pick my heart up off the floor...love comes down without devotion..." I shook my head at the loud scream singing, done by the guitarist. My smoke was out, and it was time to go in.

Entering into the barn was like walking in a "young adult" bar. Smoke filled air, empty bottles everywhere. Someone always brought a make shift bar, for "mixed" drinks. I loved the music, but had a hard time dealing with the people. A big stage, with speakers, amps, and every kind of instrument you can imagine. Microphones galore. Lights hung awkwardly from rafters, and they sort of resembled large holiday lights. I swung the door open, and was hit by the heat coming out. I searched around, seeing that almost the entire group was there. Even with all of their significant others. I saw Sean first, and went to say hello.

"Sean! Hey!" I hugged him, probably a little too closely. "How're you doing?" I was surprised that I was happy to see him.

"Hey Jane," he rubbed his forehead. "I'm good. Glad you came tonight." He looked me in the eye, and turned his gaze toward Michael, who was busily beating away on the drums. I could see the beads of sweat pouring off of him, and he caught my gaze, and winked at me. "Did you talk to Mike yet?" he turned back towards me.

"No, not yet. Just walked in. Sort of curious to see what it's all about, really." I couldn't help my tone, but I knew that this was no secret to Sean. I shrugged, and patted his shoulder. "Let's make the best of whatever this night holds." I smiled at him, and headed to get a drink. On my way over, the song finished, and the set broke. I imagined that the time was drawing near. Just at that moment, I felt a hand on my shoulder.

"Hey," he said. His hand was gently placed on my shoulder, as if he were treating me like I was breakable. "I decided to make it a party." He pointed around the room at the extra people.

"I see that. I'm sure they're all enjoying the music." I had to give him that. They were decent at music, and that part did make for a festive evening. "What're you guys playing next?" I smiled at him.

"Well…" he paused. "That's sort of a surprise. Are you…up for the mic?" He looked at me, and smiled the joker grin. I instantly raised an eyebrow, and cocked my head to the side. *Is this for real? He doesn't share the limelight. Ever. Did hell freeze over?*

"Michael, I don't think that's a good idea. I don't want to fight with you tonight, and that always ends up with fighting!" I couldn't hide my growing uncertainty.

"Janie, look at me." He was slightly firmer with his hand, and turned me back toward his face. I could smell the whiskey, but he was very calm. "I'm serious. I want you up there with me. I know how much you love it, and…" he stopped. Smiled very big, and continued, "I know I'm a dick. I've got issues, and I want to fix them. It's not going to happen overnight, but I can do it. For you, anyway." He brushed my cheek with his hand, and I couldn't help pulling away.

"Whoa, Michael..." I stepped back. *Is this happening?* "I'd love to share the stage with you...it's been so long." I paused, and inhaled then exhaled slowly. "But I think we need to talk about the rest later." I could see the look on his face changing, and he was trying so hard to keep his control. Trying to deflect the situation, I asked, "So, when are we on?" and smiled as big as I could. I saw his expression change, it swung with my energy. The crowd of people started to cheer, and chant for the band to come back. He took my hand, and led us back up to stage.

Walking on to the stage, and facing the crowd of forty brought me the rush just like my swim meets. I longed for those butterflies, *and they really helped me fly away from the bad...* The lights were hot, and bright. The rest of the barn looked so dark from out there. That helped confirm how much of me Michael could really see when he was playing. I couldn't believe this was all happening. This wasn't the usual Michael, and I couldn't help but wonder if he was really attempting to change things. I headed straight for the microphone, and repositioned it to my size. The band surrounded, and started to discuss the song selection. I knew most all of the songs, so I wasn't too worried on their choice.

"I think we should do some GNR..." Preston suggested. "It always sounds better with Jane." He waited for responses.

"GNR, or Kid? Or..." Michael turned to me. "Maybe you've got an idea?" He cocked the joker smile, and I suddenly knew this was a game. *Singing? AND choosing the song? I hope this clears up any doubt you may have had that his intentions were...normal.* I was slightly astonished, as were the rest of the band, that he had ever even let those words escape his mouth.

"I, uhh...let me think a second." I leaned on the mic, and closed my eyes. One pick, one song to sing...and so many choices. I just let my thoughts flow, and they were instantly at work, in cars, and in his eyes. I swore, that in that moment, I could smell him in the air. Gabe would never know this, but this song was going to be for him. And a little for me, too. "I've got it! Let's do 'Picture'!! Everyone knows that one well." I glanced at Preston, who was nodding, as was everyone else. I turned to Michael, whose face was suddenly ashen.

"Whoa, 'Picture' huh? Deep one, Janes." He reached for his sticks, and headed for his stool. He grabbed his microphone and began to speak to the crowd. "Alright friends, looks like we've got a little duet for you this evening. Our guest singer has returned to help us entertain you TONIGHT!" His voice bellowed with excitement. *Is that...happiness that you're there? No. I couldn't have been. This is so confusing.* "Alright, boys, let's go." He turned to me, and smiled. "You ready, Janie?"

"Mm hmmm" I responded into the microphone. The music started, and I got comfortable on my stool. The smoke in the air was thick, and I glanced over at Michael as he started to sing. I knew that he understood this song, and that made me feel a little bad. But only a little. My mouth opened, and it all flowed out. "...everyone knows but they won't tell..." I was singing my heart out, and it felt so amazing. "...I put your picture away. I wonder where you've been. I can't look at you while I'm lying next to him..." The emotion was pouring out in my words, and a glance at the crowd showed me that they were into it, too. Looking towards Michael during the instrumental showed me he was pained. The V shape on his forehead was very prominent.

"...you've reminded me of brighter days..." he sang, and I filled the holes myself.

He stared at me deeply, as if this were telling him truths that he had hoped would disappear. "...I swear I've changed my ways...I just called to say I want you, to come back home..." as we both repeated the lyrics, I stared blankly into his face. For such an emotional song, there wasn't much looking back at me. *See, Janie...only a game for him. Just nice, normal manipulations to get what he wants.* And somehow I was okay with that, which reminded me quickly of the issue at hand. Sometime tonight we'd talk, and I could be done with this. He stood to stand, and speak. I clapped along with the crowd. What an amazing feeling this was, and I wished that there was some way to keep this as a part of my life. "Give it up for Janie everybody!!" The crowd cheered, and clapped.

"Thanks everyone!!" This feeling was amazing. I loved the cheering, and now they were all chanting, "encore!" I turned towards Michael, who was shaking his head in disbelief.

"I can't believe this Janie...how about one more song? Then we can talk?" He motioned to the guys to come join in on song discussion. "I'm picking this one, then I'm taking a break, and Sean can sit in for a while." The band all agreed with Mike, and Sean joined the group.

"Hey Janes! That was amazing!! You need to join practice more!" He said exuberantly.

"Yeah, she does. That way we could be together more." He darted his stare towards Sean, who just looked at the ground. "Let's not forget our roles, here, friends." He fidgeted with his stick bag, and pulled out the special black set. "I think we'll play...Stairway to Heaven." Everyone nodded, and resumed their places. The music started pretty quickly, I absolutely loved the song. He looked my direction one last time before we started to sing, and it was blank. I was surprised he had chosen this song, as it had special meaning to me.

With a more upbeat song, movement was necessary, and I found myself dancing, singing, and shaking my tambourine. There was a silence coming from the crowd as they fell into the trap of our version of the song. The version of the song that let me pour my heart into the music, and my soul into the night. Few had heard us perform this, and he knew of my anxiety. I looked up at him, and shook my head. He opened the first verse, and I closed my eyes to fall into the music.

As if I were on auto pilot, the words just flowed freely from my lips. No extra thought, no extra pressure...just beautiful music. Looking around at the smiles, and the dancing, and my friends up playing music with me, it was amazing. I turned towards Michael as I belted out my favorite verse. "...yes, there are two paths you can go by, but in the long run. There's still time to change the road you're on...mmmm....it makes me wonder..." The chants and cheers kept me going strong, and I was on fire. In the instrumental, I turned to take a quick drink of water, and met Michael's gaze.

"You having fun showing off?" he asked, in the most distant, hateful voice I had heard for hours. *Hmm, a sneak peek of what your evening looks like? Lovely...* I could feel my mouth fall open slightly, and my eyes wince a little. The song was almost over, just another verse to go.

"No, Michael. Stop it." I said firmly, and turned back towards the crowd, as if nothing had happened. I pushed through my sudden discomfort, and got through the rest of the song. No matter what happened after this point- I'd always remember it, and getting to cross this off of my bucket list.

19

Some of the guys' girlfriends came over after we finished to chat, and I idly attempted to make conversation. Only waiting for Michael, so that we could go talk. Someone handed me a drink, and I drank it within seconds. It was strong, and I shuddered. I saw Michael coming towards us, and I parted the group to meet him. "Excuse me girls, I've got to be going. It was great seeing you all." I waved as I walked away, and towards Michael.

"Come, Janie. Let's go for a walk." He reached his hand out, and took my hand in his. He started walking toward the gazebo, by the pond. He stepped up onto the stairs, and assisted me up into the wooden swing in the dark. He sat down first, and pulled me down next to him. He stopped touching me, and in the dark, it felt like he was miles away. "I can't believe you acted like that in front of our friends." I heard him exhale, and the swing moved as he shifted around.

"I'm not sure what you mean, Michael. You asked me to sing with you." I could feel my walls start to go up around me, and my anxiety was climbing.

"Sing! Yes! Dance like a hooker?! Flirt with the...whole crowd?!" his voice got louder and louder. I couldn't take it any longer.

"Michael stop!" I said, almost pleading. "I don't want to do this anymore...all this fighting, I'm just so tired of it." The swing was still, and I couldn't hear him breathe anymore. "Don't you ever just want a normal relationship?" My thoughts ran wild. *Keep going, Janie. Get it all out while you can. You can do this.* "Don't you want me to be here because I want to be? Not because I'm forced to be?" I could feel the tears coming to my eyes, and I couldn't hold them back. "I'm just not going to do this anymore, Mike. If your behavior doesn't change..." I sniffed my nose, and was suddenly cut off.

The swing shifted, and suddenly I could feel his body heat right next to me. Every hair on my body rose, and a chill went through my body. Before I could cover, or protect myself, his hand was around my throat, and his mouth was next to my ear. He wasn't choking me, yet, but holding steady pressure that made me unable to move, or swallow. His breathing was rough, and he was starting to chuckle to himself. He drew a long breath in, and I closed my eyes and wished for the best.

"You're not doing this anymore?" He breathed heavily in between sentences. "You think this is your choice, if you want to do this, or not?

You think I care about what you want? After the way you acted tonight?" His grip tightened, and his other hand crushed my breast through my shirt. I couldn't help the small whimper that escaped through my lips, and it only fed his hate. "I think you'll do exactly as I want you to." He said, as he ripped my shirt down to expose my chest. All while never letting go of the choke hold on my throat.

"P-please Mike, I-I..." I tried to muster out some words, but his grip was too tight to breathe and talk. Before I could speak again, he grabbed my legs, and flipped me over. He released my throat, and I drew in the biggest breath I had for minutes. It stung my lungs inhaling the cool fall air. He held my face down to the swing, and rested his elbow on my back.

"I've told you before, Janes." his voice was eerie, and so empty. "You're stuck with me." As he uttered those words, I heard his zipper, and then his pants hit the floor. He leaned into me, and added, "For Always." And thrust. "Forever." And thrust again.

My tears were so hot rolling down my cheeks and nose, and they were pouring out of me. I couldn't believe that this is how the night had ended up. *Don't even start with that... you knew damn well how this night would turn out, and still you tried. And now look at you. Face pushed down on the swing, full of the world's biggest dicks cock. I hate it when you give up. even more when giving up seems to be the moments best option...* There was so much emotion inside of me, and the fire inside my heart was burning so hot, that I couldn't hide my pleasure. I was so confused. I didn't want this at all, tears were pouring out of my eyes...but I was so close to coming.

He never took his hand off of my throat, and every time I had to breathe, it hurt. With each thrust, my breath left my body. I could feel myself starting to tighten and clench, and I tried with all of my might to restrain from coming all over him. I couldn't give him the satisfaction of that, after all of this. I could feel him shifting, altering his speed, and varying how hard he was ramming into me. His grip tightened, as if he were getting close himself. I found that holding my breath made the clenching stop, and I tried to go limp.

"Ohh..." he groaned. "Don't you go soft on me now, baby..." he shifted his grip on my neck, and pushed harder into my core. He was using his cock as a weapon, and it hurt in more ways than I could even admit. "I want you to feel me on you..." he gritted his teeth, and inhaled through them at the same time. "Forever."

As he said those words, he pounded into me harder than before, and I could feel a sudden warm feeling throughout my crotch. Everything went numb at that moment, and he threw his body backwards and then reached forward and squeezed my throat harder, completely cutting off my breath while he came. He pulled out of me, and flopped on the swing. Tears were still flowing freely out of my eyes, but I was sure to make no sounds. I could still feel the warmth in my crotch, and I wasn't sure if it was just pieces of him left behind, or something else.

I reached for my pants, and he grabbed my hands. "I didn't say you were going anywhere yet. You're mine today. You agreed." He kept hold of my hand, and reached down and picked up our clothes. "Come on, let's go down to the water." He pulled me along with him, clutching my shirt closed. I turned back to look towards the barn, where the band was loudly playing. As I stepped over the hill, and the barn began to disappear, I went numb. *Don't lose yourself, Janie... keep a level head. Get away from...* The thoughts were so repetitive, and I knew there was no way I was getting out of this until he was done. Michael kept peering back at me, with that goddamn grin, gauging my reaction. I tried to stay as stone faced as possible.

20

As we approached the water, the moon's light reflected off of us, and all our things. I could now see what the warmth I had felt was. I was bleeding all over the place, or had been at least. He threw our things down on the sand next to the water, and tried to pull me to get in. "No, Michael. I don't want to go in the pond..." my voice was so quiet, in between sobs, I plead. "Please."

"Aww," he came towards me and I froze. He noticed my tension, and chuckled. "Aw, why are you scared of me?" The joker smile returned, and in the moonlight, I could tell that he was getting excited again. "You think I'm going to..." he reached out and squeezed my breast, very hard. "hurt you?" He smiled, and forced me to the ground. He used his torso to keep me still, while he shifted all my tattered and torn shreds of clothing that were left, out of the way. "Come on Janie, you can tell what I need." He moaned into my ear, and the sound made me nauseous.

I didn't have any fight left tonight, and all I could do was stare at the stars, and wonder what I had done to deserve this. His body weight was crushing my chest, but there was no way I was going to let him see that it was hurting me. He slid his fingers back inside me, and started twisting them around. Even though I could feel exactly what parts of me wanted to do, my head wasn't anywhere near the present situation. The night sky was such a deep, dark blue, and the moon seemed farther away than normal. There were a few crickets chirping, and the fall air was crisp, and chilly. I suddenly wished I had brought my jacket, because I was getting cold.

"Me, Janie. Look. At. Me." he said, as he reached up, and turned my face back toward his own. He searched my eyes for something, and at this point I wasn't sure what he was looking for. He held my face still, knowing that I would return to the stars if he let it go. He planted his lips on mine, and probed my mouth with his tongue. He was apparently unhappy with his access, so he shifted his weight, and when he did, I groaned. The pressure sliding in and out of my abdomen increased, and he was slamming into me again. His breathing was ragged, and I knew it was almost over. *You mean you hope it's almost over. Jesus Janie, get off the ground! Get out of here!* Easier said than done, but I knew that's exactly what I should've been doing. He slammed into me one last time, and let out the ugliest noise. "Ahh... that's better." He smirked at me.

I shuddered. I scrambled to grab my clothes out of the sand, and put them on as quickly as I could. It was so dark that I couldn't see how I looked, and I'm thankful for that. Tears were burning my eyes again, and it was hard to muffle the sobs. I had so many thoughts running through my head. So many things that I needed to say. I sat down to put my shoes on, and my rear end was very sore. I gasped when I landed, and a sob escaped my mouth. Michael instantly turned around and came towards me.

"Good. So I've left my mark on you then?" he smiled so big, all of this teeth were showing. I tied both shoes, and reached for my shirt, to see if it was salvageable.

"Michael," I muttered. "This was not okay in the slightest, and you know that. I'm leaving here, and I'm never coming back out here. You don't own me, you NEVER will. I AM DONE!!" I was screaming now. "THIS is OVER!! Leave me alone." I stormed off towards my car, which wasn't too far away from the gazebo and pond. It angered me that I couldn't say goodbye to my friends in the barn, but that would've only prolonged my own torture. *You're doing it, Janie! Keep walking, faster! He looks shocked! Do this for you, no more for him. Nothing. Nothing more for him. This plan will work, and you're following it beautifully.* I heard his footsteps behind me, but not in a hurry. The tears were freely raining down my face now. I was still numb, and willing myself to run to the car.

"Whatever Janie!" Michael yelled towards me. "I'll be back playing with our friends, if you decide to pull your head out of your ass!" I turned my head around long enough to see him turn his head, and wave me on. And that's exactly what I was going to start doing. Moving on... I got in the car, and headed straight home. I knew Mom and Dad were gone, so no worries of running into them, thankfully.

When I hit the driveway, I couldn't run in the house fast enough. I locked all of the doors, and the sobs started to set in louder. I ran into the shower as if I were on fire, and turned the knob until it would turn no more. Steam was pouring out of the water when I climbed in, and I screamed in agony. So many levels had burned in my soul tonight, that I wasn't sure that I knew myself anymore. Scrubbing Michael off of me was a chore. I could smell him, and taste him on me after these episodes for hours, and hours. As I was scrubbing, I noted the dried red in between my thighs. I was still a little numb, so cleaned my sensitive areas carefully. Even the soft wash cloth felt like sandpaper.

As I climbed into bed, I couldn't help but think, and re-think the entire night. It had started so well, and had so much promise. Singing on stage, oh my. *there's just nothing quite like the cheering from people, and the smiles on their faces while you're performing.* Definitely something I'd always wanted to do. And I did love those boys on stage, on some strange level. *All of them.* But no more putting myself in these situations. I closed my eyes, and my head hit the pillow. Tears on my pillow made my cheeks cold for a little while. As I drifted off to sleep... *I dreamed that I lived with someone. And in my dream, I couldn't see who it was, but that it was a man, and they had dark hair. I felt so peaceful, and so happy in the dream. This man was happy, too, and he came up and held me in the warmest, most loving embrace. I was so warm, and so safe...and I was out.*

21

Waking up Monday morning was a relief, as I had so much to look forward to. I had slept the day away on Sunday, having momentary bits of complete emotional breakdowns. My body had recovered much better than my brain had, and I could deal with that. I was so excited to get to be with Gabe tonight, alone. Away from everyone. And best of all, not inside a car... When I pulled into the lot, I parked next to his car. I had instant butterflies, which made forgetting about my horrible weekend so much easier.

"Hey Janie!!" Simon's voice rang over the entire store, and he threw a big wave into the air. Adorable and enlightening, and a much needed friend.

"Hey buddy!" I yelled back, sending back the same, large ridiculous wave. "How are you?" I asked as I approached him.

"I'm good today. Glad I get to see you today. How has...Mike been?" he asked very hesitantly. I knew I owed them all a little explanation, but I didn't want to divulge the physical and mental toll it's cost me thus far. I motioned Simon to follow me to my office, and I would explain there.

"Come in, close the door, please." I sat in my chair, and started organizing my desk. "Everything is going as I expected, and my plan is working. This past weekend was my last time attending band practice, and out with the whole group." My eyes throbbed remembering all the tears that fell dwelling on the events of the weekend.

"I see" he said, and sat in the chair next to my desk. He reached out, and put his hand on mine. "I'm glad it's working... But... Are you okay?" He sighed. I didn't know how to answer this part.

"I'll be alright. Thanks for caring, and sticking through this with me." I pulled my hand free, and put it on top of his. "But, now I've got to get some work done! Gabe and I are...going out tonight." I noticed that Simon's smile had gotten quite large at my comment, and then I imagined that it only matched my own.

"Alright, back to work for me! See you around!" He headed back outside to load the delivery trucks. I finished organizing my desk from the weekend paper work, and dove in to the invoices. When I finally stopped to take a break, it was already almost time to close. I was beyond excited now, and started shutting my office down a bit early. I grabbed my purse, and headed to freshen up a little before our night.

As I was walking down the hallway to the ladies' bathroom door, I was grabbed, and pulled into a dark stock room. Gabe's arms were so identifiable to me, all I could do was melt into him, and smile. His hands traced the outline of my bra strap through the back of my shirt, and down to my waist.

"Hey baby, just making sure we're still on for tonight, and see if you wanted anything to drink." I couldn't resist, leaning into him, and locking my lips with his. One taste was not enough, and I needed more even now. I stopped to breathe, and look into his eyes. He was so with me already, that my heart, mind and body were wrapped around him tightly. I smothered his mouth with mine, and probed into his mouth with my tongue. He tasted deliciously sweet, soft, and so warm. I stopped kissing him, and leaned into his embrace. "I'll take that as a yes." His arms wrapped around me a little tighter. "You ok, baby?" He asked gently.

"Yes, as long as I'm with you... I'm fine." It was the truth. Just being near him burned all of my bad thoughts away. Gabe gave me the energy, strength, and hope I needed to finish this task at hand. And even though it may not have started as feeling quite this much, I really hope that he'll stick around when everything's calmed down, and normal again. I couldn't help but smile, as I patted his back, and turned to go finish up my jobs for the day.

As I walked back through the copy room, I felt my pager buzz. Glancing down at the number, I already knew it was Michael. I wasn't ready to talk to him, but new if I wanted this night to be smooth, and quiet, I would have to appease him just enough. I placed my documents in the copy machine, and dialed his number on the phone that was next to me. It seemed to ring forever before he finally answered. Once I heard his voice, I could feel the 'V' in my forehead form.

"Hello?" he said, in a calmer tone, for him.

"You paged?" I said about as cold as an arctic winter's day. I'm not sure what exactly he expects from me anymore, and if this doesn't show him that it's nothing, then I'm not sure what will. *Janie, honey...you think that if you have a mean tone with him that he will ease up? Leave you alone? Just stick with the plan, lady. The plan...*

"Yeah, I did. We need to talk," he paused. The silence was heavy, and so uncomfortable. "You know I'm sorry about the other night. I was drinking, and I didn't-" I couldn't stand anymore of his nonsensical babble.

"Drinking?! You're sorry?! Michael, if you were ever sorry, you would've stopped doing that to me months ago!" I was shaking my head, and now gritting my teeth. The copy machine was on copy 39 of 65. This conversation would be over by the time the copies were made. "You are something else, you know that?? Nothing at all like you use to be." I said as flatly as possible.

"Well, people change, Janie. You've changed, too, you know." He chuckled. *Why does he always feel the need to chuckle??? It only pisses me off more.* "I miss you, and I want to see you." He waited for my response.

"Unfortunately, I've got plans tonight." I paused, searching internally for the courage I needed to push out the rest. "And quite frankly, I'm not really missing you." I could hear his breathing change, and the tense way he was gritting his teeth into the phone. "I'm not missing being raped. I'm not missing being pushed around. I don't miss the yelling, the screaming, or the accusations."

"Don't ever say that I raped you, you bitch!! You wanted it, and you know it." He was almost hyperventilating over the phone. I had enraged him with the truth.

"That IS the truth, Mike. No means 'No,' or did you miss that part in life? Anyway, I'm busy tonight. Maybe some other time." Oh! Yes! Looking down, I noticed I was on 63 of 65 copies. "Talk to you some other time, Mike." I couldn't help keep the smile off of my face. I know he could hear it in my words, too.

"Don't you dare hang up on me, bitch. I'll find--" I slammed the phone down harder than ever. It echoed through the backroom and offices so much that another coworker asked if I was ok. I piled up my copies, and headed back towards my office. I neatly restacked all of my documents, prepping then for tomorrow's work day. I heard some commotion out by the time clocks, and stuck my head out to see what was going on.

Simon saw me checking, and headed over to me.

22

"Hey Janes! We're all taking off for today. Finished a little early, that way we can get a jump start on tomorrow. I'll see you then!" He patted my shoulder as he turned away. "Oh! Almost forgot! Hope you have fun tonight with Gabe!!" He winked, and was gone in a flash. All I could do was smile.

I gathered up my things, and headed for the bathroom for a wardrobe change. Off went the khaki's, and on went the mini skirt. Off went the button up, long sleeve work polo, and on went the low cut tank top, and lace cover up. A quick refresher of the deodorant, and perfume, and I was ready to go to Gabe's. I turned the lights out, and headed towards the front offices to wait for him. It was only a moment or two before I saw him coming, and my smile grew even larger.

"Hey! Sweet Cheeks!" He hugged me, and whisked me around in a circle. "Do you want to follow me? Ride with? It's up to you!" He waited while I thought about it. I hadn't really thought of where to leave the car, and with Michael's most recent threats, I wasn't sure it was safe to leave the car anywhere. *You're right. Take the car with you, this way you can leave when you want to.*

"I'll just follow you." I smiled, and asked "will we be leaving soon?" I couldn't wait to be alone with him.

"Yeah, let me just grab my jacket, and we can go. I'll lock up, if you want to head out to the cars." He turned and smiled. The gleam in his eye told me that he was just as excited as I was about our upcoming "date" together. I nodded, and headed out the front doors to our cars. I climbed in mine, and had enough time to rifle through the CD's to find the perfect songs for the ride.

It was Jewel. Her songs always speak to me perfectly when my emotions were running on high. The first song was more than fitting, and I couldn't help smile through the lyrics at him as he climbed into his own car. *Soon you will see. You were meant for me, and I was meant for you...* The lyrics gave me chills. I had to keep reminding myself about just what this situation was, and that I may be falling in a little too deep. I could feel the 'V' form on my forehead. This was getting to be so stressful... I shook my head to refocus on following the apparent race car driver I was behind, and changed the song. It changed to another Jewel song, even more fitting than the last. *Show me one man who knows his own heart, to him I shall belong... kiss the flame...* I smiled when he turned onto a side street, and slowed for a brief moment.

Gabe was a fast driver. I didn't know that the drive would be quite so long, but it was scenic, so that made it an easy drive. First the highway for a few miles, and then a quick jump into the country. I hadn't really done the country scene much, but I couldn't help roll the windows down and let the chilly air in. Things seemed so peaceful out here, and I wondered if this was more of what I needed. The entire time my head was spinning with thoughts of what was going to happen tonight. I hoped that it was everything that I needed, and everything that I desired. When Gabe reached his driveway, he turned on his turn signal, and slowed way down.

His driveway was secluded, long and winding. As we drove, we passed their small pond, and a very large barn. We came to the quaint cottage house moments later, that he rented with two of his friends. I hung back a bit, and waited for Gabe to park his own car, and he motioned for me to take the spot next to his. I parked, and grabbed my bag and drink. I couldn't wipe the smile off of my face for anything. As I walked up to the house, I looked back towards the main road. I liked the fact that there was a certain level of seclusion behind the trees, and that calmed me.

"Come on, baby..." he held the screen door open for me. "Make yourself at home. My room is

to the left, and there's a bathroom attached, too."
He smiled, and slowly wiped his bottom lip with his finger.

I stepped through the door, somewhat in awe. The cottage was so clean for a house with three men in it, and organized as well. Walking through the living room and dining room, I set my bag and drink down on the kitchen counter, and headed back into the living room to sit down. I really liked the open floor plan, in that the living room, kitchen, and dining room were all connected. I stood, to go scope out where the bathroom was.

"Give me just a few minutes here, and I'll get some snacks and drinks, too." He dashed off around the corner before I could say a word, and then suddenly reappeared in the kitchen. "Oh, and the stereo system is great in here. Feel free to go through the CD's, and pick us out something to listen to." That was perfect, of course I'd love to pick out some music.

I got up to check out the CD selection, which from the couch, looked to be very large. I noticed photos scattering the walls of trips the roommates had taken together, parties and such. In every photo he looked so happy, and I internally hoped that I wasn't going to be what screwed anything up for him. I glanced over at him, balancing all sorts of things in his hands. Trying to make everything as perfect as he could, for me. For us. I sighed, and continued through the CD's. I pulled some out, and set them in a pile next to the player. Wilco, Dave Matthews Band, Fleetwood Mac, and Salt N' Pepa, and a few others. *Oh Janie, you're going to try to read him through his music? Such a clever girl you are. I think you already know which he'll pick though. Just as he knows the same about you...* "Hey Gabe," I turned towards him and smiled. "Need any help?" He was drying his hands on a towel, and coming up to me.

"Nope, I've got it all set. Want a drink?" He turned and pointed. "I've got some wine, and beer. You told me nothing fancy, so I kept it simple." He smiled, and headed back to the food. "I'm starving, so I'm gonna eat." He grabbed two plates from the shelves, and motioned me over. "Please, come join me." *If you insist, you excellent specimen of a man.* I headed over to the counter and saw all sorts of finger foods there. I grabbed a beer, and some snacks, and took a seat next to him at the table. Just then, he wrinkled his forehead, and looked around like something was off. "The music...I forgot to turn it on!"

"Oh, I left a pile of CD's I like next to the radio. You pick one of those to put in, ok?" I glanced over my shoulder to make sure that he heard me, and indeed he did. He was going through the pile smirking at my different choices. He selected one, and got it set up to play.

"Of course, it was a good selection, too. Hope you liked which I picked." He sat back down at the table, and we made little conversation while we both stuffed our faces. I thought it was cute that every time I lifted my eyes from the food to glance at him, he was already looking at me. The songs started, and it was Wilco. The mellow music set the mood, and as we took our drinks into the living room, he stopped to dim the lights a little.

The couch was pretty comfortable, and he sat a cushion away from me. He reached for my thigh, and gently put his hand down. "Thought we could chat for a bit, and drink a little. If you want to."

I smiled, and put my hand over his, "Sure," I scooted closer to him. "anything that involves staying here with you." I could feel my face get hot, and flushed. Just then, his hand came up and brushed my cheek.

"I love knowing that thoughts of me make your cheeks all red..." he scooted closer to me. "You have the same effect on me, Janes." *Oh, nicknames... try not to melt, too much more, with all of these cute names...* He stood to head towards the bar, and motioned to the multitude of beverages to choose from. I winced.

"I'm not really sure of drinks...I've really only ever had beer, and Cosmo's." I giggled. "So, you pick something for me. Be gentle." He nodded, and started mixing away. He returned momentarily with a beer for himself, and a drink for me.

"This is a Tom Collins," he hands me the cup, lingering as our hands touched around the glass. "Tell me if you like it. Got myself my favorite beer, too." He smiled, and took a big drink. Sipping on my drink, it was good. *A little tart, and a little sweet...* and it had a cherry. *MMMmmm....*

I was becoming more and more enraptured by this man, and between the beer, our conversations about everything under the sun, and my throbbing libido, I wanted him now more than ever. I watched as he slunk around the living room to change the CD. I saw him grab the DMB, and I melted even more. He slowly walked back over as the music started. He sat back next to me, closer than before. I could tell that he was being more than meticulous with his moves, and I appreciated that.

"Janie, I'm so glad you're finally here," he said in a whisper in my ear. His breathe was hitting the perfect spot, because I was suddenly covered in goose bumps. "If you're not ready, or don't want to, I-" There was just no need for him to finish that sentence. Or to go anywhere near those topics tonight. I grabbed his head, and pulled him into a very deep, passionate kiss.

"I'm exactly where I want to be, doing exactly what I want to be doing, Gabe." I leaned towards the table to take a quick swig of my beer, fully knowing that leaning over gave him the full view of my neck, chest, and abdomen. I heard him swallow hard, and inhale sharply. "Do you like what you see?" I smirked, and leaned towards his mouth.

"Yes," he kissed me once. "And I *need* more." His mouth was all over mine, down my neck, all over my shoulders. I could feel his desire pouring out of him, and it was all flowing straight into me. Suddenly he stood up, and reached out for my hand. I could feel my eyebrow raise at him, as I smirked at the notion. Before I could make any second thought, my hand was in his, and I was following him closely through the kitchen, down the hallway, and to his bedroom.

Entering through the door, he walked me over, and sat me on his bed. A queen size, with a maroon and red comforter. I kicked my shoes off on the floor, and reclined myself onto his pillows. My lack of hesitation was slightly startling, but Gabe always brought me a comfort I couldn't even begin to describe. I looked at him, and he looked nervous.

23

"So, this is my bedroom." he stood unsteadily in the middle of the room. "And you are on my bed..." he said, almost to himself, as if not even believing this was happening between us now.

"I am, and I wish that you would join me." I patted the bed next to me, and pulled my knees up to a bent position. "Don't hold back, Gabe. I know you can feel this, too." I sat up and reached my hand out to him. He took it with little hesitation.

"Ok, baby." he dropped my hand, took his shirt off, and flung it on the floor. He climbed onto the bed, and slowly up to my face. His body was hovering over mine, and both of our bodies were on fire. He deliberately leaned into kiss my mouth, making sure that no other part of him was touching me. I almost couldn't withstand the temptation. He was gazing into my eyes, kissing me like I was his... *Oh my God, who knew how perfect this would feel?* I searched his eyes, until I saw what I thought was the same gleam that I had.

Then, he drew his knees up so that they were both next to my hips, and he was sitting on my thighs. He slowly began to pull my arms out of my lace jacket, one at a time. He lowered my hands, and placed them on his thighs. *Look at him, Janes...he hasn't looked away from you once. His eyes are so deep, like an abyss... He wants to love you so bad.* I wanted him so badly that I was starting to shake. He was reaching for my tank top strap, and noticed the shaking. Instantly, he sat back on his heels.

"Please don't stop, Gabe." I pulled him back towards me.

"But you're shaking. Are you okay?" he had a 'V' on his forehead. I could tell he was genuinely concerned.

"I'm shaking from my want of you..." I pulled his hands, and put them on my chest. "I want you." I squeezed his hands over my breasts. "I need you." His breathing was changing, and he went back to pulling my straps down my arms. My tank top now loosely rested around my belly, exposing my red bra.

He leaned down to me, so our chests were touching, and kissed my mouth hard. "You are so exquisite..." he sighed into my mouth as we kissed. His hands felt all over me, taking careful time with each breast, and each nipple. He sat up a little on my legs, and adjusted his pants. I saw the bulge, and raised my knee so he couldn't sit back down. I reached for his zipper, and unzipped. Then unbuttoned, and slid his pants down to his thighs. Even through his boxers, he was ready for me. I put my finger on the tip of his member, and watched his eyes roll back, and his dick throb. I ran my finger slowly down his shaft, all the way around the base, to his balls. "Ohh, Janie..." he managed to get out.

He pushed me back just enough so he could slide my mini skirt off, and it slid off with ease. I sat back and let him strip my undies off, too. Once I was back upright again, I pulled his boxers down to reveal his massive erection. Grabbing his shaft, I wrapped each finger around his girth slowly. Each time making him convulse with the feeling. I felt his hand run from my backside, around to my front, and in between my legs. His fingers were hot, and quick to find my hot spots. Once he found my clit, he worked it between his fingers. My hips started to move back and forth with his motion.

"Oh God, Janie." he inhaled sharply in my ear. "You are so amazing..." he grabbed my head and fisted my hair. I tipped my hips towards him, and he slid his fingers inside me. He wiggled his fingers from side to side, back and forth, and in ways I didn't know existed.

"MMMmmm..." was all I could muster. His cock was hard and hot in my hand, and he was taking such great consideration and time ensuring that he got me off with every part of him. And I couldn't wait for every piece he'd give me.

He slowly stopped, and laid me back down onto the bed. He turned himself around, and laid down next to me so that his face was at my crotch, and mine with his. There was no way I could hold myself back. I grabbed him, and sucked him so far into my mouth. I couldn't get enough. His hands dug into my hips, as he pulled my hot center into his mouth. I'd never felt anything quite this hot, or right. We were all tongues, mouths... Sucking, probing, pulling, and lots of rubbing. I broke the suction and pulled myself back to the pillows. He came and laid next to me, and we both just stared at each other.

"More, please..." he whispered into my ear, as he nuzzled my neck. *Yes, more indeed.* He rolled back over on top of me, and I more than willingly spread myself open for him. I was dripping wet, so sliding in was no problem. He felt huge, but fit so perfectly inside me. I could tell he was thinking, because he was sitting so still inside of me. I could feel each pulse, and twitch that his shaft made.

"You ok?" I asked quietly. I put my hand on his cheek, and ran it down his chest, to his hip, and squeezed gently.

"Oh yeah," he gasped. "So good... just adjusting." He looked directly in my eyes, "more perfect than anything." He leaned in, and engulfed my mouth with his. As he kissed me deeper, he pulled back, and thrust deeply into me. Making me moan loudly into his mouth. Each thrust was deliberate, as if he were climbing inside of me. This is exactly what I've been waiting for. What I knew was going to happen between us. He thrust again, I moaned, and it all clicked.

I threw my hands onto his shoulders, and dug my nails in. He sped up with thrusts, and lifted my legs in different ways. He knew what he was doing, and it was all about us both. While he fucked me, his hands traveled all over my body. We were insatiable together. We worked perfectly like a well-oiled, and aged machine. My body was starting to tingle all over. I knew I was close to the edge.

"You first, baby," he breathed heavily in my ear. Looking in his eyes made me fall completely over, and explode all over him. The clenching went on and on. My whole body was shaking, and my breath was trembling. Gabe leaned towards me, and gently began kissing my face. Slowly down my neck, to my chest. Ever so gently, he began thrusting again. At a perfect pace, with little pressure. He leaned to my ear, licked and blew light air into it, and asked "can I come in you?"

I turned, and looked directly in his eyes. He asked. I locked my heels tightly around his waist, so he couldn't leave- even if he tried. I smiled very big at him. I reached for his chin, and grasped it with my hand. I pulled him to my mouth, and whispered, "yes..." as I kissed him deeply.

The deep kiss, and the gentle thrusting had him quickly. His body tensed in my arms, and beads of sweat poured off of him. His pace quickened as he came all over, filling my insides with his hot spray. We laid together there, just catching our breath for a few minutes. I couldn't help but bask in the glory for a few moments. This is what it was supposed to be. I could feel the pull of my heart, and I knew what had happened.

"Hey, love..." he rolled towards me, and turned me to face him. He smiled the brightest smile, and gently ran his fingers down my cheek. "Thank you for tonight." He leaned in and kissed me deeply. *Oh God don't make this night end!!* I kissed him back, and tightened my grip. This was perfect.

"Thank you, too." I buried my head in his neck. "You have no idea how long I've waited for-" his fingers covered my mouth.

"I absolutely know, because I had to wait that long, too. But baby, it was so worth it." He wrapped his arms around me, and I turned so his warmth was covering my back. We just lay there, being perfectly sated with each other. In love.

24

I awoke early this next morning, with the sun shining right into my eyes. Looking next to me, he was still sleeping soundly. *Had all my dreams come true in one night?* Still wishing this could never end, I grabbed my bag and headed for the bathroom. Once I was safely in, I checked my pager. 11 missed pages, all from Michael. This made me sigh loudly. I rinsed my face in the sink, and freshened up the best I could. I could hear Gabe rustling around in the bedroom, so I opened the bathroom door. "Good morning" I said to him, and smiled. I could feel my cheeks flush. Looking at him made me instantly think of hours before... Worshiping each other for hours.

"I could wake up to you every day." he shook his head, and fell back to bed. "I'd be the luckiest guy in the world." He smiled, and covered his face with his arm. I could feel my face flush with his comment, and subsequent face cover. *Don't be stunned! You could feel the same thing he felt last night, and he's hooked just like you are.* I was lost in my thoughts, and didn't notice that he had risen and was now standing almost nose to nose with me. He wrapped my face in his warm hands, and stared straight into my soul. "I meant it all." He kissed me deeply. "Every touch, every word, everything." He pulled me in to him, and a buried my face in his neck. We stood there for what seemed like hours. I wanted this. Every day. Just then, my heart panged at the thought of our arrangement. Was it still just an arrangement? Or now had it turned into more?

I finished getting ready, sharing the counter space in the bathroom with Gabe. "I could get use to this, you know..." I half joked, as I nudged him with my behind. He looked at me in the mirror, and dropped his pants. An instant smile plastered itself on my face, and my heart began to race.

"Don't joke about that, Janes..." looking down, and back up at me in the mirror, he added, "we're both obviously ready for every day, love." His smile was as large as my own. And just as we were both reminiscing of hours before, my pager went off. Always perfect timing on some things in this life, have to love it. To my surprise, he reached for my bag, and pulled out the pager. He scrolled through the buttons, and his eyebrows rose very high.

"Dare I ask what's the matter?" I was hesitant, but figured that Michael was behind his expression. I slowly started picking up my make-up, putting it back in the bag quietly, waiting for him to say something. Anything.

"Fourteen. At least one an hour. Sometimes more, and maybe... coded?" He turned and looked at me, almost asking the question. All I could do was sigh, and tears welded up in my eyes. Doing my best to hold them in, I nodded at him. My head sank, as I zipped up my bag. "Janie, look at me." He turned me, and pulled me into a half hug. *Why does he always have to look at me like this when he wants to talk? I'm melting here...* "I told you I'd help you with this problem," he shook the pager in his hand while he talked. "Please keep me filled in on this. Always." I pulled away a little, and held his hand. I hated that he was so involved in this.

"I don't want this to tarnish this...to hurt us." I looked down to collect myself. All the thoughts were spinning in my head, and they all wanted to jump out at Gabe. *Courage, I need you now...* Just then, his hand gently pulled my chin up, and my eyes met his again.

"Say whatever you have to say. Don't hold back." He kissed my cheek, and smiled. This type of respect was unhinging.

"I'm trying so desperately to leave my past in the past, and now it's trying to mingle with my... my future." His grasp tightened on my hand. "What I feel when I'm with you there are almost no words for. I feel so safe with you. Respected. I trust you.

I've had some of the best times of my life this past month. And when this all started, I honestly just needed help finding my way out. And I've found that." I brushed his cheek with my hand, and looked as deeply into him as I could. "But I'm afraid I've found more." His arms were around me almost before my sentence had finished. His embrace was crushing me, but not with strength. It was whatever had just sparked, and lit, between us. "Wait!" I giggled, "I'm not done talking yet!!"

"Oh, I'm sorry, love. Keep going." He had a coy smile, and just when I started to finish, his lips were over mine again. "Janes, enough with this "past" talk...let's just work on the future." His smile was huge now. He released me long enough to button his shirt. "Want to run some errands with me?" *Do you really have to ask!?*

"Yes! I'd love to. In fact," I tapped my finger on the counter. "I'd like to request a trip to the cell phone store." Looking at the counter, at the black pager, with its stupid red flashing light...*I was done with this, too*. "Yes, definitely time for an upgrade." Gabe turned and smiled at me.

"I know just the place to go. Check out my cell while I drive, and see if you like the features." We headed towards the door, and climbed in the car together. I wondered momentarily if he had noticed the childish, completely smitten smile that was written across my face. I turned to look at him, to see if he had caught any of my internal monolog, and to my astonishment, he had the same smile on his own face.

We spent the entire day together, and I upgraded myself into the times with a cell phone. Gabe was quite ecstatic with this, and even programmed it for me, and put his picture in it. He had taken me to lunch, and back to my car. There was a lot of kissing, even more hugging, and some deep, quiet stares all day long. We both had Wednesday off, so we made plans to call, and see each other at work on Thursday.

25

I spent most of the day watching Lifetime movies, and eating cookies. I was still recalling the night with Gabe, detail for detail. My parents were gone for work again, although this time together. I was tired of being alone in this house, considering the things that had happened in it recently. Since then, I've made sure to double and triple check locks on everything that opens. The phone rang, and I jumped through the ceiling.

"Hello?" I cautiously answered.

"Hello honey!" my mom's cheerful voice came through, and I almost cried. "How's everything going at the house?"

"Everything's great! When will you be home? I've got some things I need to go over with you, need a little input on." I could hear her shuffling in the background. She was always working.

"We'll be back on Saturday, I think. I'll verify with your father when he's back in here. Oh, I miss you!! How are you? Seems like I only get to catch up with you over the phone. I'm so sorry, hon."

"It's ok, mom. Works, work. I understand." I tried to be reassuring. When really all I wanted was them home. I hated feeling so vulnerable, and alone. "I'm good. Spent a lot of time with Gabe these past few weeks…" I waited, and heard her inhale a little sharply.

"I've heard you mention him quite a few times. You've worked with him for quite a while, haven't you?"

"Yes, at the Phoenix. He's wonderful, and I bet you'll get to meet him soon." I could feel the smile in my voice.

"Are you smiling honey? This is wonderful…I'm so glad he's making you happy. But," she hesitated, and I instantly knew where her head was going. "…Michael?" she asked.

"Well…" I sighed loudly. *Aww shit…all of it? Some of it? None of it? Now or never.* "He's not the greatest guy, mom. I'm tired of all of his games, and I'm seeking other options." I nodded at myself with the answer.

"Well, that seems logical. You're not married to him, Michael I mean. So you can do whatever you need to, and I'll back you one hundred percent." I smiled, and wondered if she read in between the lines again.

"Thanks, mom. I may end up spending the night with Gabe, or maybe have him stay here with me one night until you're back." I braced myself for the answer.

"What a good idea. He's a little older, too, right? I feel good about him already."

"Yes, he's older. Mature. Respectful." I sighed again. "Wonderful." My mom laughed loudly, and mumbled something to someone in the background.

"Well honey, I've got another meeting. 9 o'clock where you are, 6 o'clock here. I'll check in with you tomorrow!" Just then I smacked my forehead.

"Mom! I got a cell phone yesterday, too. I'll text your cell my number. Have a good trip, and tell Dad I said hi & love you!"

"I will, goodnight Janie." My heart pulled when I heard the phone hang up. Alone again. I gathered up my junk, and headed to the outdoor room to have a little smoke. I thought maybe that would calm my nerves a little bit. Since getting the cell phone, and disconnecting the pager, I've had a constant feeling of being watched. I turned the radio on, and the black light. I rolled a joint, perfectly, the first time. I was always that friend who could roll one for anyone on the spot. First inhale burned my throat, and drew a huge cough. While coughing, my cell phone started ringing.

"Hello?" I half answered while choking to death.

"Janes?!" a half panicked voice said. "You ok?!" It was Gabe! My heart jumped back up into my chest, and almost immediately, my nerves relaxed a bit.

"I'm so glad you called..." I paused, I didn't mean to make it sound so pitiful. "I mean; I'm having a strange night. And I hate being by myself here. Can we talk for a while? Keep me company?" I inhaled deeply, and I hoped he was okay with this.

"Of course, sweet cheeks. Anything for you. Tell me about your day, and then tell me you're going to save some of that green you're smoking for when we're together sometime." I laughed out loud. We talked for hours. About things that I wasn't sure I wanted to know, but then so glad that we could be this open with each other. *Is it possible that this just keeps getting better, and better?*

26

Waking up Thursday morning was easy. I slept like a rock, and it was much needed sleep. I dreamt of Gabe all night long, and woke to him in my head, with a giant smile on my face. I had slept in a little, so in a rush, got ready for work. I quickly scurried through the kitchen, and packed a quick lunch. Grabbed an extra pizza for Gabe, picked up my bag and keys. I unlocked my car doors, and as I got in, noticed a piece of paper underneath my windshield wiper. I swallowed hard, and looked around to make sure I was alone. I grabbed the paper, and quickly locked myself in the car. I opened up the paper, and gasped. There was a picture of Gabe and I at the cell phone store, in an intimate embrace. The note read:

"How can this be? When you are mine."

When I parked in the lot, I didn't even remember the drive to work. Now I was worried for Gabe, beyond the worry I had for myself. I was used to Michael's torture and games, but now bringing others in to this killed me. I headed back towards the offices, and quickly paged Gabe and Simon to my office.

Within moments, Simon knocked at my door. "Hey Janes, what's doing?" I smiled at him.

"Just wait for Gabe, please. How was your week? Seems like days since I've seen you!"

"It's been good. Just hanging around, you know me!!" He laughed at himself, and I laughed with him. He was naively awkward, but one of the sweetest guys I knew. Just then, arms were around my waist, and a familiar smile crept onto my face.

"Hey, love." he whispered in my ear. "Hey, Simon." he waved at Simon. "So, both of us, huh? What's up? He asked inquisitively.

"Well, I had this left on my windshield this morning." I handed the folded note with picture to Gabe first, and then he to Simon. Gabe's face was calm, but strained.

"Wow...so he's taking pictures of you two? Like, stalking you?" Simon couldn't believe it. His facial expression said it all.

"I'm so sorry." It's all I could muster. I looked down, and noticed I was trembling. "I'm worried for you both. You need to--" Gabe whisked me into a hug. He was very in tune with me, as his hug covered the tears that had just spilled from my eyes.

"We'll be fine, Janie. And we'll protect you."
He fiercely looked at Simon. "Right, Si?" Although
the way he asked almost wasn't even a question,
more like a stated fact.

"Oh, without question. This guy is a lunatic,
and I don't like the things he's done to you." His
momentary seriousness told me he understood the
gravity of the situation, and what was now at stake.
I relaxed a little in Gabe's arms.

"See, Janie...all of this is going to be okay.
One way, or another." He smiled at me
reassuringly, but I knew that he had unanswered
questions, too.

"Thank you guys. I don't know what I'd do
without you." I looked at Gabe, and at Simon.
"Both of you. Now, back to work. Simon--
deliveries, right?"

"Yes 'mam!!" he shouted, saluted, and
hustled off to get his day done. I turned to Gabe.

"You, me and the stock inventory from the
yard, in the yard say in two hours?" His foot closed
my office door, and his hands wandered all over
my back, down to my hips, and one swung around
to my breast. His mouth covered mine, and I fell
hard into him, and promptly lost myself in the
moment.

"I cannot wait to meet you outside in two
hours. You'll be on my mind every minute until

then." He met my eyes, and looked down, and adjusted his pants. I blushed, and covered my cheeks. He blew me a kiss, and vanished out the door. Falling back dramatically in my chair seemed appropriate, so I did that quickly. I tried to focus myself on the piles of invoices that covered my desk, but the stalker note kept grabbing my attention from my bag. *What does this mean? What on earth is he up to now?*

Walking outside to meet Gabe, I took a brief stock of all the sections we would have to cover. He brought me a water bottle, and we stationed ourselves at his desk, which conveniently had a view of the whole yard. "Alright, where shall we begin?" I asked. He smiled, and shook his head. "What's wrong?"

"Oh," he started, "it's really hard to focus on work sometimes when I'm around you." He looked at the ground, and reached out and rubbed my thigh. In the past when this had happened, we would both then look around to see if anyone saw any of the intimate gestures. Now, we were both too busy staring at each other to notice if any of them even cared.

"Well, we've got to get this done, or I'll be fired and then you'll have to think about me even MORE!!" I winked at him.

"Alright, Section 316, 321 and 323 to start. Want to work together, and kill this? You write, I'll count." I nodded, and hopped off of my stool. As I walked by him, he swatted my rear, and wolf whistled. Without turning around, I shook my head as I walked to 316. We finished seven of the nine sections that needed to be completed, when an odd page came over the speakers.

"Janie, store front. Janie, wait! Gabe! YARD!" I wrinkled my face, and turned to my left to look at Gabe. He had the same puzzled expression. Why was Simon calling for us on the speaker? As I watched Gabe's expression, it began to change. The noise level in the yard rose, as well, as loud talking and yelling was coming from my right. Oh God. Hell had just arrived at work.

From across the yard, he started yelling once he spotted me. "Well, isn't this just perfect! You're both together!" His insane laughter was low, loud, and deep. Simon had followed him out, along with two of our drivers, and I was grateful for this. It was then I realized I needed to take count of this situation. I knew all of these people, and how they worked, hopefully enough to control the outcome, a little.

Michael approached the dirt section we were in the back of, leaving roughly 30 feet between us and them. Sean was trailing behind Michael, but his expression told me he did not agree with their plans. He stayed a few feet behind Michael. Gabe was now immediately to my left, our shoulders almost touched. I stepped in front of him to block him completely, a gesture that spoke more words than I would ever be able to. "Stop where you are, Michael. Don't do this here. Please." His muscles were tense, he fidgeted constantly. His fists were clenched with rage, and the vein in his forehead stood out just like I had seen so many times before. "You don't want to air our dirty laundry in public."

"No, Janie. You're doing a hell of a job of that yourself. I know you got my message." Michael's glare shot straight into my head, and it hurt. "Out in public all over this asshole, and now telling me not to be pissed?" The joker smile appeared for all to see. It was so sickening. He stepped towards me, and without hesitation, Gabe swung me around so I was now behind him. Simon was at Gabe's side in a second. "Oh, you've got body guards, do you?" He turned to Gabe, "I'll fight you, you piece of shit."

"Yeah? Hmm. Well, I'm going to suggest that you back up, and take off. I know your story, Michael, and it's not one we're at all fond of here at the Phoenix." *Are you kidding me?! Is Gabe taunting Mike?! Oh my God I'm in love.* I couldn't help but smirk.

"How the fuck would you know if Janie has business with me? She is my girlfriend. You've got no business butting in!!!" Michael's finger was pointing sternly at Gabe. "Janie? Why are you just standing there? With HIM?!" Watching Michael's face and all his anger was very upsetting. He never could see what his actions did to others, and he didn't care, either. Just then, Gabe's strong, warm hand was around mine, and gave it a squeeze. I knew what it meant, and I intertwined my fingers within his, tightly.

"Michael," I stepped up next to Gabe. "I've told you multiple times in the last few weeks, and I'll repeat it again now. In front of all these people," I took a breath. Then time froze, or it seemed to, at least.

I realized then that this part from my childhood, my past, and so many memories were now going to be poisoned with this forever. The good times that Michael and I had had when we were younger, and all our group of friends... *I guess they were never truly my friends. Hell, I only stayed out of fear and convenience, and I guess they all stayed around him for the same reasons.* There were specific times popping into my memory, almost as if I was banishing them good-bye forever. I could feel my eyes getting hot, tears were brewing. I squeezed the warm hand I held for strength. It squeezed back. I then thought of all the arguments. How they each turned in to a fight. Some with punishments, some with fierce force. *The threats.* I remembered the promises. *With the threats.* I thought of the music, and how much I'd miss that part of my life. I squeezed that hand again for support. It squeezed back, and didn't let go. Not even in the face of hell standing in front of us, he still held tight. I opened my eyes, and looked at Michael.

"I'm not your anything anymore. And you know this. Taking pictures of me in public is stalking, you know." I paused, he was enraged. He gritted his teeth while I continued. "There's no need for you to be here, or anywhere where I reside from this point on. I would appreciate if you would leave my friends and I alone. My affairs are no longer your business or worry." At that moment, my back felt suddenly much lighter. But then it felt like there was a knife digging in my back, and at any moment, it was going to pierce through my abdomen.

"Biggest mistake yet, Janes." He shook his head, and rubbed his goatee. "You'll be done with me when hell freezes over. And You," he turned towards Gabe. "Your biggest mistake was touching her. You signed your death certificate when you fucked her. I hope it was worth it." Gabe's hand tensed, and tries to get away to lunge. I held his hand tighter, and closer. "This is disgusting to watch...you touching him. You make me so fucking sick. I'll see you later." As he quickly turned to go, I was thankful that this hadn't turned into something worse. But Michael doesn't make idle threats. Ever.

27

We all went to the break room to regroup, and I went to cry. I needed the release, badly. Everyone was silent for a while, and then Simon broke the ice.

"Well, that went well." he paused, and looked at both of us, and giggled a little. All I could do was shake my head.

"It's ok, baby." Gabe said, and patted my back. "He can make all the threats he wants. It doesn't really scare me. I've got friends at home, and friends at work. My concern is for you. The way he looks at you...like he owns you. It was hard to watch." He was rubbing my back now, slow and steady. *He'll understand when he comes knocking on his door Janie. He's a guy, there's no way you could make him understand what Michael's really like...*

"I'm scared too," I said through tears. "My parents won't be home until Saturday. He probably knows that, oh God…" I cried harder, not knowing what to do. I wanted to die. This was crossing so many comfort level lines now, it was too much to take. Gabe wrapped his arms around me, and let me cry. I wasn't focused on what they were saying, but he and Simon were in deep talks for a few minutes until I calmed down. I felt him shift around, and heard the numbers being pushed on his cell phone. He was rubbing my back in the same rhythm, over and over, while he waited for whoever to answer.

"Hey Greg, it's me." He paused, and stopped rubbing. "Remember my situation, well, that needs to happen. Yes, sooner is best." I listened as they finished their conversation, but my thoughts were scattered.

"Janes," he started. "I'd like you to come and stay with me the next few nights. Until your parents are back home, at least. Would you do that for me?" With tears flowing down my cheeks, I looked him dead in the eyes. Was he really asking me this?

"Are you sure? It's such a risk for you… and your house." Even though it sounded silly, it still needed to be asked.

"Yes, I talked it over with Simon, and my roommate Greg knows of the situation. Everyone's on board. Let us keep you safe." He was serious, and this was by far the biggest gesture of love I'd ever felt in my life.

*   *   *   *   *

When we got to my house, Gabe went up and checked things out first. Out front, everything was quiet. No noise on the street, but it was cold, and no one enjoyed being outside when it was like this. I was tired of waiting by myself in the car. I got out, and ran into the house. Locking all the doors behind me, I quickly ran around and packed up a large bag of things. I dead bolted the house as we would if we were all leaving for vacation together, and called my mom from the house.

"Hello? She answered on the 3rd ring. "What's up honey?" She sounded busy, but I had to get this out.

"Hey Mom, I just wanted you to have my cell number. I'm going to stay at Gabe's until you're home. Michael's not acting right, and made some threats. We can discuss it when you're home." I paused.

"Are you okay honey?! I can get on the next plane and be there in four hours!" She was out of breath with worry.

"No, Mom, do your work. I feel much better staying with Gabe. He's here now helping me pack my bag, and then we're heading to his place."

"Is his place safe, honey?" She sounded completely petrified.

"Oh, yes, two other roommates. And it's way out in the country, you know, by the old city grave yards. I'll be okay. They won't let anything happen to me." I tried to be as reassuring as possible, but even I was unsure.

"Ok honey, please make sure that Gabe has my cell phone numbers, too. Text me updates. I love you, Janes."

"I will. Love you too, Mom. Night." I hung up the phone, and turned to Gabe. His arms always new just when to find me. And I seem to fit so perfectly in them. I headed towards the bathroom to pack my toiletry bag, while Gabe wandered around our living room. It was riddled with pictures from my childhood, and of my parents.

"Hey Janes, are all these pictures you?" He sounded surprised that all these were of one child. It dawned on me then that we still had a lot to learn about each other, and I was so eager to learn about his family, too. I zipped up my bag, and headed downstairs to show him some of the pictures.

"Yeah, they're all of me. What can I say? Only child, spoiled rotten." I smiled at him, and he went back to looking at pictures. I cautiously watched his expressions, and he seemed genuinely interested in each picture. *That makes my heart smile.* "I'm almost ready, just a few more things and we can go." I headed to the back seasonal room, and checked the locks. The smoking room was my last stop, and I packed up some smoke. No sense in leaving it here to waste, and maybe we could get in to some trouble together at his place. After I packed it all up, I rejoined him in the living room. "Alright, let's go."

He picked up my bags for me, and we headed out the door. We were both still on edge, because as we were leaving the drive-way and a mystery cars headlights flashed behind us, we both gasped. Our eyes met, and I reached for his hand.

"Thanks, again, Gabe. You're doing so much for me. I can't say thank you enough." I squeezed his hand, and he lifted it to his mouth, and kissed my fingers gently.

28

Our drive was reasonably quick, or it seemed to be with his fast race car driving skills. It was quite warm on this fall evening, and I was almost hot in my coat. He carried all my bags up to the porch, and briefly stopped.

"Ok, babe, time to meet the guys. They should be on their best behavior; however, I can make no promises BUT for the fact that you are more than safe here." I nodded, and followed him closely behind.

When we walked in, the aroma of Italian lingered in the air. I instantly noticed that the kitchen island was covered with dinner, and it looked to be waiting for the two of us. Gabe put my bags in his room, and reappeared next to me. He took my hand and led me into the kitchen.

"Janie, meet Greg," he turned and pointed, "and this is Aaron. My forever roommates." He smiled, and I smiled at both of the men. Greg was tall and thin, and his face was stern. Aaron had a huge, goofy smile which immediately eased my tension. Aaron was very large, almost like a wall.

"Hi, guys. It's nice to meet you." I paused, and added, "thank you for being so accommodating with all of this." Aaron quickly came over and patted my back. *Whoa, this one is touchy. Personal space, fella.*

"It's great to finally meet you, Janie. Gabe's mentioned some pretty great things about you." He chuckled, and punched Gabe's shoulder. "And you're welcome here whenever, and we'll protect you however we can." His hand was back on my shoulder, and his honest words made that shoulder pat okay to deal with.

"Hi Janie," Greg approached more cautiously. "I'm Greg. Are you hungry? We made dinner." He seemed nice enough, but made me a little nervous.

"That's really sweet of you both, and I'm starving." It was nice to sit with people for once, while eating. With my parents always gone, it seemed like I was always eating alone. The talk around the table was of current events, school, and of work. I finished first, and cleared my area. "Thank you again, guys. It's been nice to get to know you a little tonight. I'm going to go lay down for a while. Goodnight." As I turned to walk away, Gabe grabbed my hand and pulled me back towards him. He stayed sitting, but wrapped his arms around my waist, and kissed my belly. *Is this guy for real? Even in front of his friends? This is amazing...*

"I'll be in in a little while, Janes." He looked at me sweetly, and turned back to his friends. This all seemed so normal, unlike the rest of the day's events. It dawned on me then that normal was not something I was used to, and I wasn't even sure what my next move would be. Should be. I headed to the bathroom, and changed into more comfortable clothes. I sat on his big bed, and waited for him. I flipped through the channels, and left it on some CBS television police and fire fighter show. Still thinking about the day, I picked up my cell to check the messages. I had two text messages from my mom. I was still adjusting to this new world of technology, as just days ago, I was still answering pages. *Aren't you just hilarious tonight, internal monolog?* Too much stress made my head extra full, and semi-psychotic. Or that's how I felt. Then the door opened, and Gabe appeared.

"Hey love, you comfortable?" His smile was perfect, and he stripped his shirt off. Oh my, this was perfect. He headed towards the bed, and plopped down beside me. "Whatcha watching? Anything good?" He rubbed my thigh ever so gently.

"I have no idea, you pick something." I hesitated, then pressed on. "Or, we can have some fun with this green I brought with me." I raised my eyebrow and turned to face him with a baggie of the good stuff. His eyes lit up like a child on Christmas day.

"Oh baby! Yeah! Let's!" He was genuinely excited, almost jittery. This made me smile, and feel very relaxed. "It's been so long since I've gotten to partake. Let's turn on the radio, and some mood lighting for this. I'll open the window." He scooted around the room quickly, and prepped the area for our partaking. I opened the baggie, filled and precisely rolled the joint, and lit it up. The inhale was perfect, and smooth.

"Here you go, Gabe." I passed it to him. He looked it over in astonishment.

"You are perfect, aren't you??" His look changed from shocked, to awe, to love. I must've looked shocked at his comment, because he went on, "you've rolled me a perfect joint! On the first try!" He took a long draw off of the doobie, and relaxed on the bed next to me. He shook his head, as if shaking bad thoughts out. "What a day we've had today, and here you are. Again. In my bed!" *Wait, I thought this was a good thing? Oh please don't let me over stay my welcome.* "Even though the circumstances aren't the best, I'm really glad you're back." He turned, exhaled, and kissed my cheek.

"Aww, Gabe..." I started to giggle, and it was uncontrollable. "I'm so sorry, I can't stop laughing!!" My laughter was contagious, because seconds later, Gabe was hysterically laughing at my laughing. God, this was so perfect. I could feel my mental change, and the calm set in. After ten minutes, I finally quieted enough to talk. "I don't even remember what was so funny. But, I'm so glad I'm here with you, too." I covered my face with his pillow, and added, "Honestly, it's the only place I want to be. Dreamt of being." There was silence, but I could feel him shifting around me. Then the music came on, and it was soothing and mellow Lifehouse. "Ga-," he cut me off with his finger over my lips.

"Shhh... just listen to this song for me. And roll over so I can rub your back." I did as he demanded. It was a beautiful song, and I was surprised that I had never heard of the band before now. The lyrics were very deep, and telling. *I wonder if he really knows what this song is saying to me...and if he really feels this way.* Certain lyrics began to stick in my head. *...you are the light, into my soul... you are my purpose, you're everything...* The song was called 'Everything,' the chorus told me that. It was beautiful. Not to mention the entire time his warm hands were all over my back, my shoulders, and my hips. I leaned into his hands, and one came around under my shirt to my stomach. The touch of his hand across my soft skin gave me full body goose bumps. The music wasn't helping; I was throbbing in all the right areas. *...would you tell me, how could it be, any better than this? How can I stand here and not be moved by you...*

I couldn't take not looking at him as the music pace picked up, and the words grew to be even more meaningful. His eyes told me most everything I needed to know, and in that moment, I wanted to feel him all over me. I reached up towards his face, and stroked his cheeks with the back of my fingers. I loved feeling the stubble on his face, and running my hands through his hair. He slowly lifted his hands to my chest, and softly held my chest. I placed my hands over his own, and squeezed his hands on my breasts. I needed to feel him, more than ever. He reciprocated those feelings quickly.

Using his hands that were still cupped over each breast, he crushed my back into his chest. All while hoisting my shirt over my head. His body was so hot, and so defined. Just being skin to skin set off massive internal fireworks that I couldn't even begin to understand. His mouth came down first on my neck, and bit down my shoulder blade. My undies were now soaked, and I wanted him badly. I turned so I could face him, and he pulled us both down into a side laying position.

His mouth pounded mine, and the kisses were so passionate, deep, yet gentle and delicate. He dipped his head down to suckle on my nipples, and that made me inhale sharply. He then leaned to my ear and whispered, "can we keep going?" his breath was ending in my ear. I nodded fiercely. *Yes, YES! Oh Please Yes!!*

I pushed him onto his back, and rolled on top of him. I shimmied my pajama pants off, and pulled his pants down as far as I could. He chuckled when he realized that I could only get them down to his thighs, and offered his assistance.

"I'm sorry, baby. Let me get those for you." His sly smile told me all I needed to know. He slid his pants off completely, and I pinned him back down to the bed. *Oh, Janes, you're on top. In charge. This doesn't ever happen to you...what will you choose to do? Fuck him hard, you know you want to...* I lowered my lips to his, and kissed him hard. Using my feet, I pushed his legs together under me. I sat on top of his cock, and it throbbed beneath me. He was moaning now. "Ohh Janie..." His hands fisted my hair, and our lips crushed together like waves hitting the sand. Relentless. Passionate. I palmed him in my hands, and raised my hips to take him fully inside me.

As I slid down his hard shaft, his whole body pulsed beneath me. He looked so wild eyed, and I could feel myself falling farther for Gabe. He rocked his hips in a slow but firm rhythm, and my whole body began to tense with each move. I matched each move he made, thrust for thrust. I could feel the blood surge through his hot member when he was deep inside me, and I secretly wished

I could keep him there forever. I didn't know I existed in the depths that he was discovering tonight. Suddenly, he flipped us over, so I was under him. He brushed my hair out of my face, and lightly kissed my entire face. He laced his fingers in my hair, and held the top of my head. His thrusts were deeper, and more forceful. My fuse had been lit, and each hard pump hit the spot just right. I was so close to coming that my nails dug in to his back, my legs fell completely open making me his for the taking.

His pumps got faster, and he was looking directly into my eyes. That alone brought me back to the edge, again, only moments after my head had just exploded. *Is this much pleasure illegal?* He sat back on the bed, grabbing my hips for leverage. He drove his cock deeper inside with each penetration, making me scream his name repeatedly. His moans got louder, and I felt his body tense, and release. I could feel him throbbing inside me. I wrapped my legs around him, and my arms around him, too. He relaxed into this position, and we regained our breath together.

After a few moments, we collected ourselves and laid back down for bed. I couldn't stop smiling, and Gabe kept pointing out my "after sex" face. As I lay down in the bed with him, and I felt him curl around me, I felt so protected. So loved. I just laid there, and thought about everything for the longest time. Soon his breathe was heavy, and his hands were twitching. He was sound asleep. I intertwined my fingers with his. *I'd do anything to keep this forever...* As my eyes fluttered closed, I couldn't help share my last thought aloud. "I think I love you, Gabe..."

29

Waking up next to him felt amazing, and very unreal. He was still asleep when I woke up, and headed for the shower for work. I was in there a few minutes before there was a knock on the bathroom door, "Hey Janes? Can I come in?" *Did he always have to be this polite? Love.*

"Of course you can! It's your bathroom!" I giggled from inside the shower. Moments later, his head had poked through the door.

"Can I really push my luck, and ask to get in with you?" He gave me the cutest smile he could muster.

"I suppose." I stepped out of his way, and he entered. "Are we going to carpool now, too?" I couldn't help ask. I looked at him, as I thought he'd have some sort of silly come back. Instead, he stood tall as he washed his body.

"You know, that's a good idea. We'll take my car." I was shocked, and I thought my face was going to fall off next. "That way it's not as obvious where you are." *Oh, he had a plan. Just a plan. Not an invite. DAMN!*

"Ok, that sounds great to me. I don't take too long to get ready, so we'll be on time." I continued to shave my legs, and he continued to finish rinsing off. We finished at the same time, and he pulled our towels into the shower. Looking up, our eyes met. There were those ornery smiles again. The little smirks you get when the butterflies are so good and hot that you're instantly addicted to the source that brings them to you in the first place.

"I love the way the sparks fly between us, Janie. It's so undeniable." His voice was low, and very serious. He never stopped drying off. And I never broke the stare while I quickly dressed. I nodded in agreement, and blushed. "You're so beautiful, do you get that? That's why he's mad for you. You're it. I see that now..." he pulled his boxers on. Leaning into my ear, he whispered "I know that now." That left me breathless. He disappeared to get dressed.

I waited for him in the living room, where Aaron had taken up playing the PlayStation. He turned long enough to give me a wave, and winked at me. *Who knows what the wink was for?* When Gabe emerged, he escorted me to his car. And we headed into work.

*   *   *   *   *

The day flew by, and we ended up going out to a movie and dinner. Back at his place, I decided that I had better call my mom and check in. They were due back home tomorrow evening, and I couldn't wait to see them. I sat in Gabe's big lounge chair, and sank into its softness. She answered in one ring.

"Honey! Oh, I'm so glad that you called!! I've hoped that you were okay, and you didn't answer all of my texts! I was so worried!" Waiting for her to take a breath, I cut in when I could.

"I'm sorry, Mom. Gabe's roommates made us a huge feast for dinner last night, and we stayed up talking and stuff. It was a really great night, and I really, really needed it."

"That's wonderful, Jane. I filled your Dad in, and he definitely wants to talk about all this when we're home." She paused, and added "And, are we allowed to meet Gabe? He really does sound sweet." She giggled a little, as if being able to sense my giant smile on the other end of the phone.

"Oh Mom, yes, you will meet Gabe. I hope you like him..." I sighed heavily.

"Because you really like him, don't you, honey?" She already knew, and I loved her for that. "Have you heard from Michael at all?"

"Well, not really. He doesn't have my cell number, and I don't think he knows where I've been, at Gabe's. Work today went well, no visits today. Small steps, I guess." I shrugged my shoulders, as I wasn't sure what else could be said about that.

"We just want you safe, hon. So you're staying with Gabe again tonight, right?" I could tell that she hoped I was.

"Yes, definitely. Probably more in the future, too. I'm still planning on coming home tomorrow night to see you guys though! I can't wait!" I really was excited. It seemed like forever ago I had a hug from my mom.

"Ok, that sounds wonderful! I'll text you when we land, and then it'll just be an hour or so after that! I love you, honey. Tell Gabe I said Thank you for keeping you safe!" she laughed at herself.

"I will mom. Love you too. Night." As I hung up, Gabe emerged. It was late, and I was exhausted. I grabbed one of Gabe's shirts out of his laundry, and slid it on. He smiled when he saw what I was wearing. I climbed into bed, and he laid down right next to me. His arms wrapped around me, and his warmth rocked me to sleep. My eyes were so heavy, that I knew morning would come before I was ready.

*　　*　　*　　*　　*

I woke up disoriented, and not sure where I was. I had a terrible feeling that I couldn't shake. Next to me, Gabe was sleeping soundly. The clock told me it was 4:36am. I must've had a nightmare, but I couldn't remember the details. There was a lot of running, and hiding. *But from who?* I laid back down, and tried to relax myself back to sleep. My mind was wandering, and horrible visions of Michael and the past were creeping in my head. *Don't think about him! You've been doing so well with all of this…keep your head about you!* I rolled over on to my side to try and hide my upcoming tears. At least they were the silent kind, so I wouldn't disturb Gabe.

"Baby?" His voice said still half asleep. "What's wrong?" I knew I wasn't going to be able to hide my emotion from him, so I rolled over and faced him. I was glad it was so dark, and hoped that he couldn't see the tears.

"I just had a bad dream. I'm sorry to have woken you." His hands came and gently rubbed my arms.

"It's ok, Janes." he turned me back over, so my back was against his chest. "You're safe here." His voice was more awake now, and he rubbed my back with one hand, and held on to me with the other. "Do you want to tell me about it?" I figured that he probably had some idea, but being that it was dark and we were alone...I knew I should.

"I get these feelings sometimes, like something bad is going to happen. I dream that he is everywhere, and I can't get away." I stifled the sobs, and tried to stay calm. "Or, at least I think it's him. Sometimes I can't see who I'm running from, and I run for what seems like forever." He tightened his hold on me, and kissed my head.

"It's all going to be okay, love. Look at how far this situation has come in a month. I bet in another month, it will all almost be a thing of the past." I caught my breath, *a thing of the past?* As if he could feel my tension, he added, "the only thing that won't be a thing of the past is us."

He propped himself up on his elbow, and leaned over me to my face. His mouth was quick to find mine, this time with a hunger that I hadn't felt come out of him before. His kiss was so deep, that I had to turn over and reposition myself to be able to take his tongue in that far. Once I flipped over, I could feel his erection pressing into my side. I reached down, and grasped his hard, hot member and pumped my hand around him. He moaned loudly, and shimmied out of his pants. He slid my panties down, and separated my legs.

As his head skirted the outside of my deepest depths, I dug my heels into his hips making him sink into me. I let out a sigh of pleasure as his rhythm first started slowly. I could feel ever inch, every vein throb when things were slow. He wrapped his arms around my shoulders, and thrust deeper than ever. His face was buried in my neck, and he squeezed me with every plunge. I started to clench around him, and his speed increased. His teeth gritted together, and I could feel him shoot his home brew into me.

Laying with him calmed me more than anything else ever could. We wrapped up in blankets, and in each other, and we both fell back asleep. *Here's to a good dream, Janes...*

30

When my eyes opened, it was light outside. I turned my head to check the clock, and it was just after 9am. I decided to get up, slowly and carefully, as to not wake up my sleeping stud. I wanted to attempt a breakfast for him, if they had anything remotely breakfast like in the house. I managed to find some eggs, bread, cheese, and bacon. Breakfast sandwiches would have to do. Half way through my cooking, he emerged from the bedroom.

"Good morning," I said cheerfully. He walked straight over and kissed me square on the lips.

"No more dreams?" He asked perplexingly. I shook my head no, and kissed him again.

"You seem to have scared them all away. For now," I turned back to making his sandwich, piling the bacon pretty high. "Here's breakfast for you...hope you like bacon." I winked at him as I handed it over.

"Thank you, baby. That's very thoughtful of you." He shifted to the kitchen island, and sat on a bar stool. He patted the one next to him, and asked, "can you sit so we can chat?" I grabbed my plate, and headed over to him.

"I forgot to tell you that my mom says thanks for all of this...protection. And..." I hesitated, and then let it go. "They want to meet you. Pretty bad." I cringed, and looked over for his reaction. To my surprise, he was smiling.

"Is that so?" he laughed. "Well, sort of fits with this conversation then." He cleared his throat. "We've known each other for quite a while, and these past few weeks that we've really gotten to know each other have been amazing. Even considering the situation, I don't think I would change much of this."

My head started to spin. This was going to be the end. He was going to give me the "it's not you, it's me" speech. *Fuck. I knew this was too good to be true.* I started to tremble involuntarily. I hoped I could last through the rest of this without falling to pieces.

"I would love to meet your parents, Janie. And your friends. Your aunts. Your long lost family members. And I'd like you to meet mine..." his voice trailed off, and slowly he turned his head to check my reaction.

I couldn't move. *Did you hear that?!* When I opened my mouth to speak the first time, nothing came out. I smiled at him, and he smiled back. "So, you want to meet them?" He laughed out loud.

"Are you speechless, Janes?" He paused, and continued. "Yes, I want to meet your parents. And I'd like to meet them as your man." I shook my head back and forth; I was at a loss of words.

"Gabe, I--" suddenly I was scared. "I'm afraid it might be too soon... I don't want you too wrapped up in all of this with Michael. Until it's all really done with, you know?" I paused, "I hope that came out right." He put his hand on my leg.

"Yes, baby, I completely understand. We'll go slow. There's no need to rush at all. But I want you to know that you're welcome here whenever you'd like. I'd love to spend every minute with you if I could." He kissed my cheek, and finished his breakfast.

"I want that, too, Gabe. And I appreciate that you'll go slow. I just need to be sure that everything is done with Michael before I fall into...you." I blushed, and he put his hands on my face. "I'd like for you to take me home in a bit, and I'll leave my car here. If that's ok." He knew that it was my wish to stay hidden just awhile longer.

"Absolutely, love. Anything. Will you come back tomorrow, and stay the night? Please?" *How could I refuse a face like that?*

"Of course I will…. I'm not going to be able to focus on anything else until I'm back with you, you know. You're like my personal panacea." He smiled very wide, and smacked my ass.

We spent the next hour re-packing my bags, and cleaning his room. The car ride back to my parents' house was very quiet, but our fingers were interlocked the whole ride. He escorted me up to the house once we arrived, and checked all around the perimeter. Everything looked kosher, so there was no reason for him to stay. *Although I wished he would anyway.*

"Alrighty, babe… I'll text you this evening and we can chat if you'd like." He wrapped his arms around me, and hugged tightly.

"Ok, I'll look forward to it." I leaned in, and our lips locked. Neither one of us was eager to end this kiss. So it went on, and on, and on forever standing in the doorway. Head over heels was an understatement, and I couldn't break this kiss if I tried. His hands made their way under my shirt, and he gave each breast a tiny squeeze. I smiled, and our kiss broke for now. "I'll see you later, Gabe. Thanks again…for everything." He kissed my cheek, and got back in his car and took off. After I locked up, I headed up to take a relaxing bath, and ease my worry filled mind.

31

The bubbles in the bath smelled like roses, and it was more than wonderful to relax in a scalding hot bath. My mind was wandering everywhere, but it hung most on my last few nights with Gabe. It brought an instant smile to my face, even in the bathtub. I didn't have to work until Monday now, and spending tomorrow with him again made me very happy. *This is exactly what you need. To be focusing on the positive things, and forgetting your past. The past has been pretty quiet these past few days. I wonder if it will continue this way, or revert back to how it was.* As my mind wandered more, the song changed on the radio to Led Zeppelin, and my stomach got tight.

I went for the razor to shave my legs, and waited for the song to end. 'Communication Breakdown' was blaring still, and now I found some irony in the song. *It sounds louder? Is it louder? What the fuck?* I hated the song so much, that it kept getting louder and louder in my head. I quickly shaved one leg, and reached for the soap for the other. The next thing I knew, I couldn't breathe, and my head was throbbing. My eyes were closed, and I was looking into the dark. But I didn't feel alone.

I opened my eyes enough to see his blurry outline through what seemed like a cloudy lens. Until I gasped, and realized I was underwater. Being held underwater. Michael. *What the fuck!? How did he get in here?! This is it...oh my God.* He let me come up from the water, and I was desperate for air. My chest was heaving up and down, and he sat back next to the tub. I reached up for my head, right to the spot where it was burning now...and I felt the opening on my scalp.

"What did you do to me?" I screamed at him.

"Just a small ounce of what you truly deserve." I saw his joker grin briefly before he smacked me across the face with his fist. "You're such a fucking whore. Did you think I wouldn't see you with him? Standing there, locking lips with each other, like no one else existed." He gritted his teeth, and I could see his fists clenching. "I warned you, and I warned you." He reached for me, and I pulled away to the back of the shower. "Now, Janie, that's just going to piss me off. Get over here. Now." *Maybe if you just give in. Let him have what he wants, and he'll go.*

I swallowed hard, and repositioned to where I was in the bath, but now hugging my knees. His hand reached out again, and ended up on my shoulder. I slowly turned my head to look at his face, and as I did, his other fist popped me in my eye. *FUCK!!!* The instant burn and headache that came were atrocious. I couldn't see, and my eye wouldn't open. *Get out of this bathtub, NOW!* I needed to get out of the bathtub.

"Michael! STOP! Please let me out of the tub. It's getting cold." I tried to plead with him. I hoped that there was some shred of morals left in him, or some ounce of the "love" that he had supposedly felt for me. "What do you want from me?" I held in the sobs the best I could.

He grabbed both of my arms, and lifted me straight out of the tub. He turned so I was over the bathroom rug, and dropped me on the floor. I landed on my wrist, and now that burned, too. I pulled myself into the corner, and he promptly pulled me back out. I tried to cover myself, and every time I did, he would shift me so I couldn't. *Silent Tears. Protect yourself however you can. Don't hold back. Mom. Dad. Gabe. I did love him, and now I wish I would've told him before I died.* Stop.

I opened my only working eye, to see Michael staring at me smiling. I glared at him, and held my head. The blood was making quite a mess all over the floor, and myself. Almost everything in the bathroom had been smeared with blood, and there were pink and red stains everywhere. I tried to get up, and to my surprise, he let me stay standing.

I stumbled to my feet, and it took a few seconds to get my balance. My head was very cloudy, and it was hard to focus.

"Michael," I tried to speak. "Please don't. Can't we just talk? Or-" He cut me off, as he forced me to bend over the counter top. My face was pressed on to the sink, and I had enough leverage to block my head from hitting the water spout. He had one arm across my back, and held me down hard. He was fumbling with his pants. *Just like old times.* They dropped to the floor.

He spread my legs apart with his foot, and took off his gloves. He slammed straight into my mind, and it ripped apart. Silent sobs were screaming from my chest, and blood stained tears were rolling like thunder down the sink. I felt things pulling and tearing in my crotch, and it burned. Every thrust was harder than the last. He was hissing through his gritted teeth, grinding my face into the cold counter top. He pulled out so far I thought he had finished, until he rammed in harder than ever in my life. Everything around me turned red, and all I could see was red.

I screamed out in pain, and something pierced my shoulder. *Ouch!* And again. I started to turn my body, but the pains kept happening. *I'm burning...like I'm on fire.* The pain was so blinding, that I had to will myself to breathe. He then punched the side of my face with his hand, and my head throbbed so hard, I was sure it was going to explode. Then the red went to black, and my mind began to wander... *It's so sunny outside, I wish I would've brought my sunglasses. Gabe said to meet him by the swings, in the park. Look! There he is! I wrapped my arms around him, and he instantly warmed my soul. His lips were so gentle, and so caring, on mine. I never wanted this to end. Wait, Gabe! Don't go! Stop! Why are you walking away? I need you! Please don't leave me here! I'm scared to death!*

Suddenly the dream was over, and the black was back. My head hurt beyond belief, my body was on fire, and I couldn't move. I could feel my chest heaving, and gasping, for air, but pulling a breath in felt like an elephant sitting on my chest, and was impossible. I could feel the darkness swallowing me again, and I fought to stay in the lighter dark as long as I could. I gasped again, and with the failed breath, I forgot to try to stay awake.

Wake up Janie! GET UP JANIE! I tried to open my eyes, someone was yelling my name. Where am I? In the darkness, I reached up for my head. It was moist, and it hurt very badly. I shifted my weight, and leaned to the left. My arm gave out, and my entire side burned. Suddenly I was gasping for air, I shifted back to my right, and my breath came back to me. *Oh my God. Oh Jesus. Cell*

Phone. I sat for another minute, remembering more of what had happened. *Michael was here. Is he still here? Oh God, please don't let me die here.*

I was sure I had recollected most of the events, but I had no idea of the time. I knew my bath had started around 5 o'clock, but it was dark outside now. I slowly stood, using the bathroom counter top as a crutch. *It must be nearly...midnight? It feels so late...I'm soo tired.* I reached for the light switch, and flicked it on. I winced in the light, as it made my eyes feel like blowing up. It took a moment to acclimate to the lighting, and once I opened my eyes, I saw the carnage.

32

Blinking slowly, I turned my head around the bathroom. There were pools of red everywhere. My head was throbbing, burning...*and, is it wet?* I tried to focus, and remembered that Michael had been there. My heart started to beat out of my chest, and I couldn't catch my breath. Just then, I heard something crash in another part of the house. I cautiously limped towards the door, and closed it quickly. I turned the lock, and opened the closet door against it, so it was impossible to open. *Calm down. Just breathe.* There was no life in my legs, I could not stand any longer. I collapsed to the floor, and all went black.

Suddenly, I heard a noise. The familiar ding told me that I had a message on my phone. *Your phone!! Pick up your phone!!* I reached out, and tried to feel the floor around me, but the only thing I felt was a minding stinging pain going up and down my left arm. I quickly recoiled that arm against my chest, and tried to focus not on the internal fireball of pain that was coursing through my veins. I leaned out again, this time with my right hand, and felt underneath clothes, and towels for my phone. Something hard hit my finger, and I jumped back in fear. *No one is in here with you. It's okay. Just get your phone, and call anyone.* I picked up the object, which was indeed the phone. I could barely make out the blinking green light that was flashing.

My fingers fumbled for the keys, and I lit the screen. I squinted to read the messages, or who they were from. But my eyes wouldn't focus well enough. I hit whatever text was on top, and tried to type a message. I could feel the waves of sleep coming back to overtake me again, and I fought to finish typing. I hoped that the letters I was pushing made enough sense to get help. *Please help...* I knew the bottom corner button was the 'send' button, and once it was pushed, I leaned my head back against the wall and closed my eyes.

Ahead of me is a large building, and I'm walking right in. I know I'm dreaming now, and I can't wake myself up. I'm scared, but there's someone over there! Hey! Hello? Can you hear me? Where am I? Why am I here? I don't want to be here! Please, can you help me?!

I heard something, something loud. It startled me awake, and I started coughing and gasping for air. Abruptly, there was a figure in the doorway. I tried to scream, and push myself away from the door. Until I heard a heartfelt gasp, and that calmed me long enough to listen through the pounding in my head.

"Oh, my God...Janie? Honey..." I could hear him struggling with the door. "Janie? It's me, it's Gabe." In between sobs, I could hear him rattling the door. "Baby? Can you move? You're safe now, I swear. Please baby," he shook the doors. *It's Gabe. To save me.* I tried to scoot over to the door, and leaned on my left arm. I quickly collapsed, and Gabe moaned as if he was in pain. "Oh Janie! Don't lean on your left side sweetie, please. Use your right arm, just a bit farther." It was so wonderful to hear someone I loved. "That's it, now reach out, and close the closet door. You can do it, love." As I leaned to the side, I felt the door, and pushed it closed. I felt myself start to collapse, but I never hit the floor.

His arms were around me, and I could hear him on the phone. He was frantic. "It's on Blue Hallow Ct., I'm not sure of the numbers, but my Probe is out front." There were pauses in between his words, and I was lost in them. "Yes, she's breathing, but barely. No, not keeping consciousness at all." I tried to open my eyes to look at him, but it was so hard. My eyes were so heavy. "She's got an open wound on the top of her head, lost too much blood." He was sobbing. I felt him shift me around, and my body was on fire, everywhere. I was listening to his breathing, and silently trying to make my breathing match his. His breath would hitch, and I would get anxious.

"She's got more blood on her back, should I check? Ok, one second." He gently leaned me onto his knees, and my chin rested on him comfortably. He dabbed my shoulder with a towel, and gasped. And sobbed. "Oh my God..." his voice trailed off, and his breath hitched. "She's been stabbed. Many Times. OH, please hurry!" His pain was making me sad, and I tried again to open my eyes. This time one opened, and I saw his beautiful face. He turned to me, and semi smiled. "Hey love, stay with me, ok?" I nodded, and tears flowed from one eye. I found his hand with my own, and I clutched it. The blackness was surrounding me again, but this time I wasn't as afraid.

"Stay with me..." I managed to push out in a whisper, as the darkness engulfed me again.

*   *   *   *   *

When I woke up, I was uncomfortable. I tried moving, but couldn't. I tried opening my eyes, and to my shock, they opened. I slowly looked around, and the night started to flood back. *Oh my*

God, Michael! My chest started to burn, and I couldn't catch my breath. Suddenly, there was a hand on mine, and a kiss on my forehead. *Gabe.*

"Shhh, it's alright baby. You're safe now. I'm here, and your parents are on their way." He stroked my hair, while my breath regained it's slow, labored speed. I cleared my throat slowly.

"I'm... sorry..." I cleared my throat again. "Thank... You..." I tried to smile at him. But the tears loomed again, and they were pouring down my face. "So... scared..." I closed my eyes to forget, and his arms were around me, so tightly, and gently at the same time.

"Don't you ever apologize for any of this. You didn't deserve this. Stop worrying, love. I swear I'm never leaving your side." He stroked my forehead so softly, so rhythmically that I fell back asleep.

*   *   *   *   *

My head felt so heavy, and my eyes wouldn't open. But I could clearly here everyone that was around me. I could feel them, too. I let their voices fill my head, and I was calm knowing I wasn't alone. Gabe was talking, and he seemed to be very anxious. There was another deep voice, but I couldn't place who's it was. Then I heard a female voice come in, and I knew it was my Mom. *He must be with mom and dad.*

"Yeah, I had been texting her, and she's normally very fast to respond to me. When a few hours had gone by, I started to worry, and tried calling. She didn't answer. I waited another hour, and then I got the text from her." I could hear him rustling around with his phone. "This is what she wrote, and I immediately got in my car and drove over here. And found her..." He started sobbing again. I did remember texting him. *'hurt, hes here.'*

"It's ok, son..." my Dad said. "We're so thankful you got there when you did. She's going to be alright, just relax and breathe." I could hear his hand patting Gabe on the back, trying to calm him.

"I'm also sorry we had to meet like this. Janie and I...well, we've had a relationship for a while now." There was a big pause of silence in the room. *Oh my God...can't believe he said that! Some explaining will surely be warranted!* "I know," he paused. "Michael." He frowned. "It was a pretty bad situation, and there were a few of us at work that she had confided in. We were helping, doing it "her way," and she had ended it with him a few days ago. I should've known he would do something like this. I should've had her stay with me." I couldn't take this just listening stuff anymore. I tried, once again, to peel my eyelids open. Again, one opened. *Thank God.* Seeing was believing. There was Gabe, in my Dad's arms...and my Mom looking over both of them with adoring eyes. *Oh please let this be real... how is this possible that in a matter of months this man has made his way into my life, saved me, and loved me this much? This is all just so different...*

I coughed, and cleared my throat. Before I could even try to speak, all of them were gathered around my bedside. I smiled at them. "Hi." Was all I could get out for now, but I was so happy to be awake. My Dad rushed off, and reappeared with the nurse. She was smiling at me, and checked my pulse.

"Well, her pulse is almost normal. Let me check the chest tube drainage, and radiology will come to x-ray her arm and wrist. All things considered, she's doing very well." She turned to me, "Hi Sweetie, you thirsty?" She beamed, and offered me a few ice chips. *The Best coldest things, ever!!* I nodded, and accepted more. Finally, I felt like I could talk more.

"What did... he do... to.... Me?" I asked. The nurse looked at my parents, at Gabe, and then back at me. The nurse looked very gravely into my eyes.

"We stitched up a five inch wound on the top of your head, and we're still not sure what did it. Your lung was punctured by a knife, and you were stabbed multiple times in the back." She sighed heavily. "And, it looks like your arm may be broken, and there were signs of sexual assault." She bent down, and looked directly into my eyes. "But you're going to be fine now. You're awake, safe, and we'll get you all taken care of. I promise." The tears stung my eyes, because as she was talking, I was remembering the night with Michael... *I remember begging him not to, but he did anyway.* Suddenly, I couldn't find my breath. I was underwater all over again, and grasping at the sheets. I couldn't make myself relax, and suddenly, a warmth came over me. The nurse was still there, rubbing my arm slowly.

"That better honey? I don't want you to be anxious. Tell me if you are. Doc already called in orders, and you look much calmer now." I smiled at her, feeling warm-brained and drugged out of my mind. *But calm, Janes, soo relaxed now...*

33

"Honey," my mom called as she headed over to my hospital bed. "Can I ask you a question?" I could feel my forehead instantly wrinkle, but her face remained calm. I nodded at her. "Why didn't you ever tell us about Michael?" She sat on the edge of my bed, and waited. I couldn't talk at first. There was too much emotion, and too much hurt. *But you owe her an explanation...and you know it.* Her face was pure sorrow, and sadness. But I couldn't give her the answer she wanted, because truth be told, I had no idea.

My voice was raspy, and shook when I spoke. The doctor's said that the chest tube was draining properly, and no infection was present in any of the wounds. They kept repeating over and over how lucky I was to have made it. I sighed. "Mom, I'm sorry." Catching my breath had become easier, but I was still slow to talk. "I never thought...he would do anything... Like this." I shook my head. "My friends, Gabe... were always there. Always strong. Love them." I coughed, and my chest felt like it was being stabbed with each lung convulsion that propelled out of my mouth. The coughs were deep, and each brought tears to my eyes.

"Paul," she turned to my dad. "Please go find the nurse, and tell her Janie needs more pain meds." He smiled at both of us, and headed out of the room. She rubbed my forehead, and then my thigh. "I'm very thankful for your friends, especially Gabe." She smiled widely. "He's very sweet... and handsome." I could feel my cheeks flush, and my face got hot. *Yes, he's delicious, and I want him to be mine!* My mom laughed loudly. I smiled. "Well, now I know how to bring color to those cheeks! He's a keeper, I think." I nodded at her.

"Yes, makes me very.... Happy." I heard commotion at the door, and my Dad and nurse both entered.

"Hello Janie, how are you doing? I've got some more pain meds for you, honey." This nurse was older, and very sweet. Soft spoken, and a soft touch. Made all the needle pokes, prods, and exams a little more tolerable. "Want to try sitting up a bit, Janie? I could raise the head of your bed."

"Yes... please...." I smiled at her. She slowly raised the head of my bed, and the pressure in my chest lessened. I let out a long breath, and the room went silent. I couldn't talk right then, so I raised my hand and gave them the thumbs up.

"There you are, honey. You call me when you need anything! I'm right outside." She threw away her trash, and headed out the door. My Dad settled back into reading his book, and my mom returned to my bedside.

"You feeling okay?" Her voice was concerned.

"Yeah... drugs are good." I smiled goofy at her. "How long... am I here?" I tried to scoot myself up, but the slight movement of my left arm turned on a fire deep within my body. It took away my breath, my words, and my focus. A moan escaped my lips, and my mom's hands were on me, steadying me.

"Easy there, honey." She sighed, as I calmed down and caught my breath. "Well, radiology said that your wrist is definitely broken, and they'll be in to set it sometime this afternoon. The chest tube will come out this evening, I think, depending on your oxygen levels and progress. Doctor said earlier that he thought it would be no issue, that you were doing great." She half smiled, trying to help me find the positives. "So, a few more days, then you're free." Suddenly, a voice I recognized returned.

"And when you're free... I owe you a date." his smile was huge. He set down a duffle bag, pillow, and his coat. He brought the teddy bear over to me, and set it on the bed. "I'm so glad to see you... and sitting up a bit!" His arms were so warm, and my face fit right into his neck. He smelled so wonderfully, I never wanted him to go.

"Hello, Gabe!" My Mom said cheerfully. She patted his back, and he turned and hugged her. *Perfect!* "Honey, Gabe would like to stay the night here with you, and after our talk earlier...I'm sure you're ok with that?" My smile almost broke my face.

"Yes...." I turned and squeezed his hand. "Please stay..." I could tell by the look in his eyes that he wasn't going to be going anywhere. That made me feel so relaxed, that my thoughts ran wild. *MMmm... I really want to wrap myself around him....*

Just then, the radiologist and doctors came in, and the atmosphere in the room changed. "Hello Janie," Doctor Bruschi said. "We're going to set your wrist in a cast now, and we'll have to reposition the bones. It's going to hurt, and we're going to give you a shot of pain medicine right before, so it will take effect immediately." He turned towards my family, and Gabe. "It's not going to be pretty in here for a little while. It's your choice to stay or leave, or up to Janie, of course." My family nodded, and the Doctor pressed on. "After we set the wrist, we're going to remove the chest tube. Your oxygen levels have stayed up, and your breathing is becoming more regular. That won't be as bothersome to you, Janie, as the wrist will be." He smiled, and patted my thigh. "And finally," he chuckled. "I know, as if all of this wasn't enough... first, let me say how brave, and strong you are, young lady. You'll need that strength to get you through this. After you're comfortable tonight, the police will be in for your statement about what happened to you."

I could feel my cheeks flush, and my breathing quickened. The Doctor motioned for the nurse, and she hooked a vial up to my IV, and pushed the liquid in.

"Don't panic, honey. Your family can stay with you through all of this, I promise." He motioned, and Gabe squeezed my hand. "We're going to set your wrist now, Janie. I need you to keep breathing."

As he spoke, I got lost in the fog of medicine. I could hear their voices, and the pressures from things pushing and pulling me. Suddenly, a crack, and a vibration started in my body that I couldn't control. The pain was immense, and surged through me. I couldn't even tell what hurt, only that everything hurt. I heard voices talking, and I tried to focus to listen.

"The bone is set! Hold her through the seizure! It's only from the pain, looks like it's slowing." More commotion. "Here you are, Janie...can you hear me honey?" I focused first on my breathing, in and out. Next the pain, and pushing it to the back of my head again. Now my eyes... they were so heavy. I pulled them, and willed them to open, and slowly it was happening. *I felt scared, and alone. Many sets of eyes wide open were staring back at me, all holding their breathe. Everyone was so on edge, and that was making me nervous...*

34

Finally, they stayed open. I was still surrounded by nurses and doctors, but felt safe. I could see that they were still wrapping my arm in the cast, but now it did not hurt as bad. *Thank God.* The nurse finished wrapping the cast, and it set very quickly. Now that I couldn't move it, it felt much better. I smiled at the thought, and someone giggled.

"What are you thinking about, love?" Gabe asked softly, and low. It wasn't just my face that got hot when he said that in my ear.

"Good drugs..." I winked at him. He laughed, and kissed my forehead. "Doctor says I've got to move, so they can lower your bed to get that tube out. I'll just be over by the window." He kissed my hand, and my eyes closed again.

When I awoke again, I scanned the room. Empty. *Hmm, wonder where everyone is?* I was sitting up more than before, and my breathing was much easier. I breathed in deeper, and then deeper, and then...*FUCK!* Ok, that was enough. I looked at my wrist, and forearm... which were now in a white cast. I wiggled my fingers, and all ten of them were still there. *Thank God.* I reached up, and felt the top of my head. There were staples and stitches down the center and side of my scalp, covered with some sort of ointment. I lifted the sheet, and saw the large gauze bandage on my left side. My heart sank. This must have been where the chest tube was.

"Don't be scared by those, love." His calming voice came flowing from across the room. Who knows how long he had been there, watching me take stock of my injuries. "That side one isn't so bad, the tube slid right out." He slowly approached the bed. Almost cautiously, and I wondered if I was scary.

"How does my back look?" I asked. His expression told me that it wasn't great.

"Well, you've got pretty big stab wounds. They're all stitched up, but were pretty swollen." He sat at the end of my bed. I rubbed my forehead with my hand. There was so much to take in. "Now that all the tubes are out, all you have to do is heal. Your parents will be back up in a little bit...the detectives are meeting with them now. I really like your parents..." he chuckled. "You should know; I did tell them about us." He looked down at his hands, and slowly up to me. He met my smile.

"I know you did. I heard you." I reached for him, and he scooted closer to me. "It was like I was lost in a dark room, but I could hear everything. And feel everything. You made me feel so relaxed..." I moved my hand, so I could link my fingers with his. "Thank you for saving me...for coming when I needed you." My eyes filled with tears, and he threw his arms around me.

"Oh, baby... I knew something was off. I could feel it. But until I got your text, I thought I was just being irrational, and missing you." His hug was abruptly firmer. "I have such deep feelings for you, Janes. I swear I'll never let anything like this happen again." *Oh Gabe, I love you...*

Just then, my parents both reentered the room. "Sorry to interrupt," my dad began. "But the detectives are here, and want to know if you're ready to give your statement." All eyes were on me. I wasn't sure how I felt about everyone hearing this, but I knew it was going to come out at some point. I nodded, and squeezed Gabe's hand. My dad turned, and opened the door.

Two female detectives appeared, and showed us all their badges. They nodded at my parents, and turned towards me. Both of the women looked very friendly, but not much like detectives. Their long brown hair, both pulled back into a tight pony tail, and teeth beaming white.

"Hi Janie," she extended her arm, and we shook hands. "I'm Detective Knox, and this is Special Investigator Maddox. Or, Betsy and Lucy if you prefer." I couldn't help but smile at their perfection. But I knew what they were there for, and my heart was beating so fast.

"We're here to get your statement about what happened to you three nights ago. Can I sit?" She motioned towards the foot of my bed, and I bent my legs so she would have room. "Are you comfortable? We aren't here to bring you any worry or trouble, we're simply getting things on record, and seeing that whoever did this to you is brought to justice." I could feel the 'v' form on my forehead.

My eyes darted around the room. My heart pained for what my family would hear when I started talking. For what Gabe would hear, and what he would think. *But this is something that needs to be done... be strong, you can do this.* I turned back toward the detectives, and squeezed Gabe's hand. He was now in a chair next to my bed. His fingers were still intertwined with mine, giving me the quiet strength I needed to go back to that afternoon...

"Alright Janie," Detective Knox pulled out her tape recorder. "This will be recorded, but if you need a break, to stop, a drink--anything. Just say so. We're here for you, always keep that in the back of your mind." She smiled as if she were truly concerned. She then spoke into the tape recorder with my name, the date, time, and all people who were present. Hearing all of that made it all real, and a chill shook me to the bone. "Whenever you're ready, Janie." I sighed heavily, and closed my eyes.

"I remember spending that afternoon with Gabe." I turned at looked at him, and smiled. "I had spent a few days with him while my parents were out of town. When he dropped me off, we had a," I paused and cleared my throat. "We had a moment on the patio, and as he walked away, I remember turning around and locking the doors." *Flood gates. Get it out. The truth, girl.* "I was diligent to lock the doors because this was not the first time he had done this. Been in the house when I've not known, and inflicted..." I heard her gasp, and saw her head crash into her hands. *Oh no, your poor mother....*

"It's okay, Janie. Your mom will be strong enough to handle this, for you. Just take a moment to catch your breath, honey." the investigator said. I collected myself quietly, and sent my mom an apologetic expression.

"A little while ago, I had been home alone and he had snuck in through the basement room window. He was angry with me then, too." I paused to catch my breath, and take a quick drink.

"Janie," the Detective asked questioningly, "maybe we can clarify something now on tape. Do you know who did this to you?" Her stare was piercing. I nodded, and my breath hitched. Gabe squeezed my hand.

"Yes, I know who this was." I closed my eyes. "It was Michael Comaro. My ex-lover, ex-boyfriend, ex-best friend." I swallowed hard at the admission.

"Do you know why he would do this to you, honey?" the investigator asked.

"We started dating about a year ago, and things went south soon after. I could never find the right time, or way to end things with him. I finally had the right way out, or at least one that felt safe a few months ago. I started hanging around more and more with my friends from work, and Gabe. And less and less, and finally ended things with him. He didn't take it well, and made a lot of threats. Not only to me, but to my coworkers, and to Gabe." I hung my head, and shook it back and forth. "He did this to me because he promised he would, if I ever left him." There was a silence that overcame the room in a hush.

"I'm sorry that this has happened to you, honey." the Special Investigator said. She rested her hand gently on my leg, and looked directly in my eyes. "We will see to it that he pays for this, and that you are protected." As if she could read my mind. Michael would find out that I was reporting this, and he would hunt me down.

"Are you okay to continue with your story?" the detective pressed on. I nodded.

35

"So, that afternoon, Gabe took me home, I locked up the house, and went straight for the bath. I had music on, and I was reliving my previous nights." I blushed, and I felt a squeeze of my fingers.

"So you weren't focused on your surroundings, in other words." the detective pointed out.

"No, I wasn't. I was just taking a bath, waiting until it was time to talk to Gabe again." I smiled at my mom. Now her face was happier, and a small smile appeared to cross her cheeks. The Detective turned to Gabe.

"You must be Gabe." She extended her arm, and he shook her hand. He nodded.

"Yes, I'm Gabriel Lazarus. I work with Janes, uhh, Janie, at the Phoenix. We've been….an item for a few months now." He blushed at his own statement.

"Did you ever have any encounters with Michael Comaro? Or were you present during any of the times Janie has spoken of?" they waited for his response.

"Yes, there were instances that Michael injected himself into our work life. As for the instances that she has mentioned so far, no. I was not present, but I was the one to find her after this attack." He rubbed his forehead with his free hand. He looked positively ill.

"Ok, we'll go into that more with you in a little bit." Detective Knox turned back to me, "alright Janie, let's keep going. You were in the bathtub. Go back to that point, and let's go all the way through it." She smiled idly, while I slowed my breath, and closed my eyes. Going back to that point was hard. Certain spots were just black memories, and I couldn't keep them straight. I wrinkled my forehead.

"Yes, I was in the bathtub. I remember that I was getting ready to shave my legs, when I noticed that the music seemed to be getting louder." I paused, and looked down at my lap.

"Ok, Janie, when you say it was getting louder, what exactly do you mean?" The Detective asked.

"The volume was increasing.... Slowly at first. Then almost deafening when I was underwater." I waited for more questions. She took notes, and re-read what she wrote.

"Do you remember what song it was?"

Come on, think! You hated the song that was on…. It just kept getting louder… "It was 'Communication Breakdown,' I remember now." I nodded to myself, and took a drink. "I was shaving, one leg…" I whipped the sheets back from my legs, and felt them both. One leg was definitely hairier, and the other had a day's worth of stubble. "See?" I pointed.

"Confirms that…only one leg shaved." The Detective noted.

"Then suddenly, everything was black." There were sighs, and gasps happening around the room. Gabe's hand was still on me, but his face was ashen, and covered with his other hand. "I remember thinking that it was dark, but I couldn't take a breath. I soon realized that he was holding me under the water." I swallowed hard.

"What did you do when you realized this, Miss Taylor?" The Detective asked.

"I struggled, and tried to lift myself up, even though he was pushing me back down. He finally let me out of the water, and I came up and took huge breaths of air. My head felt hot, like fire. When I touched it, I could feel the gash." I tentatively reached up to feel the spot, and now the staples met my fingers. I shook my head, and pressed on. The Detective nodded, and smiled idly. "I couldn't believe what he had done, and I started to ask why he was doing this. He told me that I deserved it, and that I was a fucking whore." The Detective raised her hand.

"Did he call you names often? Was he very jealous?"

"Yes, the names came every time he was angry. Which was often, here lately. And yes, he was jealous of everything." I put my head down, and my eyes stared at my wrapped up wrist.

"Ok, honey. Keep going," the Investigator pressed on.

"He lifted me out of the bathtub, and dropped me on the floor." I lifted my left wrist and arm in the air. "That's how this happened. When I landed, it was directly onto my wrist. It felt like my arm was instantly on fire. The first time I tried to stand up, he punched me in the eye, and I fell back down. When I coward in the corner, he pulled me out, and stood me up. I think." I paused to think, and wrinkled my forehead again. The Special Investigator opted to take a break.

"I'd like to state we are taking a break, pausing the tape." She turned towards my family. "Is everyone doing alright? I know this is a lot to hear. You are all remarkably strong. Your family seems so wonderful, I'm sorry to have had to meet you all like this." She smiled at them again, and turned towards me. "Alright, honey. Can you keep going? Need a break? Anything?" I could feel how much she cared for victims. I appreciated that. *Victim. That's a dirty word. You can do this. Draw strength from your supporters.*

"No, I'm alright. Can we keep going now? I really want to get this out, and over with." I smiled at them both, and they nodded. With a quick push, the tape recorder was back on, and the Detective spoke into it to restart the tape.

"We are back on, beginning after the suspected wrist break." She nodded at me, with a stern face.

"I sat on the floor, and he poked at me. Made fun of me. I remember his joker smile never left his face. There was blood everywhere. I didn't even recognize the bathroom." My head shook back and forth from remembering the horror that was before me. "Only one of my eyes were opening at that point, so I looked at him, and begged him to stop. He didn't, but instead stood me up again, and bent me over the counter top. We were right by the sink, because I had to cover my head wound from being rammed into the water spout. I heard his zipper go down, and I-" I couldn't help but pause. The Detective reached for the recorder, but I stopped her hand, and shook my head. I was okay, just felt terrible for my family, and Gabe.

"I'm just sorry that they're listening to this...like this. I'm sorry." I sighed loudly.

"Did he rape you, Miss Taylor?" Her voice was grim. I nodded.

"Yes." Tears fell from my eyes. "Once I heard the zipper, his foot spread my feet apart on the floor. He was always quick, I mean, every time he took advantage me. Normally if I was just quiet, he would go away. This time, the last time he rammed into me, I felt the sharpest, hottest pain in my side, and on my back. Over and over, but I couldn't focus on any one thing. He was everywhere, and everything was spinning." My forehead was wrinkled, and my voice was no longer shaking. *You can do it. Keep going...* Their pens were frantically writing on their notepads.

"I stumbled back, and he must've punched the side of my face... because then my whole head hurt, and I was on the ground. I saw his boots, then everything went dim." I shifted in the bed, and adjusted my hospital gown. "Once I was awake again, it took a while to remember what was going on, and get my bearings. If I hadn't heard the ding from a text message, I may have sat there forever. I found my phone, but couldn't see to text. Just pushed some keys, and hoped for the best. Luckily," I reached for Gabe's now sweaty hand. He looked pale, and very sick. "this guy, my knight-in-shining armor came and busted the door down." He smiled up at me a little, and I smiled back, and wiped my tears on my gown.

"I didn't technically break the door. I calmed you down, and talked you over to it. You managed to push the closet door closed, which was holding the other door open only an inch." He patted my leg, and turned to the Detective. "I thought it was genius. If he was still in there, she had protected herself enough to keep him out." The Detective smiled.

"Yes, Gabriel, you're right. She's a very smart girl. Now Janie, a few questions. Ok?" I nodded toward her. "Were there any specific words exchanged between you and Michael Comaro while these events were happening? And when I ask this, I mean quotes that you can remember?" she had her pen ready, as well. I thought for a few minutes. It was so hard to remember specifics, especially words.

"He said," I made quote fingers with my hands. ""I warned you, I warned you," and then he also said, "this is just an ounce of what you deserve." I think that's about all he said, that I can fully remember." They both nodded at me, and the Special Investigator picked up the tape recorder, and spoke into it.

"Ending the victim's statement, at 8:36pm. Detective Knox and Lucy Maddox done." She clicked the button, and came and sat back down on my bed. "Janie, remember to keep your wits about you. Don't ever think this was your fault, because it wasn't. This is going to get pretty crazy for a while for you with meeting with the Prosecutor, but he'll try and keep you out the spotlight, and all media off of this. I'll see to that, I promise." I smiled at her, and tried to believe her.

"Thank you for giving your statement, Janie. You don't realize how strong you've been by just telling us what happened. It takes some weeks, or months to be able to do that. Here are our cards, and extras. Take them, keep them on you. Both of our cell phone numbers are on the back. Program them in your cell. If you see him, call one of us. If he's too close, call 911." She turned and pointed at each person. "Don't hesitate to call us. EVER. He's already shown what he's willing to do, and I don't want to test him. Understand?" She turned back to me.

"Yes, thank you Detective." She shook my good hand, and they headed out of the door. *Again, even though I had stopped talking about it, it was running through my head like a play-by-play. But now only of Michael's different expressions. It was all I could do not to sob, and to just keep calm. My nerves were wearing down low...*

36

I instantly relaxed in the bed, but scanning the room, all I saw was turmoil. *OH God... your statement broke your family. And Gabe... he's in pieces.* I took a quick drink. Stretched my neck muscles, and spoke. "Hey guys, please don't do this." They all slowly looked up at me. "Don't sit there, and think the 'wonder' thoughts. Don't think you could've stopped this. Don't kid yourselves. We just have to move forward. I can do it, if you can..." I looked around the room. My Dad's eyes met mine first.

"You're right, Janes. But I'll always be sorry that I wasn't there to protect you. I'm your Dad, that's just how it is." I smiled at him, I understood. I stared harder at my mom, who was now just blankly staring at me.

"Oh honey," she was shaking. "I'm just so damn angry at him! I want to go kill him! I'm sickened that he had us fooled. I can't believe that I treated him so well. I'll work on it...it's just a shock to hear all of this. I love you, Janes." she stood, and smiled. I turned to Gabe, he was still pale.

"I know that was hard to hear... I know you knew, but I always tried to save you from the details. I hope you can still--" like the typical Gabriel, he cut me off. He had tears in his eyes, but they never fell.

"Don't even say it. This is the worst situation I've ever had to deal with." he scooted closer to the bed, and clasped my good hand in his. "And all I know, is that I have this giant desire to protect you from everything, and anything I need to. Earlier, when I went to get my night bag," a tear fell. "I ran through the house, threw all sorts of random things in my bag, and rushed back here. Being away from you felt like half of me was gone. I can't do it." He put his head on my hands on the bed. I looked over at my mom, who was crying like a baby, with the biggest smile on her face. She nodded at me, she knew what I was thinking. Then she stepped forward, and spoke up.

"Well Janie, Dad and I are going to head home. We've got some security things to work out at the house, so I think we're going with Gabe's plan for a while." I wrinkled my forehead, and Gabe's head slowly raised. "Oh, bet he didn't tell you." She giggled. "We'll let him fill you in. We're starving. You two have a good night, and call if anything comes up, just because, whatever." She smiled, and kissed my head. My dad kissed my head, and scoped out the staples while he was there.

Once they were out the door, I relaxed a little bit more. But it didn't look like Gabe had. I patted his head.

"So, you were saying…" I rubbed his hair. It was so soft…I wished we were back at his place, and that none of this ever happened. He slowly sat back up, and looked at me.

"What your mom mentioned…it's solely up to you. Okay?" He looked worried now, and that made me apprehensive.

"Ah, this must be 'Gabe's plan?' Ok, I'm ready to hear it." *Or at least I think I'm ready to hear this.*

"Yes, my plan is that you'll come stay with me and the guys. While the investigation is done, while court stuff happens…however long it takes." He paused, and I opened my mouth to talk. His finger quickly covered it, "wait. I've got lots of reasons. One of the big ones being that one of the guys will always be home, considering their different work shifts. Your parents also liked this idea. They are trained in hand to hand combat, and with guns. They also liked that." he laughed a little. I couldn't help but smile. "And then I can take care of you while you heal. We don't have to worry about him finding you, and if he does, he'll be met with force. We already have a security system, and.." he sat on the bed with me. "I get to spend time with you. Lots and lots of time..." His smile was now huge. *Is this happening?* I sighed, and paused for a few minutes. I pretended like I was in deep thought, just a little teasing from the girl laid up in the bed.

"Where do I sign up for this great deal?" I joked with him. He carefully reached around me, and gave me a gentle hug. I giggled.

"I love hearing that.... You laughing." He nuzzled my neck. "God, I've missed you... I can't wait until you're feeling better." I couldn't help but squeeze him with my good arm. I wasn't feeling too bad, actually. Just very stiff. Having Gabe almost laying in my bed wasn't helping the situation!

"Hey, I've got a favor." he instantly sat back, and waited to hear. "I'd love a shower. Can you find out if I'm allowed to have one?" His eyes lit up, and he disappeared out of the room. Moments later, he returned with a trash bag to put over my cast.

"Shower, allowed! But I insisted that you'd want my help over the nurses... I hope I was right." He smiled, questioningly. I nodded. *That sounds like fun...* "Need me to help you get out of the bed?" He leaned towards me.

"Let me see how far I can go myself. But, please stay close. Really close." I smirked at him. I shifted my legs around the side of the bed. They fell out from under the sheets, and were covered with blood spots, and deep bruises. I gasped at them, but kept going. Using my good arm, I reached to put my feet on the floor. My ribs felt extra stretched, so I held them with my arm with the cast. I was able to stand, to my surprise. Gabe smiled very big at me, and I was smiling very big at myself.

"You're doing great, baby. Can you walk into the bathroom?" He repositioned behind me. "I'm right behind you, arms at your sides. Just say the word, and I've got you." I felt so safe, and secure. I slowly hobbled over to the bathroom, and made it to the bench in the walk-in shower. I plopped down, and started to strip off the gown. I managed to get it over the cast, but needed help with the rest.

"Could you pull it off for me?" I smiled, knowing that I was about to be naked in front of Gabe. He reached down, and gently slid it off of my shoulder. "Turn it on, nice and hot."

He reached in, and obliged. In the mirror, I saw my face. A black eye, a giant gash on my head, bruises everywhere... I turned to the side in the mirror. Under the bandages on my back were the stab wounds. *That one is hard to digest... I can't believe he did that to me.* I shook the thought out of my head, and angled myself to be in the hot water spray. It felt so good. Suddenly, I felt his hands gently soaping my back.

"If you want me to stop, just say so." His hands shook. "I don't want to hurt you...just figured you couldn't reach back here." His eyes were so focused on avoiding any sore spots, that he was oblivious to everything else.

"You're fine. I like your hands on me...I just wish I wasn't so tainted and gross." I winced at my own words. *I know he knew what I meant.* I could feel him shaking his head behind me. Then, his hands slowly dropped to my lower back. He spread his fingers out at my waist, and slowly reached towards my stomach. His warm hands were setting off all sorts of tingles, and setting fire to each spot he touched all over my body. Soon he reached my chest, and he slowly and gently cupped my breasts. His hands went higher, and he crossed his arms gently over my chest, and hugged. *He's so wonderful! This is amazing...*

"You're not tainted, or gross. Or dirty. You're Janie." He smiled. "You're my Janie." He gently kissed the back of my neck, and I could feel his arousal kick in. "Oh dear... We'd better get you cleaned at back to bed, love. Before..." he chuckled. "Anything crazy happens." He leaned his hips into mine, and I could feel his hot, hard crotch rub against my rear. I sighed loudly.

"Oh my..." I leaned back into him. "I can't wait to be out of this place!" I leaned forward again, hoping to regain focus on the shower. "Could you wash my hair? Lifting my arms, I mean arm, isn't working for me right now." I turned to him with my defeated look. *Damn this shower for being so difficult. Damn Gabe for being so Goddamn hot!* I sighed again.

He got the shampoo, and lathered up his hands. He gently washed around the wound on my head, but it really was feeling much better. He massaged the unbroken parts of my scalp, and it felt so good. "Baby," he began. He slowly massaged circles into the base of my neck, and it made all the hairs on my arms stand straight up. "Are you sure you're okay with coming to stay with me? I just…. Don't want to pressure you, or move to quickly." He stopped massaging, and waited for my response.

There was really no reason not to be okay with this idea. I would not be at home, the place where I was attacked. It wouldn't be as easy for Michael to find me at Gabe's. The guys were always home, so I would always have protection. *Not to mention… you're in love with Gabe!* I couldn't hold back my smile, and he nudged me when he saw it.

"Yes, I'm perfectly fine with staying with you. I can't wait, in fact!" I used my good hand to hold the shower massager, and try to rinse my hair. Instead I ended up spraying Gabe, the wall, the towels, and half of my hospital room with water. "Damnnit!!! Oh come on!" I dropped the massager on the ground. It was safer there.

"Oh baby! I'm soaked!" He roared with laughter. "So is... everything!" He was literally busting out laughing. *OH, how cute is he?* I smiled at my own internal monolog. She was always right. He helped me out of the slippery bathroom, and into some sweats and a t-shirt. I tried to get comfortable in the hospital bed, but it was so cold. "Honey, you really did try to flood the place. This is awesome..." he was still chuckling to himself.

"Well, at least I can still provide some entertainment." I had a random flash of work, and Simon. "Oh no. Please tell me you let Simon know what was going on?!" I could tell by the way his face dropped, that he hadn't. "It's ok," I pleaded. "It's been a hell of a few days... a favor though? Can you call him for me, and just tell him we're alright? Please?" he instantly threw on his dry t-shirt, and headed over towards the bed. He plopped down, and looked for his number.

"I'll absolutely call him. Just give me a minute...then bed, ok?" he sort of smiled.

"Yes, sounds perfect. One last favor?" thought I'd push my luck just a little bit. "Will you lay with me for a while?" I scooted over, and patted the bed.

"Oh Janes, of course I will." He disappeared into the hallway to call Simon for me. My eyes were so heavy, that I barely felt him climb into the hospital bed with me. His warmth instantly calmed me, and let me rest safely.

37

When I woke up, it was morning. I felt the bed next to me, and it was empty. My heart instantly started to race. I sat up, and frantically searched the room. I saw his bag packed on the couch, along with my bag. That was now also packed neatly, right next to his. I sat up slowly, and noted that my ribs didn't seem to hurt quite as much today. *Thank God...* I checked around, and no one seemed to be near. I slowly stood, and step by slow step walked to the bathroom. I forgot how good peeing felt. On my way back to bed, I snagged my cell phone from the table.

I started to scroll through all my missed messages, and texts. I finally read the texts that Gabe had sent before it all happened. They truly did sound worried. *Poor guy.* I decided to send my mom a quick text. I typed quickly for only having one "good" arm. *But both of your thumbs are still good, girl.* I chuckled at myself.

Hey mom, I'm up and feeling better, I think. Not sure of the plan, will update soon. XO

As I settled back into bed, Gabe and the doctor came in. Gabe was beaming.

"Hello, Miss Taylor." The doctor was always so professional. "I wanted to go over your discharge instructions, if that's ok." *Getting out? Already?* I nodded. "Your sides will heal over the next few weeks. If they become itchy, use vitamin A capsules, broken open, or cortisone cream. That should be all you need there. The stitches in your back wounds will dissolve on their own. The plastic surgeon did a great job, and the scars will be very thin. May I look at your head wound, Miss Taylor?" He checked my face.

"Yes, of course." I said without hesitation. I leaned my head towards him. He promptly put on a glove, and gently poked around the area.

"I would like to take the staples out before you leave in a bit, and put a thin layer of liquid stitch over it as well. The stitches will dissolve, and there are many of those in up there, too..." he smiled. "I didn't want you to think your brains would leak out or anything." He quietly chuckled. I could feel my eyebrow raising at him, but I laughed anyway. "Is that okay with you, Janie?"

"Absolutely, Doc." I smiled back. He quickly took off the glove, and jotted down some notes.

"Alright Janie, I think you're good to go. I'll have the nurse come in and remove the staples, and seal you up. Basically take it easy. I mean, really easy. You're not cleared for work for 10 days." He dug in his pocket, and pulled out a card. He wrote on the back, quickly. "This is my cell number. Same that my daughters have." He pushed the card into my hand, and closed his hands around mine. "Please follow through with all of this Janie. I know, it's a lot. You're strong, I can tell. You keep this card, and if ever you can't reach anyone... I'll always answer." He patted my shoulder. "Thanks for being a good patient." And that was it. He turned and left. I turned back to Gabe, who was still smiling.

"Well, I'm glad you're getting sprung from here! I already packed most everything up. Greg said he'll go to the store for us when we're home. So, we'll get you comfortable in no time, love!" He sure was chipper. I wasn't sure how I was feeling at this point. My body felt better, not perfect, but I was moving, at least. But my head felt cloudy, and I could feel my anxiety starting to shine through. I took a few deep breaths quietly, hoping the feelings would pass.

The nurse came back quickly, and first put some numbing agent on my head. She only waited a few seconds, and started on the staples. I could feel the pressure, and a little sting in parts. But otherwise, it wasn't too bad. There were eleven staples. The liquid stitch she used burned like a hot campfire, but squinting my eyes seemed to make the pain lessen.

"Alright honey!" She said, as she handed me the paperwork. "Just need you to sign here, take these directions and medicines with you. And go home to rest, and relax." I took her pen, and the papers, and signed by all of the 'X's. "Thank you, Janie. Take care now, honey!" Lydia was by far the nicest nurse I had in all the days I was there. I turned to Gabe.

"Do I have shoes?" He wrinkled his forehead, and looked in the bag. His face changed, and he started to laugh.

"No, love, it looks like no shoes." He shook his head. "Can't believe I didn't think about shoes!!" I couldn't help but smile.

"It's alright. The socks will do for a car ride." I stood up, and started to walk out to exit. My head was swirling with so many thoughts. Some good, some bad. I tried to stop and focus on the fact that I was going home with Gabe. That I was going to be living with him for now. That I would soon have meetings with Prosecutors, lawyers, and the courts. *What if he finds you?* The thoughts were creeping in slowly. I shook my head, and focused on walking out of the hospital.

"Here baby," Gabe leaned me against the side of the wall by the door. "I'll go get the car, be right back." He turned as he walked away. "Don't move," and winked. I watched him throw our things into the car, and drive up to get me. I climbed in slowly, and I cautiously buckled my seatbelt. I just wanted to get to his house. "What do you want to listen to?" He handed me his CD case, and I flipped through it. It was a good half hour drive back to his place from the hospital. Jim Croce sounded the best, so I popped it in. It was more mellow, so I relaxed and leaned over in my seat. I suddenly felt so exhausted, like I had just run a marathon.

"I'm just going to close my eyes...I'm so tired." I patted his arm. He put his hand on my thigh, and gently rubbed it back and forth. I drifted to sleep....

38

He woke me up when we were parked in the driveway. I loved the way his country house looked next to the little pond. I made a mental note to check that out in my time out here. *Maybe there were fish?* I tried to wake myself up a little, but just couldn't. Gabe opened my car door, and reached for my hands. I weakly grabbed on.

"Hey baby," he looked in my eyes. "Are you okay? What do you need?" I held his hands weakly, and smiled.

"Just tired..." I yawned. I leaned in to him, and rested my head on his chest.

"Well, let's get you out of the car then." He wrestled around with the door, and my rather wet-noodle like body, and scooped me up in his arms. I clung to his neck. "I gotcha babe, just relax." I could feel him moving quickly, and he yelled to someone. "Door G," he stepped in. "Thanks man." It was easier to leave my eyes closed. *What if they ask questions? Do they know?*

He carried me into his bedroom, which had been semi rearranged to fit a comfortable lounge chair, with his big bed, the whole TV set up, and a chest with my stuff in it. He laid me down in clean, fresh sheets. They were so soft, I couldn't help grind my legs against them. He covered me up slowly, but I could feel his eyes staring into me more than normal. *He's just trying to read you, relax.*

"Baby?" he gently asked. "Greg's going to the store. I need to know a few things..." he smiled.

"I need smoke, popsicles, chicken soup, and iced tea." I said without opening my eyes. "Is that possible?" I now opened one eye to gauge his reaction. He smiled very big.

"Oh yeah, no problem. I'll get extra. I'll be back in a bit. I'll just be out in the living room in you need me." He kissed my forehead, and I instantly smiled.

"Ok, I'll be asleep." I rolled back over on to my only good side. My eyes were heavy, and the meds they gave me for home were strong. It put me into a semi-conscious state. I could hear Gabe talking to someone...*probably a roommate. There are two, remember? Greg and.... And? Can't remember!* I listened closely to them. Whoever was talking to him was trying to be quiet, but I could hear pieces. "...it's pretty bad..." was said a few times. There were a lot of "...I'm sorry's," too. Then it was quiet, and I fell asleep.

Hours later I woke and it was dusk. The lights were dimming outside, and the sun was just setting. My eyes were staying open this time, and I didn't feel like I was half dead. I took a breath, and smelled something good. I stood up slowly, and sat up. The pain was excruciating, and I tried to just plow through it. I took my time getting my bearings. I could hear the guys in the living room, and it eased my mind. *You're safe. Just breathe.* I went to the chest, and opened it. Oh my... *had he done this himself?* All my important things, and my favorite brush.... right in front of me. My smile was uncontrollable. I brushed through my hair, and headed out to the living room. When I turned the corner, I was met by two pairs of wide eyes, and one pair of loving eyes. Who were suddenly rushing to me.

"You ok, baby?!" he said frantically. I scrunched up my face.

"Yeah, I'm just done sleeping now. Something smelled really good....and I heard you guys." I shrugged. He wrapped his warm arms around me.

"Well, I suppose you could join us. Are you hungry? Greg got all of your list, plus a ton of extras." He paused, and turned me. He looked in my eyes for a few seconds. "You don't look too *medicine* drugged. Are you?" I shook my head.

"I'm alright now. How long did I sleep for? Feels like…. days." The guys giggled.

"You were out for about 7 hours." He looked at me empathetically. "I figured you needed it. You were so peaceful, I checked on you a few times." He smiled. I patted his cheek with my broken hand.

"Thank you," I turned to the guys. "And you Greg, and you Aaron. I'm not sure what I'd do without you right now." I smiled at them. "I'll do what I can around here to help out, for sure, too." The guys all giggled.

"Come join us," Greg said. "We may have tapped into your smoke before you woke up…" he laughed out loud. Then Aaron busted out laughing. Greg turned back to me and asked, "Would you like some?" *Oh, absolutely!!!*

I took the bong, and slowly inhaled. Each inhale of the smoke stung my lung badly. It burned, and was almost intolerable. But it was also bringing a certain calm over my stomach, and the "sick" feeling started to turn to hunger. I took another hit, and that was all they could take. The coughing that commenced brought tears to my eyes, and had all my manly protectors ready to help however they could. Gabe's hand stroked my back gently until the fit ceased.

I quietly sat in the circle with the guys, and passed the bong around. It was funny to listen to their inside jokes, and silly stories. There was no pressure to be someone else, or to even speak. *So this is how normal friends function? They chat, sit together, and don't fight. Interesting...* After about half an hour of smoking, Gabe leaned over towards me and asked if I was hungry.

"I am starving... what is there to eat????" My hunger was almost uncontrollable. All the guys busted out laughing, which made me laugh. The extreme laughing was just too much, and my side started to pull. I quickly hunched over to avoid the pulling feeling. "Damn it." I mumbled under my breath in a whisper. "Gabe, could you just pile some food on a plate, and I'll eat whatever. I can't move right now." I winced the awkward position I stayed in.

"Of course, just one minute." And it was literally one minute, and he was back with a pile of chicken, rice, and vegetables. It looked and tasted wonderfully. I couldn't have asked for a better meal.

"MMmm," I swallowed. "My compliments to the chef!" I pushed more gigantic piles into my mouth at light speed. My stomach was getting full, but that wasn't stopping me. Gabe approached again with a hand full of pills, and put his hand out for me to take them. I picked up the antibiotic, and one of the two pain pills. He gave me a questioning gaze. "It's good. Two makes me sleep for a day." I smiled, and winked. He shook his head. I finished my dinner, and watching the rest of a game show. I patted Gabe's leg, and stood to head to bed. I leaned down, and kissed his cheek. His hands gently brushed both of my nipples through my shirt, and they instantly got hard from the attention.

I stood to leave, and was met by Greg's shielded eyes, and Aaron's eyes glued to my chest. I looked down to see that my mostly white shirt did not hide my sudden turned on feelings from Gabe's hands. *OOooops.* "Well," I covered my chest. "Guess this makes me an official roommate. Jesus, guys. I'm sorry. I'm going to bed." I grabbed the bowl, smoke, and lighters. There was a simultaneous, "G'Night Janes" from the boys, followed by hysterical laughter.

"I'll be there in a minute, babe," and a gentle smack on the butt on my way through the room from Gabe. I smiled at him, and headed to the bathroom, and listened to the boy's chatter and giggle amongst themselves.

I stood there for minutes, staring at the bathtub. I so badly wanted to take a bath, but for whatever reason, the bathtub was making me panic. *This is about ridiculous. He's not here, and you're perfectly safe. Come on, honey...relax.* I took a few deep breaths, and turned on the water to extra hot. I took my robe in with me, and stripped and sat in the bath, as it filled up. The hot water felt so good on my skin. Even on the tender, healing areas. My body looked terrible. Covered in bruises. Scabs, cuts, stitches. I gently washed the scabs, and relaxed back in the tub. There was a knock on the bathroom door, very gentle.

"Hey, love...it's just me. Can I come in?" My heart sped up at the sound of his voice, and again my nipples hardened.

"Yeah, you can." I turned my head to the side, and smiled when he entered. I wiggled my finger at him, and he stuck his tongue out playfully. He headed over to the counter, and began washing his face, and brushing his teeth. *Hmm, must be his nightly routine. He's so adorable...* He was barely paying me any attention, or so I thought. I caught his eyes on me in the mirror, sneakily staring down at me. It made my crotch throb.

"Do you think you're about ready to get out?" I looked at my hands, and my fingers were really wrinkly.

"Sure, will you grab me a towel?" He nodded, and went to the closet for a big, fluffy towel. He held it out for me, and wrapped it around me as I got out. His arms lingered around me a little longer than a normal hug, and I could hear him breathing me in. His touch was making my skin hot, and my thoughts were definitely not of resting. I pulled away long enough to dry off. He took a step back, and took account of the situation. I let my towel fall open to dry my hair, then rewrapped it to brush my hair. His eyes were still directly on me. I smiled, coyly at him.

"You're so beautiful…" the words just rolled out of his mouth, while it hung open still gaping at me. I took his hands, and pulled him with me to bed. I could feel his apprehension with my injuries, and his slight pull away.

"Please don't," I clawed into his skin. "I need you. I really need you." It was almost a beg. "Promise I'll stop if something hurts. Please?" My fingers pressed into his skin. His eyes bore deep into mine, and seconds later, his mouth was around mine. His hands stroked my back, and gently over my wounds. There were constant shutters flowing through my back, and my muscle were tense all over.

His tongue was desperate in my mouth, dipping into the deepest realms. Sometimes I forgot that just kissing Gabe was better than… *ice cream.* Moans were starting to escape my lips, as his lips scaled down my neck and on to my shoulders. The loudest came when his teeth grazed my shoulder blade. He gently laid me back on the bed, and kissed down my abdomen. I closed my eyes, and tried to focus on my breathing. His mouth was too demanding, and once he closed around my hot spot, there was no turning the nerves off. I rested my cast above my head, and got lost in the moment.

His fingers spun, while his tongue twirled. It was like a superbly crafted machine, perfect at what it did. He slowly pulled his fingers out of me, and gave me a slight nibble on my sensitive places before biting all the way up my back to my neck. His mouth lingered over my ear.

"You sure about this baby?" I pulled his hands to my chest, and hugged them. Then put them on my breasts, and squeezed. I frantically nodded, and stared into his eyes. There were no words exchanged after that point. His mouth was back on mine, and he was pushing into me. It was the fullest feeling I had had since the last time I was with Gabe. My tensions left, my head relaxed, and I could focus on him thrusting into me. My walls began to clench, and I could feel myself coming all over his big cock. Watching his face while I came turned me on. *Do you see what you do to him, Janie? Look at the way he reacts to your body.* I could see when he felt each clench, which only made me clench harder. I wanted more. I needed more. I dug my finger nails into his rear.

He pushed into me like he was searching for a treasure. It was relentless, hard, and perfect. We were both drenched in sweat, and all sorts of bodily fluids. I felt him grip my hips harder, and I felt him change pace. I reached around him, and gently grasped onto his balls, and pulled. His roar was unstoppable, and he pushed in as deep as he could get. The fill of his throb pulsating through me and filling me up was the final calm I needed.

He cleaned us both off with towels, gently as ever. He found me a large t-shirt, and some new undies. He turned on some music, and lit a candle.

"How about some smoke before bed?" He smiled, and crawled into bed next to me. While he got it ready, he spoke. "I'm really liking having you here…. I can't get enough of you." I could feel my cheeks turn flush, and hot.

39

The morning sun light beamed into the room, and woke me up softly. His arm was draped over my waist, and he was still half asleep. I was so thirsty, that I almost couldn't breathe. I scooted up on the bed so I was closer to sitting, and reached for my drink. The water was lukewarm tap water now, and I sort of wished it was ice cold like the night before. I couldn't stop drinking it, and now my belly was feeling very full, and watery. I slowed down a little bit to catch my breath, and give my stomach a break. It was relentless though. This thirst was not going way. I nudged Gabe.

"Hey Gabe?" I gently rubbed his arm. His head rose quickly, and he checked me out to make sure I was alright.

"What's up baby?" he said with a very raspy, sexy voice. He was sitting up now, rubbing the goo from his eyes.

"I'm too thirsty, it won't go away. And now my stomach is upset... from drinking too much water." I shifted on the bed. "I think I need my nausea meds now, if you could, please." I pointed over to the chest and the bag of medicine. He nodded, and grabbed the medicine. I took the one pill out of his hand, and swallowed it with only a sip of water.

"Hey, why don't you try this, too?" I reached down, and handed me the pipe. Pre-filled, ready to go. "I'll be right back. Want some juice?" That sounded delicious.

"Yes, please." I smoked a little bit, my lungs stung at the first touch of the smoke. After three inhales, my stomach was calming, and my mind was quiet. I relaxed back on the bed, and my eyes closed again. *The room was dark, and I wasn't alone. I could feel him coming closer, and I was getting cold. I didn't know what to do. I was screaming for help. As loud as I could. No one was coming, but him. I needed to get away from him. "Help!! Help!!"*

Just then, I felt the gentle shaking. At first, I recoiled at the touch. *Wake up. It's not him! Relax...* I opened an eye to see Gabe, with one hand gently caressing my hand.

"Shhh, it's okay love. It's just me, I'm sorry I scared you." He smiled reassuringly. Now I knew what was happening, I smiled back.

"I'm sorry, I must've fallen asleep back into a nightmare." Tears started to sting my eyes, and I covered my forehead with my hand. I tried to quietly sob into my hand, but it was useless. I didn't want to deal with having Michael in my head when I slept...*why am I torturing myself? I just want him to GO AWAY.* I sobbed, and Gabe's arms stayed around me. He didn't speak, only offered support. Eventually I calmed, and he started to rub my back.

"Janes, you don't need to apologize. I knew what the "side effects would be," for lack of a better word right now...sorry..." he turned to see if I was offended. I wasn't, and smiled at him. "I knew what could happen...your anxiety, nightmares, mistrust- especially of men... I was prepared. I am prepared. I talked this over with your parents many times, and I've texted with your mom daily." He turned, and pushed the hair out of my face, and behind my ear. "I know I can help you through this. I want to help you though this...I'm not going anywhere." He gently kissed my cheek.

"Thank you for being so understanding...and for being You." I cleared my throat. "What time is it? I'm still so thirsty." I searched the room for water. I didn't see my cup anywhere. "Where's my-" Gabe was there with the glass of...*apple juice?*

"One of your medicines causes the thirst. The pharmacist suggested trying a juice rather than just water. So, let's give it a try. It's ice cold." He handed me the glass, and I drank, and drank....and drank. The apple juice was perfect. While I drank, he spoke. "As for time, it's about 1:45pm. You fell back asleep at about 8:30am. I went in to work for a little while, and Greg stayed and watched over you." I smiled.

"How was everyone at work?" I asked, suddenly a little more excited than before. His face told me he knew I was going to ask, and he was ready to update me.

"Actually, some of them are stopping over later for some food, and some *calm* visiting." He checked my face for reaction, only to see that my smile went from ear to ear. "So, I guess that's a yes?" He chuckled, as he asked.

"Oh, that would be wonderful! Simon and Heather? Bill?" I hoped that they would be there over anyone else.

"Yes, most everyone was there this morning when I went in. They're all excited to come out here to see you." He started to walk out of the room, then abruptly stopped, and turned to me. "Oh, and I did tell them all that we are....we. Together. I hope that's okay."

My eyebrow raised high in the air. *Did he just say that we are together? And he hopes it's okay? YES, and YES!* I sat and thought about this, well, pretended to, rather.

"Yes, I do suppose I like the sound of "us" together." I giggled, "I'm glad you told them. And

I'm hoping you answered all of their questions this morning, too?" I eyeballed him for the answer.

"There were a few questions, and yes, I did. But most were just about your welfare, and how you were doing. I think it'll be alright. Plus, your parents will be here, too!" With that, I bolted out of bed with the bits of energy I had reserved for...who knows what. I leapt into his arms, and hugged him tightly. *And all of this for you, Janes...* My side now hurt terribly, but it was worth it to give some thanks for the way Gabe is helping me, and being there for me.

"You're so wonderful...how did I get so lucky?" I whispered into his neck while I hugged him. He laughed at my outburst.

"Now don't you go wasting all that energy before your little party, love." He carried me back to bed. "Back to bed, I'll bring you some snacks and a movie. No one will be here for a few hours yet, so no reason for you to be up." He sternly pointed his finger at me...while undressing me with his eyes. He disappeared, and then returned quickly with a movie, and a bag of chips. It was *The Blue Lagoon.*

"Awesome! I love this movie!" He plugged it in, and set everything up for me. I came around and planted a big kiss right on my lips.

"I'll be in the kitchen for a while, making the foods for tonight. Going to do many different party foods and finger foods. That way you can choose."

"Alright, thank you... I... I.." I had completely just stumbled over my words, and I could feel my cheeks get warm. "I really appreciate it." I smiled. *Oh my! Almost slipped out there!* I quickly glanced at his face, and he was shaking his head at me. I was definitely caught on that one.

"You're welcome." He kissed me again. "Get some rest." Yes, I guess this was the idea... lots of rest. I ate some chips, and watched the first parts of the movie. Before I knew it, I was out. *I was dancing to the music, swaying back and forth. His hands were on my hips, and we swayed with the music. In between songs, I fixed my hair. The next song wasn't like the first...and I felt anxious. And scared. And paranoid. There was noise, and it was drowning out everything. Now I was terrified. I looked around the room, but couldn't see anything. But he was there...somewhere. I could feel it. I started to breathe heavily, all while searching the room. Then his hands were on me and I jumped back in retaliation...*

"Hey! Baby! Relax!" I could hear Gabe, but I was too panic stricken to move. I heard more voices, "No, stay back. Let her calm down. Have her mom come in, please." There was more mumbling. I opened my eyes slowly, while trying to calm my breathing down. It was Gabe, and he was smiling. I took a deep breath, a little too deep, and coughed quite a bit. He sat me up a little, and rubbed my back. I put my head in my hands, and looked at the sheets.

"I'm so sorry…" I fell sideways into him. His arms were around me instantly, and he comforted me.

"Gabe?" *Is that my mom?!* I heard her calling for him.

"Mom?!" I couldn't help yell her name, and she appeared in the doorway almost instantly. I reached for her. She hugged me, and I calmed.

"Hi honey, how are you feeling?" She leaned back, and checked out my face. She scanned the rest of me. "Gabe's updates are pretty detailed…so I know about the dreams." I wrinkled my nose at her.

"Pain wise I'm not too bad. But I am so tired, the littlest things completely wipe me out. I've got no stamina. And yes," I sighed. "He's telling the truth. I'm having nightmares. I just get confused, and forget what's real and what's not. Once I wake up, I'm alright. See?" I pointed at myself, and laughed.

"Oh, I've missed your laugh!! It's so good to hear! How's living with three guys?" she winked at me, and looked over her shoulder. "Looks like you've got your own personal police force." She chuckled.

"Gabe has been...incredible." I could feel my cheeks flush. "And the guys, Greg and Aaron, they're hilarious. They're helpful. I feel so safe." I looked at my mom, and she was smiling, even with her eyes. "Thanks for agreeing to this, Mom. And trusting Gabe... I think that's a really good decision on both our parts."

"It's different with him. I can see his bond to you in his eyes, even when he talks about you. And the way he is with you, and you are with him. It's still growing, still blossoming...but I think you're both in for the real deal here. If you both can stay the course." She was right. This would surely be a difficult thing to get over in the beginning of a new relationship. "Here honey, can I help you get some party clothes on?" I nodded. She went through my wardrobe chest, and pulled out some jeans, and a tank top. She knew me too well.

Gabe came in as I was changing my shirt, and I was the only one who blushed. He smiled, and so did my mother. She shook her head at my reaction, obviously having already read in between all the lines. *Oh, you are a trip tonight Janes!!*

"I just wanted to check on you, baby. How's she doing, Mrs. Taylor?" he came and leaned into my face. I wasn't sure what he was up to, then he let it be known. "It sounds like you're breathing a little hard.... Are you?" I looked into both of their faces, and nodded.

"For the past few hours. Since the chips." I shrugged my shoulders.

"Gabriel," my mom started. "you're going to call me Sam, okay? Just try it...'Sam.' It's really easy." They both laughed with each other. "Oh Janie, for days I've told him to call me Sam. He refuses, and would rather make me feel old, 'Mrs. Taylor.'" She shook her head, with an ornery smile.

"Seriously you guys??" I turned to Gabe. "Please just call her Sam. All my closest friends do." He nodded, and outstretched his hand to hers.

"Hello, Sam. I'm Gabe. It's wonderful to meet you...again." We all looked at each other in the sudden silence, and then laughed hysterically. Gabe brought in my inhalers, and I inhaled three puffs quickly. These things made me shake like I had Parkinson's disease, but they did relieve some of the chest pressure I was having. *Your nurse is taking great care of you...*

"Alright, let's go out and see some people!" I stood slowly, and moved even more slowly. On my way, I thought about my Dad...*wonder where he is?* "Mom, where's Dad?"

"Oh, he's stuck in Cleveland doing seminars. He'll be back this next weekend. I'm only home for a few days. Possibly only hours. This job, I swear..." She trailed off, and I knew that it was that love-hate relationship she had with the job for my whole life. She went on. "The security company comes tomorrow, and then I'm off again, too." She patted my back as we walked into the living room.

40

I walked into the kitchen, and I was met with clapping... *a whole loud lot of it.* I looked around and saw Simon, Heather, Greg and Aaron, Bill, Nichole, and a bunch of the guys' friends. As if it were planned, Gabe appeared with a rose. One single red rose. He raised his glass, and the entire crowd followed.

"Please raise your glass to the most courageous, smart, brave, honest, loveable, adorable, gorgeous woman I've ever met in my life...Janie. We're here to celebrate a new beginning, and we hope you have a wonderful evening." The group cheered, agreed, and drank. High fives were given, and there were smiles all around the room. His arms were around me, and he kissed me. It was the most connective kiss we've ever had, with the validation of an entire room full of people. Our friends cheered louder with each kiss.

"I can't believe you did all of this, Gabe." I shook my head. "I love it. Thank you!" I pulled him in for an even longer kiss, that may have been semi-inappropriate. My broken wrist, and arm were tired, and were starting to shake. I managed to keep my arm in between Gabe and I while we embraced. *Argh! This fucking cast!*

"Go talk with your friends, have fun. I'll bring your meds when it's time. If you need me, just yell. I'm never far baby." He kissed my cheek, and sat me down on the couch. Within seconds, I was surrounded by friends. Simon and Nichole to my right, Heather to my left. Bill had pulled up a chair in front of me, and was the first to be brave and talk to me.

"Hey Janie! Work just isn't the same without you!" he joked to himself.

"Oh Bill, I know...I'll be back soon, I promise. I think I've got 9 more required days off." I winked at him. Simon held my hand, and squeezed it.

"You sure did have me worried there, sis. My heart about fell out of my body a few times...I just didn't know what to do." I was pretty sure he was going to go on and on, and I felt bad that he hadn't been updated.

"I'm sorry Si," I began. "I was pretty out of it for a few days, and I wasn't really communicating. Gabe was doing the best he could, and he felt terrible, too, once I finally reminded him to call you." I squeezed his hand back. "That won't happen again, ok? I'll be here, with Gabe, for now.

One of the guys is always here, so I've got protection. Once I go back to work, I'll come and go with Gabe. He and my parents came up with all of these plans while I was sedated. Funny, huh?" I smirked at him.

"Wow, I just can't believe how all of this turned out. I'm sorry we couldn't stop this from happening, Janes." He put his head down, and I could tell he was very upset.

"It's okay Simon. No one saw this coming, not even me. Not like this...." I got lost in my thoughts of that night in the bathroom with Michael... *Stop losing yourself in that bathroom, Janie.* Every time I blinked I saw the red stained bathroom, and I felt trapped all over again. *It's not going to happen again. You have to know that.* I changed my thoughts quickly to avoid the anxiety from creeping in. Just then, Heather broke in.

"I'm just really glad you're here now, and safe girl." She hugged me gently, and stood up. "I'm going to get some grub!" Everyone smiled. Nichole scooted on the other side of me. Simon waved at Gabe across the room, Gabe motioned him over.

"I'll be back over in a minute Janes. I'm needed for a guy thing, apparently." His smile widened as he strolled away. Nichole held my hand, now it was just the two of us on the couch. I looked at her, and she had tears streaming down her face.

"Janie..." she composed herself enough to talk. "I'm so sorry you had to go through this. I can't believe I didn't see this about him... I'm sorry I never believed the things I had heard. Maybe if I had..." I hugged her.

"Stop it. I don't want everyone to feel this "what if I could've...," when really, I don't think I could've even predicted this was going to happen." I leaned back on the couch, and exhaled. My chest felt tight, so I stretched my arms out, and my chest cracked, and was better.

"I know...and I know how you push people away when you're upset. Friends for life, remember? Just don't do that now, please Janes. At least keep Gabe and your parents in there with you. Just promise me you'll try, and that if you ever need anything, I'm a phone call away." She kissed my cheek, and leaned back and looked at me funny. "You ok, hun?" I nodded.

"Can you find Gabe?" I smiled, and she nodded and went searching. Moments later, he appeared and was already shaking the inhaler. He held it so gently in my mouth, and spoke so calmly while I inhaled each puff. Three later, and it was eased again. "Is this okay?" He nodded.

"Doc said that once your punctured lung started to heal at the stab wounds, they wouldn't work quite as well for a few days. He said it was be marked by chest heaviness, shortness of breath, and tiring quickly." He smiled, as if proud of his diagnosis. "I think you're doing just fine, baby." He brushed the hair from my face, and simultaneously we both noticed the entire room had stopped, and were listening to us. And staring at us. *OOooops... but everyone was smiling, and happy. Including my love...* I nodded at his explanation, and asked him to bring me some foods. He nodded, and asked, "you getting tired? It's already 9, it's been a few hours. I'll call this done at any time...don't want it to be too much for you." I shook my head no.

"It's fine. I'm good. Just hungry, please?" He nodded, and disappeared. Greg came through to change CD's, and smiled at me on the couch.

"How you doing, trooper?" he sat down next to me for a minute.

"I'm alright, I guess. Pretty tired..." I yawned. "Gabe was getting me food, I think." I shrugged, and sat while my arms had tremors from the medicine.

"I'll go check on Gabe, and put a rush on that food there, Sleepy Head." He rubbed my shoulder, and turned the music down to a more medium level. I smiled at him. A few moments later, Gabe was sitting next to me, with a plate full of foods. I sat up a bit, and thankfully, it was all finger food. *He's not only amazingly handsome, he's a genius, and thoughtful, too... Did I mention a chef?* I smiled at him.

"This is soo good! You're an excellent cook." I patted his leg, and slowly chewed my bites. Then his hand was shaking my leg, and he was laughing. "What's so funny?" I asked him. I noticed my Mom was there, and she was chuckling, too. "Whhhaat???" I said.

"You're falling asleep while you're eating, honey. Mid-sentence, even." she said. I felt my cheeks flush. *How embarrassing...*

"Oh, I'm sorry. I'm just so tired..." I took a drink of water, well, I started with a drink. Then I polished off the entire glass. "And thirsty." There were eyes on me everywhere, and my anxiety was growing. I started to fidget, and Gabe was right there in my ear.

"What do you need? I can tell something's wrong... tell me." he leaned back, and smiled coyly, so no one would take any thought to what was happening.

"I don't like the audience...they're staring. I think I'm done...I'm sorry." I whispered in his ear. He smelled so wonderful. I just wanted to crawl next to him, breathe him in, and sleep for days.

"Ok, baby. Give me a few minutes, and I'll clear it all out. I'll send some over for goodbyes, and have your Mom take you to the bedroom.

Okay?" I nodded, and rested my eyes. A few minutes later, I gentle touch woke me up. It was Simon, he smiled.

"Hey Janes, just wanted to say goodbye for now. I'm counting down until you're back at work, and call me if you ever just want to chat!" He hugged me gently.

"Thank you Si," I managed to push out with a very sleepy, raspy voice. I smiled at him. He stepped aside, and headed towards the door. Nichole bent down, and gave me a brief hug.

"Call me girl, any time. And remember what I said." She smiled, and kissed me goodbye. Most everyone else were the guy's friends, and there was no need for them to end their festivities on my account. My Mom headed towards me, and I nodded frantically.

"You ready for bed, sweet girl?" She asked adoringly. I shook my head, and stood slowly.

"I'd really like a bath first." I started heading towards the bathroom, and she followed. She sat me on the side of the tub, and prepped the bathroom. She started the bath, nice and hot. She folded the towels over the side. She got me a robe, and laid it by the tub.

"This is a wonderful bathroom. Such a nice whirlpool tub." I must've missed that somewhere.

"What?" I asked.

"It's got water jets, you know, like a hot tub." She pointed to the power buttons, and controls. *Hm, well, I really missed that one!* I raised my eyebrows with excitement. She was helping me take my shirt off, and cover the cast so it wouldn't get wet.

"Those sound heavenly... I think I should try them." I smiled at her, with my eyes closed on the side of the tub. I lifted my cast at her. "Thanks for the help with the ole arm, Mom."

"OH you poor dear... ok, I'll leave you to it." She hugged me, and kissed my head. "I've always got my cell, and I'll always answer when you call me. I promise. Call whenever you need me, honey. Love you." She blew me a kiss as she closed the bathroom door. Funny thing was, every other time she had left me, I felt sort of sad and alone. This time was different. I didn't feel like I had lost anything, and I didn't feel alone. I smiled quietly at myself as I prepared for the bath.

41

I slowly stripped off the jeans, and held myself up on the counter top. It was cold against my barely covered skin. I pulled off my slippers, and then braced myself to take off the tank top. It slid off relatively easily, thankfully, and all I was left with were my bra and underwear. I slipped out of both easily, and carefully sat on the edge of the bathtub, and then pushed the 'power' button. The jets turned on, and bubbles galore. I slowly sank into it and positioned myself so that I wouldn't sink, if I fell asleep.

It felt heavenly, just as I had imagined. I sank under the water once, to soak my hair and get completely wet. Then rested my head against the headrest, and closed my eyes. Moments later, I heard a knock at the door.

"Can I come in, baby?" his voice was soft.

"Yes..." was all the talking I had. Speaking was exhausting right now, because breathing was an issue. The door opened slowly, and his head peeked around the door. He came in, and closed the door.

"The bedroom door is locked, and I'm in here. So I just wanted you to…" his words were lost, and I opened my eyes to find him staring at my chest in the tub. The air jets were hitting and making my breasts bounce from side to side, and he was mesmerized. I laughed out loud, and he refocused.

"Did you…get a little sidetracked on something?" The smile was plastered on my face, and I imagined his warmth next to me. He hid his red cheeks from me, and shook his head. I needed to feel him. "Hey…are you busy?" I asked him.

"Not really, what do you need?" He came closer to the bathtub, and leaned over the edge so he could hear my mumbles. Even though my eyes were closed and tired, my body was alive and awake on the inside. My heart was beating faster now that he was here, and I wanted to feel him on me. In me. Touching me, everywhere. I put my hand on his cheek.

"You." I smiled. "I just need you." I reached for his hand, and pulled him towards the water.

"Can I get in with you, love?" his eyes lit up, and his smile turned to deviously ornery. *Bring it on… Janie, you'd better wake up…* He slowly stripped off his shirt, and I squinted through my tired eyes to watch the whole show. There wasn't a part of him that I hadn't touched, but as my eyes were showing me...there were parts I wanted to focus on even more. My eyes focused on his pants, as he fumbled with the button on his jeans. My leg started to squirm in the water. I watched his pants drop onto the floor, and he stood before me in boxer briefs that were black. *Maybe just one bite? Delicious.* My legs writhed with need for him. I almost couldn't restrain myself, and forgot that an hour before, I had been exhausted.

He stalked towards the bathtub, and linked his thumbs under the band of his underwear. *Which now clearly say Fruit of the Loom, by the way...* They dropped to the floor, and my mouth fell open at what I saw. He stepped into the bathtub behind me, and sunk down under the water. I waited until he was situated, and then laid back onto him. *All of him...* There was no denying what was on his mind. I could feel it poking me in the back. Both of our bodies were as hot as the water, and the jets just made it all that much better. I closed my eyes on him, and tried to relax my thoughts.

The only things I could think of were us in the bath tub. Us in the bed. Us on the floor. We were everywhere around this house, and he was deep inside me in each thought. I shook my head, and tried to turn off my libido. *I want him.* It wasn't working. Parts of me were throbbing, and needing to be touched. Before I knew it....my hands were creeping their way up Gabe's thighs. I rolled myself over in the bath to find his eyes closed, and his head back... *he was hoping for this.* I smiled with my conscious at this fact, and my hands trailed up far enough to tease him. To run my fingers around his most sensitive parts and watch his breath hitch... To feel him twitch underneath me, without holding me down; letting me decide what was coming next. I climbed up to him, still between his legs, and kissed his chest. *I need this...* I kept kissing up to his neck, his face, and finally his mouth. He moaned into my mouth, and I could feel how enraptured with us he truly was.

In a flash, he pulled me onto his lap. Water splashed out of the whirlpool tub all over the place, but he didn't seem to notice. I tried to brace myself so the cast would be safe, but it was hard to do being that everything was now soaking wet. I was now sitting on top of the hardest part of him, while he nibbled and bit my nipples and breasts. His hips moved naturally under me...and it was obvious that he was as eager as I was. He pulled my head to his own, and passionately kissed me. He lifted my hips, and pulled me onto him. I slowly sank down, taking as much of him inside as I could. I tossed my head back, and moaned loudly. I could feel ever inch pulsating inside me, and I didn't ever want him to leave. I slid up and down his shaft, first slow, getting every inch. Then speeding up, creating a hot friction that was eating us both alive. He wrapped his arms around my shoulders, and pulled me onto him deeply. The depth of the thrust set of an instant orgasm, my body started to convulse, and my burning hot core tightened around him extremely hard.

"Holy shit!" he exclaimed, and I felt him pull me tighter onto his cock. He held his breath, and I felt him shoot straight into me. He gasped for air, and tried to breathe. A moment later, when he had slowed his breathing enough, he spoke. "Baby," out of breath as ever. "That was amazing." He smiled, still panting for air. I nodded, and hugged him. I was feeling overly emotional, and very attached to my Gabriel right now. *Yes, I am aware I just said he was mine. I think he is mine. So there.*

I wasn't sure how long we had laid there, but the water jets had turned off, and I was turning wrinkly. I smiled, and kissed him. I eased off of him, and quickly rewashed myself so I was clean again. He helped me sit on the side of the tub.

"Thanks," I patted his knee. "Want to watch some TV with me before bed? I've got to take meds before I can go to sleep." I smiled at him.

"Sure baby, that sounds great. Can I help you out of the tub?" I nodded, and took his hands when he extended them. He pulled me out, and right into his hot, wet body. I loved the way his skin felt on my skin. I swallowed hard.

"Gabe, I...I have to tell you something." He didn't even move, just kept hugging me.

"Ok, what's up?" One hand was at the small of my back, holding me against him. The other was at my neck, gently rubbing the very back, while holding my face to his. I swallowed hard again. *Yes. Do it.* I cleared my throat.

"I love you, Gabe. For so many reasons." He was quiet at first, and then smiled and laughed briefly. I wrinkled my face, and he scooped me up in his arms, still smiling.

"I've known that for a while, and I know you've known that I've been in love with you for weeks. I can feel it every time we touch." He smiled, kissed me, and gently laid me on the bed. "I love you, too. A lot, Janes." He rubbed my cheek, and turned on the CD player. It was *Everything,* and he turned it up.

"I'm very glad to hear that," I said while I towel dried my hair. I'd been waiting to hear him say that for what seemed like an eternity. Now that he did, it seems like it's always been love for Gabe and I. Some deep, eternal connection. *I love it.*

"I don't plan on giving you up for anything, just so you know." He smiled, and bounced on the bed next to me. He sang into my ear, *'you're all I want, you're all I need...you're everything, you're everything...you're all I want....and how can I stand here with you and not be moved by you? Would you tell me how could it be any better than this?'* This was absolutely one of my favorite songs of all

time. I couldn't stop smiling. It was so peaceful--
blissed out from being bathtub sexed, and now
being sung to. He twisted around, and rolled back
over with a baggie of green, and an inhaler. "Which
would you like first, patient?" He winked, and
smiled.

42

Before my inhalers, we decided to smoke it up a little. Gabe was quick to notice that I was calmer after a few inhales than with none. On my last inhale, my cell phone rang. I picked it up, and it was my parents' house number. I answered it slowly, so I could exhale.

"Hello?" I said cheerfully, trying not to cough. Even though my mom knew of my past times, she didn't always approve.

"Where the fuck are you, bitch?" The blood drained from my face, and my breathing accelerated to an alarming rate. My eyes were wide, and filled with tears. His voice was like knives in my head. I winced at the instant pain hearing his voice caused inside me. *Oh no...* "I know you heard me Janie. You know I'll-" Gabe snatched the phone from my hand.

"Hello?!" he screamed in the phone. "Who the fuck is this?!" The line was dead by the time he got the phone. I couldn't speak, but the tears flowed from my eyes. "Baby," he tried to calm me down. *Focus on his arms around you...* "We're safe. It's just you and me, and the guys out in the living room. It's okay. I need to know love, was that him?" I nodded frantically, and the sobs came out of some dark, deep place. "Shhh, it's alright. Can I look and see what number he called from, please?" I nodded, and handed him the phone. He got up out of bed with my phone, and his in his hand. He started to dial on his phone, and as he was leaving the room, I heard him speak... "Ah, Hello...Detective Knox? This is Gabe Lazarus, I was with Janie, ah yes, you remember. Well, a slight problem here. The sonofabitch just called her cell phone, from her parents' house. The trouble is, her parents' house is empty. I know the alarms were being installed tomorrow..."

I put my hand on my forehead, and shook my head. *What do I have to do to make this stop happening?!* I pulled a big t-shirt over my head, and curled back up on the bed. I found the pipe of smoke, and helped myself to more. *Why not?* I waited for Gabe to come back in, and it was a good fifteen minutes later. He smiled when he came back in, and stayed silent for a moment. Once he sat down, he handed me back my phone.

"I talked to the Detective, and they're going to lockdown your parents. Talked to your mom, and she's safely on her way to the next business destination. Our first court hearing will be next week, and you're not required to appear, if you don't want to. He'll be notified of the court date in the next 24 hours, due to this phone call." I hid my head under the pillows. "It's not your fault Janie, none of it. I'll do everything I can to protect you, I promise." He kissed my forehead, and we laid down to watch a movie.

"I know," I smiled. "I'm sleepy. And shaking... I hate these inhalers." I curled up in the crook of his arm, and passed out. Even dreaming was an experience with him in my head...

*   *   *   *   *

The bright lights woke me up, and Gabe right after. I wrinkled my face to check the time, and it was around 3am. I could hear the guys up in the living room, too, apparently still awake from the night before. Then there was a knock on the door. Greg's loud voice was calling for Gabe, "Uhh, you'd better come out here a minute, man." He rolled out of bed, and put on a pullover. He opened the door, and turned around once.

"Stay there." he pointed his finger at me, and closed the door. I was perplexed as to what was going on. I cautiously slinked over to the window, where I could partially see what looked like car lights shining down the driveway towards the house. But the car lights never moved. I stared into the car lights, for what, I wasn't sure. But then the overwhelming feeling of dread came over me like a black cloud. *It's Michael.*

I sank away from the window, and slowly stood to stand. I was almost down the hall, when Greg came and turned me back toward his bedroom.

"Come on, trooper. Let's get you in the back of the house for now, okay?" He smiled, but it wasn't very reassuring.

"What's going on Greg?" I stopped walking, and faced him in his doorway.

"Gabe's on the phone with Betsy, err, Detective Knox. They've been in the driveway for about an hour. Everything's okay, we're just waiting for their assistance, now." He patted my back. "I've got a cool new poker game on my computer, if you want to try it out." He grinned, and closed the door. I sat on his chair, and laid my head on his desk. I was too tired for the computer, or any other technological gadget right now.

Moments later, I could hear the sirens in the distance. And then I heard a roar of men's voice, and yelling. The knock on the door told me that the Detective was here, but I could still hear the sirens. *What the hell is going on?* I was coming out of Greg's room cautiously. I wasn't sure what I was going to walk into, but Gabe turned the corner and smiled when he saw me.

"It's ok baby. It's just the police. Come on out." He reached for my hand, and took me out to the living room. Lucky for me, the t-shirt covered me like a dress. I still stood sheepishly behind Gabe for protection.

"The suspect has taken off in a chase, but is no longer at the Lazarus household." She turned toward me. "Hey honey, sorry to meet up again like this. I'm on my way out, but you'll have police marked at the driveway on and off the next few days. That should keep everything quiet." She patted my shoulder, and I slightly smiled.

"This is getting old! I fucking hate this!" I turned and ran back into Gabe's room and collapsed on the bed. I heard voices, and mumbles, and all the locks being clicked on the front door. The buttons for the alarm being set, and then Gabe's warm arms gently rubbing my back. He laid down slowly next to me, barely touching me at all. I scooted back into him, so every part of me was touching every part of him. I sighed into my pillow. He kissed the back of my neck on and off until I fell asleep.

43

I woke up coughing terribly, unable to catch my breath for anything. He was quickly at my side shaking the inhaler, putting it to my lips. The coughs were like tiny knives that each stabbed my lung, and I couldn't stop long enough to inhale anything. I tried to motion to him that I couldn't inhale, and he caught on quickly. He timed the spray when I was gasping for air in between coughing, and it worked. Four times, for sure, and a few others just in case. I was still gasping for air, but the coughing had slowed. I sat very still, trying to calm myself to ease the pressure in my chest. The scars from the wounds on my back were throbbing with my pulse. *Jesus, what a way to wake up...* I threw my head back against the pillow, and breathed in and out slowly. I half smiled to Gabe, who was now wide awake with me at 4:56am.

"Sorry," I whisper talked to him. He just shook his head and smiled. He turned the TV back on, and found an early morning movie for me to watch. He laid back down next to me, and closed his eyes. I tried to control my body enough to just be quiet and still so he could rest. He was going back to work today for a little while, and even though Greg would be here, I was going to miss him. Even though these circumstances sucked, getting to be here with him is what I've wished for.

When the clock hit 8am, I had already woken up from another nap. I gently woke Gabe up, and kissed him gently.

"Someone told me you're going to work today. Don't want to be late, G..." *G? Well, he does seem to like nicknames... oh well.* He reached up so his palm was over my face, and patted it. And I giggled. I got up, and moved into the living room to watch some Maury show. He rolled out of bed to get ready for work. It didn't take him long to get ready, but it was plenty of time to have his lunch packed, coffee ready, and breakfast to go by the door. He saw the layout, and turned and beamed at me.

"Thank you so much! That's so sweet.... No one's ever..." he reached for me. I pulled myself off the couch, and walked over and into his hug. "That's really awesome of you, Janes." He hugged me hard. "I'll be back around 2 today, okay? Greg's here, and I've got my phone. I'm only ten minutes away. Just text if you want to talk, okay?" Tears started to prick my eyes, and I tried to hold them in. I sniffled. "It's okay baby, the day will go fast, and you'll be back in my arms again soon. I promise." I kissed him, maybe too hard for the morning goodbyes. *Some slack, I'm new at liking a relationship...* I waved out the window as he pulled away, and my heart strings pulled.

I instantly went and found my phone, and called my mom. She answered on the first ring. "Morning, Janie! How are you honey?" she was very peppy for this early in the morning.

"Oh, I'm just...bored. Gabe went to work a bit ago, now I'm just hanging out with Greg." I paused, and guessed I should fill her in, if G hadn't already. "Last night we had an incident, I guess. I missed some of it. The good parts it seems." I chuckled.

"I heard, I talked to Gabe last night. I can't believe the gusto that Michael is showing. What a dirty scumbag. I wish there was a way to keep this from happening." he sighed. "Your dad has met me here, and he's telling me to tell you he loves you. In a few days, we'll both be back for a while again. I told him all about Gabe's house, and the guys. He's very hopeful for you now, honey." I could hear her small smile. *Make that smile bigger.*

"Yes, I'm very happy here... minus all the drama...things are progressing very normally. We exchanged some pretty important words very recently." A giggled slipped through my lips. "So now all feelings have been declared."

"OH that's the best news! And your laugh! OH! I may have to speakerphone this goodness for your father, honey!" She laughed more.

"I know. Oh, one more serious thing...the Detective said last night that Michael would be served with court papers in the next 24 hours, due to this incident. So we've got police protection, which I know you know... but I think that you both should have it too, once you're home. Will you think about it?" There was a big pause, and background chatter.

"Yes honey, we'll take the protection when we're home. However, I don't think he's got much on us when we're traveling." I laughed, boy was she right on that one. Michael had never paid attention to what my parents jobs even were, or what they did. He just liked the extra time alone when they were gone for days at a time.

"I definitely agree, Mom. Well, I don't want to keep you, just wanted to check in. I'm going to go take my medicine, and watch Maury with Greg." There was so much background noise there, it was becoming hard to hear.

"OH! Honey tell Greggie I said hello!" She giggled. "We can chat later honey, my seminar is beginning now!!!" She laughed out loud, and I heard the announcer speak. "Welcome Samantha

Tay-" and the phone hung up. That was my mom. I was always first, but work was never too far behind.

I relaxed on the couch, and Greg was on the loveseat. Maury had paternity tests on, just like every other day it was on. The curtains were drawn in the living room, and my eyes were falling closed again.

"Hey Greg?" I asked.

"Yeah Trooper?" he said jokingly.

"My mom says hello. She missed you, I think." I laughed a little, and waited for his answer. He chuckled himself.

"Sam's great. Your mom, I mean. I'd love to meet your dad, too." He threw a pillow at me. "Hopefully it gets to that point with you and G?" he questioning asked me. I shrugged.

"I hope so...I really love that guy. He saved me, you know." I nodded. And sleepily added... "he's the best ever." I vaguely heard Greg agree, and tell me to go to sleep. Didn't take too much... *his face was always last I saw...*

*   *   *   *   *

His voice whispered in my ear, but spoke loudly to wake me from my dreams. My eyes opened in a flash, and I sat up quickly.

"It's okay love, it's just me. Home from work." He kissed my forehead, and added "all the work friends say hello!" and he disappeared into the bedroom. I was groggy, and still waking up. I rubbed my eyes on the couch, and yawned wide. I reached for my phone, and checked my texts. I had twenty some missed messages. Most of them were hang up calls, and I didn't recognize the numbers. I listened to the last two, and I swore I could hear Pantera playing in the background. *Oh you have got to be kidding me. Again?* I saved the two messages to my voicemail, and turned the phone off. Gabe was walking towards me, perplexed. "Why do you have your angry face on?" he sat next to me.

"I'm not angry...just tired. Still." I sighed loudly. I debated for a few more second as to whether or not I should tell him about the voicemails. And even though I knew it may sour our evening, I knew I had to. "And, he's left some voicemails." His head instantly snapped towards me, and he looked upset.

"When did he call??" I could feel the twenty questions start. I calmly put my hand over his, and smiled at him.

"Slow down there, tiger. Don't lose it yet…please. Let me explain." I propped myself up more, and tried to collect my thoughts. "So I had 25 missed calls, and voicemails. Most were hang ups, none had words. But the last two I heard something…a telltale sign of Michael. Pantera." I looked at him, and his eyebrows were bent at me. "I know, seems crazy. But I hate that band with every fiber of my being, and he knows it. He played it loudly at my parents the night he attacked me. I saved those two messages, and I'd like to send them to your phone, so you can message the Detective. But I don't want to dwell on this… please." I paused, and looked at his forlorn, lost face. He was nodding, but I wasn't sure which part he didn't agree with. "I'm having a hard enough time keeping my anxiety at rest…please just be easy with this." I rubbed his shoulder with my free hand, which happened to also be covered in plaster.

"Okay, I'll send them to the Detective. And I'll do my best to stay calm about things…it's easier to do that when I'm with you." He kissed me, at first very gently. But there was an unsaid hunger I could feel that was trying to come out. I slowly slid my hands up to his face, and held it while he kissed me. I gently stroked around his ears, and down his neck. His lips were so soft on my own, and he tasted sweet like candy. *More would be spectacular…* He pulled away from me slowly, and scanned my face. He was smiling slightly, like he wasn't sure how to gauge this situation. "Janie, what's gotten into you?" he chuckled.

I could tell he was apprehensive due to my constant drowsiness, but he was the only panacea I needed now. I traced the outline of his face with my finger, and my breath hitched. His face swooped back down to mine, and he stopped just short of letting his lips touch mine. Looking down, his lips were right above mine. His eyes were inches from mine, and they had the most crystal blue color in them. *Don't get lost in those eyes...* I tilted my chin up, and tried to grab his lips with mine. He pulled away just far enough, and I searched his face, and caught his ornery smile. I got off of the couch, and walked towards the bedroom... not before raising my eyebrow in his general direction.

44

I went to the bedroom and tried to make it onto the bed. It didn't work. I heard the door slam as I giggled and sprint tip-toed through the room. He was laughing too, and we faced each other at opposite sides of the room. Separated only by a chair. I decided to use this to my full advantage. Without a second thought, I grabbed the other chair next to me, and walled myself in with chairs. I stepped back, and made sure he was watching. My shirt came off pretty easily, revealing my black bra. His eyes focused on my boobs, and his mouth opened slightly. He looked primal, like he was starving.

Next I took off my pajama pants, steady and slow. Once they were down to my knees, I turned around to finish taking them off. One leg at a time. With each leg raise, his breath hitched. After the second leg, he readjusted his footing, and his pants on his side of the room. He took off his shirt, in return. We were both exchanging very devious, evil smiles...and it was really heating up in the bedroom. I turned back around so I was facing him, reached behind me with my arms, and unhooked my bra. I loved it when he looked at me like a meal. When I could almost see him drooling over me.... *I needed that.*

I spun a few slow circles, and at the end, released the bra I was clinging to. I stood before him in only underwear, and now blushing...waiting to see what he would do. For minutes, he stared at me. Directly at my face, and in my eyes. His breathing was deep, and erratic. He was wiggling his fingers like they were asleep. Finally, something, he licked his lips.

"You've been teasing me for so long..." he over took the chairs, all but throwing them out of the way. He pressed his body against mine, making sure to feel my breasts with his chest. He tipped my head up to his mouth, and whispered, "I can't wait any longer..." His lips overtook mine, and his tongue dove into my soul. His hand held me close to him, and also felt every inch of my body. He took extra time over my nipple, clamping on and squeezing until I held my breath. *Perfect.*

"I won't tease you, I promise. It's all yours..." I tipped my head to his shoulder, and he bared his teeth on my neck and bit. The instant throb between my legs screamed his name. My deepest depths were crying out to him, begging for his love. Without hesitation, he spun me around onto the bed. He threw me back, and thumbed my panties. With quick movements, he stripped them down my legs and tossed them aside. He slid his hands up my legs to my inner thighs, and lingered around the tops of them with his fingers. My hips writhed with want, and he took notice.

He sucked his middle finger, and pushed my legs apart with his knee. He took his wet finger, and rubbed my clit then slipped his finger inside. His face lit up when he was inside me, and he reacted every time I clenched. His cock throbbed with excitement every time I wiggled. My only thought was him on me... *taking me hard*. I reached out, and palmed his length in my hand. He gasped when I squeezed my hand around him. I began to stroke him to the rhythm he was fingering me to.

My hips gyrated under his hand, and he turned his head a bit to take notice of my need. He pulled his fingers out, and licked them off. *Oh my God...how hot was that?* He sat down on the bed next to me, and I couldn't resist temptation. I leaned over, and sucked him into my mouth.

"Ohh Janie.... oh God, yes..." he tensed, and gripped the back of my head. I bobbed up and down for a few minutes, and went a little deeper for some serious action. He gripped his headboard, and moaned louder than ever. I sat up on my knees for more leverage, as he seemed to be thoroughly enjoying himself. I double fisted, and twisted his cock in my mouth, and vacuum sucked his tip. His head fell back, and he became silent for a moment.

"Shit, Janie, I'm gonna come!!" *You got this, honey.* I kept sucking and pumping away, and I slid another hand around his balls and his dick got massively hard. Finally, release. His hot spray hit the back of my throat, and tasted of salty water. I sat back, and wiped off my face. I started to get off of the bed, and I was pulled back down. "Oh hell no you don't... we're not done yet." He rolled me back over onto my back, and trailed the first track of kisses from my knee, to my upper thigh. The second track of kisses didn't stop, and once his mouth was over my core, I could barely keep control. My hips wiggled everywhere, and he stilled me with his hands.

Once I was wet, he flipped me over, spread my legs, and teased me with his tip. In, then out. Barely in, then out. *Goddamn it!!! PLEASE!!!!* His hands coursed up and down my body, fueling my internal fire even more. *Gabe, now...fuck me....* Finally, he drove it home, and I instantly came all over him. Everything tensed, my hot liquid was all over him.

"More baby, I want more from you." *Oh sweet man, have you figured me out?* He was relentless, slamming into me. Making me form to his size, and take all of his length. I focused on him drilling me, when out of nowhere, he spanked my ass harder than ever. Another flood gate opened, and I came all over him again. This one was long, I clenched hard. He never stopped fucking me, in that entire climax. My nerves were now firing at every other thrust, and I was surely going to explode on the next push in.

"G... with me. Please." I stared into his eyes, and he understood. He changed his grip, and his thrust, and was instantly on the brink of falling over the biggest climax of all. He reared back, and struck my ass again. The stinging pain of pleasure swept through me, and I clenched on him harder than ever before. He released another load of his hot liquid inside me, and we both collapsed in a heap of hot breaths and panting.

We just lay there for quite a while, not moving, not talking. Just being with each other. This was sort of new to me, and I really liked it. He rolled off of me, and onto his side. I turned toward him so my face was cuddled in his neck. He stroked my hair, and back. After a few minutes I looked at him, to find him staring at me. He smiled, and tipped my mouth to his. It was the most romantic, full of promise kiss I'd ever had in my life. When he pulled away, he had that smile again, and I wrinkled my eyebrow.

"I love you, baby." he blushed. "It's so true... you're so perfect. So you." he shook his head, and smiled. I smiled back at him. *Gabe, you just made my life.* "I'm so glad that you're here Janes." I smiled again, and winced. I hadn't had any pain meds for almost 10 hours, and I think that may have been pushing it a little. *Bad timing, stupid pain! Way to ruin the moment!* He instantly reacted, "what can I do?" he asked.

"You could get my meds for me... I just waited too long to take them. That's all." I smiled a little, while holding my side that now hurt. And itched. He took off to get my meds, and on his way, stopped and sent his phone my voicemails. He brought back my medicine, and a big glass of water.

"Here's your stuff, my dear. Brought the biggest glass of water I could find." he chuckled as he walked to his desk. "I'm going to call the Detective now, so you can hear things, too." He smiled, and dialed on speakerphone. It didn't take long to get through to her.

"This is Knox." She answered abruptly.

"Hey Detective, it's Gabriel Lazarus." he waited for the recognition.

"Gabe! What's up? Actually, I'm glad you called." *Uh oh.* That was never a good sign.

"Well, Janie had a load of missed calls today, all went to voicemail. All hang ups, but the last two she heard music in the background." he paused.

"Go on," she seemed intrigued.

"The music was Pantera, a band that Janie hates. They'd apparently had fights over this band in the past, and she said that this band was playing loudly the night he attacked her." He looked at me sideways, and I smiled at him. I was still thinking of how we had just spent our last hours together. *Oh my, careful...you'll get all hot and bothered again.* I raised an eyebrow at the thought...maybe that would be fun?

"Ah damn, I wish he'd just leave her alone." She sighed loudly on the speakerphone. "Well, I'll file the report. I want you to know he'll be served within the next few hours. This means his world is going to get really scary, and with how he's lashing out now, I'm thinking he may be one to push the limit's a bit." I listened to her words carefully, and my heart started to break a bit.

"I understand. We will take proper precautions here tonight, and we will all stay in. Will Janie's parents be protected?" His face now very serious, and inquisitive. I was sure they were out of state, so I nodded and made the "ok" sign with hand.

"Yes, Janie's parents are out of state currently. They should be okay." She paused, "but as for you all, I'm adding a security detail. We'll put your address on rotation every hour, and you should see a marked car in your drive, and back out frequently. I know it's a hassle...but...I don't want to see you guys put through any more of this."

"Thank you, Betsy. I do appreciate it." He looked at me, and restated, "we appreciate it. Janie's on the speaker, too." I smiled at him. We really were becoming a team. And a good one at that.

"Janie! How are you doing?" She sounded truly curious.

"I'm alright, thanks for checking. I really just want all of this to be over." I didn't mind saying, but did cautiously look up to Gabe, who was nodding sympathetically to what I said.

"I'm doing my best to give you extra protection, honey. Gabe's doing an excellent job keeping me informed, which is allowing us to closely monitor and follow Mr. Camaro." She paused, and went on, "he's currently at his parents' house, and that is where they plan on serving him the documents. Our hope is that he will react a bit better with his family there, especially his parents." She seemed confident, which was good, because this conversation was making me nervous.

"I hope it works, and this starts to go smoothly. I could use a good night's sleep, and to be safe outside Gabe's house." *Absolutely.*

"Ok Detective," Gabe started. "Please keep me posted on the court documents being served, and if you find out anything. Don't leave us in the dark if he leaves that house, please." He was stern with her, and seemed to be code talking.

"Absolutely Mr. Lazarus. We will all do what needs to be done. I'll talk to you soon. Goodbye." He hung up his phone, and nodded.

45

Monday morning came quickly, and Gabe had to get ready for work. Aaron would be home today while Gabe was at work, and even though I knew I was in fully capable hands, it just wasn't my G. I was feeling unusually uneasy this morning, and short on words. Gabe bounced around the room and bathroom getting ready, and putting his work clothes on. We were both glad to wake up this morning with having no issues with Michael last night, and I hoped that this kind of quiet would continue.

"What time will you be back today, G?" I rolled towards him and asked. He stepped out of the bathroom, still buttoning his pants.

"I'm off at 2, I think. I'm just working short hours until you're back, then we'll both go back to the ole 8-4, or whatever." He smiled, and finished sliding into his shirt. I nodded, and sighed. I got up, and headed out to the kitchen. For the first morning since the incident, I could walk straight, and almost take a full breath. But for the stupid cast on my arm, you almost couldn't tell what had happened. I went to the kitchen, and grabbed a few things for Gabe's lunch. *That's good of you to make use of yourself.* A moment later, he flew out of the bedroom and to me in the kitchen. He almost ran smack into me, but instead swirled me in circles with him in his arms. I giggled a little.

"Did you make that for me?" he smiled, and pointed at the food on the counter. I nodded, and reached for a bag. Before I could, I was caught in a passionate kiss. As he broke the kiss, he stepped back and moaned with satisfaction. I smiled at him.

"Hope your lunch works..." I trailed off.

"It's perfect, thank you for making it for me. I'm gonna be late, so I have to go! I'll text you in a little while." He swung around, put his coat on, and turned back to me as he opened the garage door. "I know something's up... we can talk later, okay?" I nodded, and put my head down. "Hey!" he yelled across the room. I turned my head in time to see his big smile, a hear him say, "Love you, Baby." I shook my head, and turned to clean up my mess in the kitchen.

"Good morning," the deep, raspy voice said while it yawned. I smiled, and waved. Aaron was awake. "How are you feeling?" he asked, once he rubbed the sleep out of his eyes.

"Physically I'm doing a whole lot better." That was all I seemed to be able to get out. I wrinkled my forehead at myself, and wondered if I was losing my mind. "But, I think I'm going crazy." I looked at him frankly, and shrugged. He chuckled at my comment, and shook his head.

"Oh Janie," he began. "You're not going crazy, I promise. I've seen crazy women…you're just not one of them! I already told Gabe this, too." He poured himself some OJ, and sat at the bar while I finished cleaning the counter. "Give yourself some credit. That was a whole load of bullshit you drove through last week. Hell, the last few months it sounded like. You're strong, and you've got one of the best guys I know on your side. Head over heels, on your side." he laughed.

"Nah," I started. "Not just one of the best guys…he's got two really super roommates who are pretty damn awesome, too, if you ask me." I handed him the bagel I had toasted for him, and turned toward the bedroom. I waved at him, and told him where I'd be if he needed me.

"Thanks for the bagel, Janes!! Just yell if you need me!!" I heard the living room television turn on soon after I clicked the doorknob closed. I sat back on the bed, and turned on the radio. I plugged in some old Alanis Morissette, and went into the bathroom.

As I walked through the threshold to the bathroom, the flashing memories of my parent's bathroom came back into mind. I tried to shake the thoughts free, and locked the bathroom door. I turned on the shower to scalding, and climbed in. The water beat over my fresh scars on my back, and it stung a little. Not enough to turn down the water though. It was still hard to shower one handed, but I had perfected my methods in the past few days. The Ziploc bags truly eased the tension of the shower getting my cast wet. I shaved my legs, and underarms. Looking down at the tub made me smirk, I couldn't help think of what G and I were doing in there just days before. I turned the water off, and slowly stepped out, careful as not to slip. Suddenly, and wave of tiredness came over me, and I thought I was going to pass out. I quickly unlocked the bathroom door, wrapped my towel around me, and climbed into bed. I was asleep before I remembered to turn the bathroom light off...

*   *   *   *   *

I woke up to commotion outside the house, and I was instantly terrified. I checked the time, and it was 1:36pm. *Gabe's at work until 2.* I grabbed his t-shirt, and pulled it on. I couldn't process what was happening, and I wasn't sure what to do. I looked out the window again, only to see Aaron standing in the driveway near the house, screaming at something down the driveway towards the road. He looked frustrated, and his face was angry red. He threw his arms in the air, and turned to come inside. I waited until the door closed, and then I heard him arm the alarm system.

Peeking my head out the door, I quietly called for him. "Aaron? Are you in here?" My voice was shaking, and I could barely take standing on my wobbly feet. A second later, he appeared in the hallway.

"Everything's okay, Janie. I'm not sure what you could hear of that..." he rustled around with his phone, and flipped it out. He was still short of breath, and looked very mad. While he dialed, he turned and asked, "what did you EVER see in that douche? Sorry Janes, but Jesus..." he paused, and turned back to the wall. "Gabe, hey. Yeah, I handled it. But he says he'll be back. Greg's due home by 7, I'm staying home. I'm not missing this arsehole again. Ok, sounds good. See ya." He turned back towards me. "Gabe's heading home now. I've got to call the Detective real quick. Nothing to worry about, okay? I promise... he's not going to get near you. Ever." He said sternly, and left the room. I pulled my knees up to my chest on the bed, and cried. This was just insane, and I wasn't even really sure that had happened. The radio provided me little comfort until I heard the car door in the driveway.

"Janie?" he spoke quietly as he opened the door. He saw me curled up on the bed, and instantly came to my side. He pulled me off of myself, and onto him. "It's okay, baby, you have to trust us." He cradled my face in his hands. Tears still dripped down my cheeks.

"I know." I said in between cries. "I do trust you, and the guys. I just don't want to deal with him anymore! I just want him to disappear!" My sobs took over everything. He held me tighter, and calmly patted my back. A few minutes later, I had calmed again. He was still holding me, although we had reclined a bit in bed. He played with my hair with his fingers.

"It will be over soon, Janie. I trust that the system will work this out. We have to trust in something, right?" He sat up so he could look at me. "I want you to understand that even after we've gotten rid of that asshole, I'm still going to be here. Then we can just be us... together." He smiled, and kissed my lips. "Just focus on that future, okay? And let me try to take care of the rest of this bullshit." He hugged me, and lifted me up. I nodded at him. *He's right. He's what you want...what you've wanted since day one. Don't lose sight of that now.* "Do you have enough energy to eat? Greg's bringing home take-out." He took my hand, and lead me out to the living room.

He sat on the couch, and patted the seat next to him. I grabbed a blanket, and curled up next to him.

Aaron spoke up quietly, "Hey G, do you want some?" there were hushed man giggles, and I quickly opened my eyes to see what was happening.

"Hey!!" I yelled, and smiled. "How's about we share?" I stuck a hand out of the blanket, and took the joint in my hand. I inspected the quality, and laughed. "I can roll one better." I said, and raised an eyebrow.

"Ohhh really? Care to prove that, Janie?" Aaron was hard, but sweet. And I was about to kick his ass in the rolling department.

"Absolutely. I'll hold this doobie while you go get more," I inhaled and shooed him away with my hand. There was a roar of laughter through the house. I looked at Gabe, and he was texting someone on his phone. *I wonder what he's up to...*

"It's just your mom, so stop with the worry, silly." Without even looking at me, he knew what I was thinking. *Oh my...he pay's attention.* "She says hello, and call her soon. But not now, because she's in a meeting. Your parents are a trip, I tell you." I was only half listening to everything now. I was laying in my man's lap, smoking some decent smoke, just trying to keep my mind empty.

"Ok, Janes...here you go." A fat sack landed in my lap, along with the rolling papers.

"Perfect. Give me..." I looked down at my cast. "Aww, fuck!" I shouted. Both men were slightly taken aback by my yell. "Sorry, this stupid cast is going to hinder my perfection!" I laughed. Gabe chuckled, and shook his head.

"Ha! No handicaps allowed!" Aaron shouted! While he fidgeted, I managed to get the smoke broken up, and in the paper. Since I still had use of all of my fingers, I put them to use. The rolling pulled and strained my sore wrist, but I knew defeating Aaron would surely set my place in the house. *Maybe gain a bit of respect from the man?* I swirled it through my fingers once, and through my lips to seal it a second time. I held up my creation in front of my nose, eyeballing its goodness.

"It'll do. It'll do." I repeated, and giggled. Gabe picked up the specimen, and quickly did the scientific "mmm hmmm" noise at it, and passed it to Aaron. Without hesitation, he quickly lit it up. To his shocking surprise, it lit on the first attempt. And perfectly all the way around the cherry tip of the joint.

"Ok, I forfeit my trophy." He passed the joint back to Gabe, and bowed on the floor by my feet. "You are the mighty roller in this house, from now on." He spoke in a silly tone, and busted out laughing at the end.

"Oh thank you, mighty sir." Everyone was a laughing, stoned mess. Greg suddenly came in through the garage carrying pizza, and all sorts of tasty treats.

"Damn guys! Thanks for waiting for me!" he said jokingly. He put all the food down on the bar, and without thinking, I bolted for the food. I hadn't felt hunger like this for weeks, and I wasn't going to miss it. There was pizza, and breadsticks, and cheese dip...MMMmmm!! It was delicious. The guys soon joined me at the bar, and stuffed their faces as well. We all went to bed soon after, and hoped for a peaceful night's rest.

46

The alarms were deafening, but it still took a few moments to come out of dreamland, and understand that those were real alarms, and that something was wrong. Then I felt Gabe's hands on me, and heard his words, "Stay here, do not move. I'll be right back." I was breathing very fast, and was now fully awake. There was commotion all through the house, and it seemed there were noises outside, too. I could hear Gabe on the phone, and Greg and Aaron were in defensive mode.

"Is she in bed??" Greg yelled to Gabe.

"Yes, I told her to stay put. She was half asleep." he replied, and added, "head's up."

"Thanks," Aaron grunted. "I can still see them Gabe, tell that Detective to get her ass here quickly, or I'm going to go solve all our problems." There were mumbles from all of them now, and suddenly loud noises. Someone was throwing things at the house...*but what?* I wanted to check out the window, but didn't want to be seen.

"God damnit! You're going to pay for that, too, motherfucker!" I heard Greg yelling now. Suddenly, sirens came out of nowhere, and the noises all stopped.

Silence over took the house, as I cautiously exited the bedroom I saw the guys all pressed against the windows, watching the action outside. Gabe was still attached to the phone, and there were now loud voices yelling outside. I could clearly hear, "get on your knees! Now!" Over and over. The police had arrived. I stepped out of the dark, and Gabe turned to me, and smiled. *How is he always so smiley in these terrible situations?* He mouthed the word "detective" at me, and pointed to the phone. I nodded. Moments later, a knock on the door.

"Good Evening, Guys," I'm Officer Rhinehouse. "All of these juveniles were caught, and we're taking them in. They must be on to our watch rotations, so we will be changing up the times we're checking on you all. We're sorry that they got through." He looked over their shoulders to me, and nodded. I tried to smile, slightly. The guys all nodded, and thanked the officer. Gabe hung up with the Detective, and turned to us with explanation.

"So, sounds like Michael paid all those high school boys to terrorize us, basically. She's got no idea where Michael is currently. After he was served yesterday, he left his parents' house late, and lost the detail." His face was grim, and he turned to me. "Do you have any ideas where he could be hiding? If you do, I have the Detective's cell to text." I could feel the lump in my throat grow, and harden. I nodded.

"I do. His brother's farm. Check in all the buildings, and down by the gazebo. Prestyn Idles house." He smiled at me, and I swallowed the lump down my throat again.

I joined the guys at the table, and put my head in my hands. Simultaneously their hands came down on my shoulder, and squeezed.

He finished texting the Detective, and turned to see his friends supporting me the best they could. He joined them, and thanked them for being so loyal to us both. I felt like an interloper in their conversation.

"Well, back to bed everyone?" he held up his cell phone. "She's going to text me after they check out those two places. Keep your phones on you at all times guys. Especially if we divert to plan b. Get some rest guys." They all waved at each other, and Gabe joined me back in bed.

His body pretty readily conformed to mine now, and I loved it. He wrapped his arms around me, and put his face in my neck. I was restless though, and couldn't lay still.

"I'm sorry… I've got to calm back down after all that." I sat up against my pillow. I always felt like there was more that needed to be said about this entire situation, but I could never find the words.

"Okay, I'm sort of awake now, too. Want to watch some tv?" He flipped through some channels, and ended up on the music channel. "Oh, I got it. One second." He disappeared into the living room, and I already had a suspicion of what he was getting. He reappeared with "the box" and lifted it in the air. "Awake enough to roll me one, rolling master?" he joked. I nodded, and quickly did my thing.

Gabe took the blunt from me, and lit it. We passed it back and forth in the dimly lit room, until suddenly, car lights lit his back wall. He stood suddenly, and hesitantly looked out the window.

"It's only the police check." He scratched his head. "Guess we're all a little on edge." He jumped back into bed. Sleep was finally coming back to me, but it was already 5am. We finished passing the blunt, and he snuffed it out. We cuddled with each other, and must've fallen back asleep, because the 8am alarm was torture.

*   *   *   *   *

"Hey baby," he rubbed my shoulder. I slowly turned over, and opened an eye. "I'm going to run into work, give the guys directions, and grab my paperwork. I shouldn't be gone long, and Greg is here, too. Okay?" I nodded, and rolled back over. I was exhausted from being up in the middle of the night, and hoped to sleep in to catch up on my sleep.

Once I was woken up though, I couldn't seem to relax enough to get back to sleep. So I got up, and threw on some jeans, and a t-shirt. This was the first day that I didn't get completely winded from just standing up, let alone getting dressed. I headed out to the kitchen, and snooped around for what I could make for dinner. I checked the freezer, and didn't find anything too exciting. I remembered there was a freezer in the garage, and headed out to check it out. On top there was a roast of some kind... *Oh, yum... time to show the boys my cooking skills.* I smiled at myself. I carried the roast back in, and managed to find some good root vegetables to throw in with the meat. After searing the meat, seasoning the crock pot, and setting it on low I headed to the couch, and plopped down.

I was just staring out the windows, watching the tree line, when I thought I saw a car near the road. The trees were still bare from the beginning of winter, so the metal of the car shown through. I sat very still, and watched the car. It didn't move, but I didn't see anyone either. I quickly texted Gabe, *how much longer?* and I went back to watching the window. I turned on the radio with the volume low, as to not wake Greg. I checked the coffee table, and found a *Rolling Stone Magazine.* Not my first choice, but it was better than the muscle magazine next to it. I was checking out the celebrity updates, when my eyes happened to catch something over the top of my knees.

47

Are my eyes deceiving me?! My phone buzzed at the same time. It was Gabe's text reply. *About 30 minutes or so* *Shit.* I looked up again, and I could see movement through the tree line, coming towards the house. I wasn't sure if this was the police doing their checks, or something worse. *Go over the facts.* The car looked green, and he didn't have any green cars. *That you know of.* The movement looked singular, and I doubted he'd come alone. *Oh really?* I continued to watch, and finally they broke the tree line.

My heart sank, and my anxiety skyrocketed. It was Sean. *Had he sent him to find me? To talk to me?* He was a good football field away from the house, and I calmly tried to think of what to do. I still didn't see anyone else approaching, or any movement in the trees. I opened the front window... *maybe talk through the window?* Sean's eyes were searching the property, and his eyes slowed when he saw me in the window. I didn't break my stare, or react to his acknowledgement. He raised his arms in a defensive position, and to me that said he came in peace. I hoped. Sean and I had an awkward past...one that Michael had always picked up on. *Positive that's why he kept us apart.* We had remained friends regardless, but it was definitely a strained relationship. For whatever reason, life always drove us apart. *So, he couldn't want to cause me harm. Not Sean...* I knew Greg was asleep, and would absolutely protest to this meeting. On the other hand, keeping myself safe and inside was definitely the smart thing to do.

Sean stopped on the walkway, far away from the window. I looked around, and there was a chair ten feet away from the window on the patio. I pointed to the chair, and nodded toward him to sit in it. I opened the window wider, and waited.

"Ok, I'm going to the chair Janie." he spoke calmly, and moved very slowly. I crossed my arms over my chest, and stood as confidently in the window as I could. Inside I was shaking, and about to throw up. My eyes darted around the yard, checking for any other movement, or cars. He noticed my apprehension, and tried to calm it.

"Janie, I'm by myself. I know you'll have a hard time believing that," he paused. "But please try." He folded his hands in his lap, and looked directly into my eyes. "I've known for months how he was with you. I'm so sorry that I didn't ever step in. I didn't know how to handle it, or what to do. Confronting him seemed... dangerous." He put his head down, "but that's no excuse. And I know that.

It's deplorable that I didn't say something. For that, I'm forever sorry." He looked back up at me. He seemed to be being honest. It felt honest in my heart.

"Sean, I appreciate your words, and I know you were between a rock and a hard place. But tell me, why are you here?" I pulled the chair over to the window, and sat down. Standing, and being so nervous, made my legs shake terribly.

"For a few reasons, honestly." He sort of smiled. "I needed to see that you were okay, and I needed to inform you of what I know." He was very to the point. I nodded.

"This is sort of awkward, Sean. I'm so glad to see you, but petrified he's put you up to something." I rubbed my hands together, and he noticed my cast. He inhaled sharply, and sat back in his chair. I wrinkled my face at him, "I don't understand why you seem shocked." He shook his head.

"Michael told us what happened...but he seems to have left out some parts." He said, pointing at my wrist. "God, Janes, I can't apologize enough...I just can't believe this." I shrugged. "Can we talk? Catch up? I'll stay right here, and you can stay in there. I don't want you to feel uncomfortable at all. I swear." He put his hand on his heart, and I couldn't say no. *Plus, he's got*

*information you need... You know, keep your
friends close, and your enemies closer.*

"Yeah, we can chat. For now, I'll stay here.
One of my protectors, Greg, is home. When he
wakes up, he will surely shit. Gabe will be home
soon, too...and will also probably shit. Just stay
calm like you are with me, and we'll be alright." I
smiled.

"I understand. So," he started. "You and
Gabe? Together?" I nodded. "I've figured that for a
little while...but how long, really?" I smirked.

"See, questions like that make me think...." I
shook my head. "But I'm not going to hide the
truth. Gabe and I have been together for quite a
while." I inhaled sharply, knowing that this may
sound odd. "Started between us a few months
back, and been very serious these past few weeks."
His face looked pained, hurt even.

"Really? Wow..." he trailed off, and got
quieter. "I honestly didn't think you'd go out on
him...but that said, considering how he was... I
could never judge you for that. Is Gabe good to
you?" he raised his eyebrow, truly questioning it.

"Absolutely perfect to me. I love him, and
he may be the first person I've truly loved." I
paused. "If he would've been different, things
wouldn't have gone like this. Feeling how a
relationship is supposed to work, what love really
is... has been such an eye opener. Michael never

loved me. He just wanted a possession, and he had that by the way he controlled me, and hurt me." I sighed. "This has been terrible. I couldn't have imagined the things he did to me... I never thought he would." Tears filled my eyes, and rolled down my cheeks.

"Can you tell me... what happened?" his questions startled me, and I adjusted in my chair. I could feel my forehead wrinkle, and I wasn't sure I was ready for that conversation yet. "I don't mean everything, just what happened that night." He pointed to my cast again. I nodded, and as I did, Greg appeared behind me.

"Who the hell are you?!" he shouted out the window. I stood up in front of the window, and put my hands up. Sean also put his hands up, and didn't move a muscle from his chair.

"Greg, listen." I held my hands up in front of him, trying to calm him a bit. "This is Sean, one of MY old friends. He's been here out there for nearly twenty minutes, and no one else has come. I've only spoken to him through the window, and he came with information about this situation, too," I pleaded. He shook his head at me, as if he didn't approve of the action. "You can stay out here, if you want. Gabe should be home anytime, too. Everything's alright." I smiled, and put my hand on his arm. He calmed, and inhaled.

"I'm texting Gabe, and I'll be here at the bar." he sat down on a stool, and scowled at Sean. I took my place back in my chair, and smiled.

"Sorry about that," I paused and laughed. "But expect it again in about 15 minutes." Sean and I both laughed a little more. "What happened? You sure you want to know?" I left it at that.

"Yeah," he nodded. "I don't want to pretend about this anymore. I need to know so I can face it. Face him someday." I nodded.

"Ok," I took a drink, and adjusted myself. "Well, you were there that day at my work when he came to prove his point. There I reminded him we were done. I distanced myself from everyone after that final band practice..." I swallowed hard. "Because that night he hurt me, too. So fast forward to that week my parents were gone, and I didn't want to be alone considering how things had been going with him. I stayed here with the guys then, and went home Saturday only because my parents were going to be home." I paused, and looked over Sean's shoulder. Gabe's car was barreling in the drive way, and into the garage. "Just a minute, please." I smiled. I turn slightly in my chair to see my angry man storm through the kitchen door, and straight towards me.

"What the hell is this guy doing here? And is that his car parked on the road?" I smiled, and nodded.

"Relax, please." I reached for him to come over. "Sean is here on his own will, to give us information, and check my welfare. I've not gone outside, and he hasn't even asked me to. We're just catching up." I patted the chair next to me. "Care to join?" My calm reaction and tone kept Gabe from going crazy. He nodded.

"I'll be right back to join you, love." He turned and nodded at Sean. I watched him stalk to the bar, and quickly get caught up from Greg. *I love those guys... my protectors. And mine is so sexy, so fine. Oh, whoa. Focus, Janie.* I turned back to Sean, and continued.

"So, Gabe dropped me off that Saturday evening, and I went to take a bath. Apparently, Michael had been in the house all day waiting for me. He attacked me while I was in the tub. Broke my face, literally broke my wrist," I held up my cast. "He raped me, beat me, and stabbed me repeatedly in the back. Collapsed my lung." I lifted the side of my shirt to show him the still healing scar. He gasped, and covered his mouth with his hand. "Oh, and my head," I bent over, and moved my hair. I ran my finger down the scar on my scalp, and the few stitches that were still half there. "He hit me with something, caused a big gash." I sat back up, and fixed my hair. I smiled as I saw Gabe sat on the couch across the table from me. I winked at him. He smiled back.

"Janie...Oh man." his voice was low, and mournful. I just sat, taking it all in, looking at both me, and Gabe. Gabe just nodded at the facts, but being Gabe, he wasn't going to stay quiet.

"So Sean, now you've got the truth. You've seen it with your own eyes. What are you doing at my house?" He crossed his arms over his chest.

"I just wanted to check on her, honestly." He rubbed his legs with his hands. "I saw Michael the evening he was served, and he was angry. He put on a great front for his parents, but they were shocked, too, at the charges. He left in a rage, and headed towards the clubhouse." I glanced at Gabe, because that was indeed one of the places where I had instructed the Detectives to go and check. Gabe nodded again at Sean. "He called me the next day and asked if I'd help him get revenge. I refused. Prestyn also refused, just so you know. I haven't heard from him since, and neither has his parents. He was making more than his fair share of idle threats though," he paused and looked directly at me. "You know better than anyone, Janes... he doesn't just threaten." I nodded, and tears flowed. "I hate seeing you cry Janie. I'm so sorry he's doing this." He put his head in his hands, and wiped his own tears away.

"I do appreciate the information, Sean, and the risk." they smiled at each other. "Listen, in about five minutes we're due for the police to check things out. They'll surely need to speak with you as your car is parked in a watch zone." Sean nodded at Gabe.

"No problem, like I said... I only wanted to check on her, and help you out. I'm sorry I was too chicken shit to help before now." The silence in the room could be cut with a knife. And sure enough, the police car rolled in and the lights flashed on. Gabe stood, and went outside and explained the situation to the officer. He also gave the officer Sean's updates for the Detective.

I stepped outside while I had a free minute to breathe fresh air, and motioned for Sean to come over. I hugged him, and I hope he felt that there were no hurt feelings.

"Can I have your cell number, Sean?" He nodded. I opened my phone, and programmed it in. "I can't give you mine right now...I'm sorry." He shook his head, and hugged me again.

"I really hope this isn't goodbye Janie... I'd love to catch up with you sometime." I nodded, and as he walked away, Gabe caught him.

"Sean!" He stopped next to him. "Thank you, for coming to visit her. I can tell you've perked her up a little more than she's been in days. Also, here is my cell number. If you ever get more information on Mr. Camaro, please forward it to me via text." He patted Sean's shoulder, and turned back to me.

Once he was next to me, he wrapped his arms around me, and held me. He nuzzled my hair, and kissed my head. Greg had joined us outside by this point, and was shaking his head at Gabe's affection. We all headed to go inside, and walked into a house that smelled of a wonderful roast.

"Who made the feast?!" Greg happily asked. I smiled, and set the table. "Aaron should be home in a bit, let's wait for him and eat together. I think we need to go over the plans." Gabe nodded, and looked towards me.

"Is that okay, baby? We all should be on the time page." He hesitantly waited for my response, as if he actually thought I'd tell him no.

"Sounds great. I'll get everything ready." And off I went, to show my kitchen skills, and impress my boys. All three of them.

48

As everyone finished licking their plates clean, the moaning and burping told me just how wonderful the food was.

"Janie, I'm so amazed. The master roller is also the master chef! Listen, if it doesn't work out--" Gabe cut him off immediately with a terrible noise.

"Don't you EVER finish that sentence, my dear friend, or it will be your last!" The wine we all had at dinner obviously loosened everyone up a bit. Gabe was laughing leisurely, with his head back and all. He looked at me, and rubbed my cheek with his finger. "Boys, I think I've found her." Mouths fell open, including my own. And the guys burst out laughing.

"What a declaration, G!!" Aaron yelled, and held his stomach he was laughing so hard. "But seriously, we'd keep her if you didn't!!" Greg applauded in agreement, and the laughter slowed. He tapped his fork on the plate.

"So... We should really cover the plans once. I want us all on the same page." We all nodded. I took a big gulp of wine. *You're gonna need that...* Gabe turned to me, and pointed to Greg.

"He's going to go over everything, just listen baby." He wrapped his arm around me, and we leaned into each other for the conversation.

"Ok, so the alarm is our first defense. If it goes off again, we meet in the living room. You too, Janes." He looked at me, and nodded. I smiled. "If we're breached, two get her out to the back shed, and car. Keys under the mat. There are guns in most all the rooms of our house. Did you know that Janie?" I shook my head no, and smiled obnoxiously at him. "What's that for?" he smiled at me.

"Oh nothing. I mean, I figured that there were guns in the house, but in every room?" I giggled and smiled at the three, smiling back at me. "I don't mind the guns. I've shot guns before." Suddenly, the three faces were taken back, and their gaping mouths told me they were shocked. "What's THAT for?" I laughed.

"Well, that makes me feel more comfortable then!!" Greg cheered, and patted Gabe's back. G nodded in agreement. "So, that's the plan. Of course, the first plan is that we keep them all out of here, and we wait for the cops." It all sounded good to me, so I agreed with everything. Gabe reached for my plates, and refilled my wine.

"Life sure has been eventful since I've met you, Janie." I winced my face, and shrugged.

"I'm sorry?" I said questioningly. "Look, I don't ask for the crazy. It just finds me." I giggled, and Aaron high fived me at the table.

"I don't mind it...because," he said, and he slammed his entire glass of wine, and quickly poured more. "I get to sleep next to the warmest, softest, most beautifulest girl in the world." A giant burst of laughter came from the two guys, and Greg's fist pounded on the table. I blushed, and drank some wine. The guys pulled out a deck of cards, but I opted out. I was exhausted. This was my first day without a nap, and I was starting to feel it. I finished off my glass of wine, and headed to the bathroom.

"Goodnight guys, love you all..." I said goofily as I walked away. To my shocking surprise, they all counted to three and yelled, "We love you too, Janes!" I laughed and stumbled into the bathroom. I needed to take a shower before bed, so I clumsily turned on the shower, and stripped quickly of my clothes. When I was taking off my shirt, I fell into the wall, and landed right on my sore and healing shoulder. "Damnnit!" I yelled at the wall, while I rubbed my shoulder. My shoulder hurt like hell now. I hated that the aches and pains I still had brought back the distant memories I wished to burn from my brain.

I stepped in, and the hot water felt so good. I leaned my head back in the stream, and let the water beat on the stitches still in my head. I gently washed my scalp, and hoped the rest of them would finally fall out with this washing. As I finished rinsing, I reached for the body wash. I lathered up a sponge, and slowly began washing my body. I let my fingers trace over the swells of my breasts, and my nipples instantly perked to attention. I stood in the water stream, and squeezed each nipple until it hurt. I moaned with pleasure. My hands and the sponge slowly trailed down my stomach, and slid between my legs. It was mere consequence that my fingers found their way inside, and slowly rubbed in and out. I was burning hot, and was in dire need of my man. I leaned my head back in the hot water spray, feeling how hot I was internally just made me want him more. My body was aching, it was throbbing. My breathing was so heavy... I was in my own little shower world.

I lifted my head slowly, and squeezed my nipple again. I could feel the clench begin, and my body start to tense. I started to stand up, and opened my eyes to see Gabe sitting on the counter, quietly watching me in the shower. Seeing him staring at me, completely enraptured with what I was doing, made me come on the spot. My moan was the loudest yet, and I fell back against the shower wall. Once I regained my breath, I looked up at him with an ornery smile, and a raised eyebrow.

"Can I have a turn now?" he asked. I nodded, and opened the curtain to him, inviting him inside. He was only sporting workout pants, and those seemed a little tight, and not really hiding his massive hard on. He slowly stripped his pants down, and his massive cock bounced up and down as he took them off. He walked towards the shower, and climbed in behind me.

The instant feeling of strength and power that I felt behind me made me tremble. His cock pressed against my ass perfectly. I could feel every inch of him, throbbing on me, begging to be in me. I pushed back into him, and slowly turned to face him. His arms clung to me, and our bodies stuck together in the water. He rubbed his chest on my chest, and moaned. His hands slid around my waist, and he pulled me into him. His mouth quickly found mine, and our tongues struggled against each other. He was hungry for me now, and I needed him.

His fingers found their way inside me, and they probed around in circles making me grind for more. He withdrew his hands, and spun me around again. He pulled my hair back, and I moaned. He bent me over, and raised my leg to the side of the tub. He threw a towel towards my arms, and pushed me onto them. He squirted some lube on his hand, and I watched him slide his hands up and down his thick shaft. *I want that...so bad.* He held onto my hips, and squeezed as he plunged into my depths.

I loved the feeling of him thrusting away, filling me with himself over and over again. I loved the sounds our bodies made when they were slapping against each other. I loved the moans that came from both of us, and the deep stares that made me come harder. He drove his hips harder, and faster, until our rhythm was down pat. I could feel him getting harder, and my insides started to shake. It wasn't long until my eyes rolled back in my head, and I floated away on clouds *all* while being fucked. My body was numb, but I could feel him squeezing my nipple. He pushes were slowing, and his grip on my hips were extreme. *He's close.* He drove in hard, and smacked my ass as hard as he could will himself to. I instantly came around him, clenching and squeezing, and squirting all over him. Moments later, he shrieked out with pleasure, and came hard. We both fell against the shower wall, and slowed our breathing.

I stood slowly, now with legs that wobbled freely and re-cleaned myself off. Gabe quickly washed his parts, and turned the water off. We both had permanent smiles on our faces, and couldn't stop looking at each other.

"Thanks baby," he said, and swatted my butt. I blushed. "God, I love that I can still make your cheeks red." He pulled me into bed, and I pulled on a large t-shirt. He flipped on the television, and I got comfortable in the crook of his arm. Between the blankets, and my Gabe, I was warm and cozy enough to sleep for days. My eyes got heavy, and before I knew it...dreamland had arrived.

49

Morning came quickly, and I woke up before our 8am alarm. I wasn't sure what time it was, but it was just starting to get light outside. The television was still on, so I rolled out of bed to go to the bathroom. I got inside, and closed the door. All of the sudden, the alarms were going off. I finished peeing, and headed for the living room. Gabe had already jumped out of bed, grabbed the gun, and was in the hallway. We met up, and the guys checked out the surroundings. The front window was broken out by a brick, but there was no sign of movement otherwise. Greg picked up the brick, and came back to the bar with us. Another loud noise towards the back of the house got everyone's attention just long enough...

His hands slid around my mouth, and the gun was at my head in a matter of seconds. The metal was cold, and it didn't help that he was pushing it into the side of my face. I gasped for a breath, and the three of them turned around in horror.

"Now I've got the prize, I guess," Michael chuckled. "Why don't we just go sit down and have a chat? Doesn't that sound like fun, Janie?" His voice was off, and in that tone. His joker grin I had not missed, and I started having flash backs of the attack. Gabe, Aaron, and Greg all exchanged glances, and looked at me. Their faces were pained, and confused. He sat the guys down, but kept me standing. "Hmm," he rubbed up and down my body. Tears poured from my eyes, silently, just like old times. I looked down at Gabe, who had to look away as to not make matters worse. "Let's see what I did to you last time." He ripped my shirt down so my shoulders were exposed. He turned me into some light so he could see the scars. He pulled the shirt down more so parts of my breasts were exposed.

"That's about enough," Gabe stood to cover me. "Stop doing this to her!" he shouted at Michael. "You tripped the alarm, you've got minutes until you're surrounded!"

Michael threw me aside, and stepped towards Gabe.

"That's exactly why I've got to decide quickly who I take with me." He looked around at each of us, and pointed his gun at us when he looked. "You know, there are some pretty terrible lies you said about me, Janie. And you'll have to pay for those, and fix them." I tried to stay calm, but I was terrified.

"Michael...I didn't file the charges. I swear." *And that's the truth, because I knew this moment would come. Now when I look at you and say this, it's the goddamn truth.* He looked at me, perplexed. "I was almost dead when they found me... whenever cases like this are taken to the hospital, they automatically file charges. I didn't want any of this for you." I swallowed hard, and tried to hold the tears inside.

"I don't believe you. You couldn't wait to ruin my life." I shook my head at him, and spun around to face him.

"Goddamn it Michael! You're fucking insane! You think I wanted to ruin your life? Are you KIDDING me?!" I was screaming at him now, and it felt great. "You were the one ripping ME apart! Raping me! Stabbing me! Fuck you!" I pushed myself on the barrel of the gun. "If you're going to shoot me, then fucking shoot me." I relaxed my arms down to my sides, and stared him in the eyes.

His joker smile was slow to sneak in, but soon was staring me in the face. Without a thought, he cold cocked me across the head. It knocked me back into Gabe, and we fell onto the couch. He quickly put his hand over my forehead, and pressed hard. Moments passed, and my head began to throb. So hard I could barely keep my eyes open.

"Come on Michael," Gabe calmly pleaded. "This doesn't make sense. You're smarter than this." The smile faded off of Michael's face. "Look at her. She's bleeding, and in pain, again. Again. Because of your choices." Gabe shook his head. "Do you have a mother?" Michael's head snapped back to Gabe, and he stepped towards both of us again.

"Don't bring my fucking mother into this. She's got nothing to do with any of this." I tried to sit up a bit, and as I moved away from Gabe's hand, the blood ran down my face. Every time I looked at Michael, the joker smile returned. He was having fun doing this to us, I could tell. He glared at me, and suddenly spoke. "Get up." He reached for me, and lifted me off the couch. He pointed to the three guys. "Don't fucking move." He started to drag me into Greg's room. I kicked, and screamed, and fought. I heard all three voices pleading on the couch.

Before I knew what was happening, I heard the gun shot ring out. My head snapped around to see Michael aiming the gun past me. Time stood still. *No.* I couldn't turn fast enough, and when I did, my heart sank. Gabe held his shoulder, and fell to the ground. I fiercely fought Michael now. *God no.* I wanted to get to Gabe, I needed to. But I couldn't...Michael kept pulling me into the bedroom. I clung to the door frame with my hands, and my feet until Greg turned towards me on his way to attend to Gabe. There was no time left, I was losing my grip. I had his attention, and said all I knew to say.

"Change the plan. Now." My hands gave way, and I fell back into the bedroom with Michael. He quickly threw me to the floor, and locked the door. He then propped a chair behind the door, making it virtually impossible to open. He turned to me.

"See? I learned this door trick from you." He smiled eerily at me. I tried to keep my cool, but I was falling apart. He stalked towards me on the floor, and kicked at me. I tried to miss the swings, but a few connected with my shins. The pain rang through my legs. "Get on the bed. Now." I just sat and stared at him on the floor. I couldn't move. He was growing impatient with my not moving, so instead just picked me up and threw me on the bed.

I tried to crawl to the pillows, and away from him, but he held my ankles. He flipped me over on the bed... looking at his face was the last thing I wanted to do. *Ugh.* He had so much rage on his face, and he was so angry... there was no talking him down. He pulled me towards him, and held my legs apart.

"Come on baby," he whispered in my ear. "Just one more for the road?" He fumbled with his pants and underwear, trying to take them down. I tried to pull myself away from him, he pulled me back, and backhanded me across the face. The slap made the right side of my face go numb. And it made me angry. Looking down, I could see him trying to make himself hard so he could get what he wanted from me. *Too bad it wasn't working...* I braced my fingers on my cast, and swung at him, hitting him across the face. The cast scratched his cheek, and left a decent sized wound. He sat back, completely shocked that I had just done that. Then the rage came. He swung at me with both hands, hitting my head, my shoulders, and punching me in the side.

"What's this? You're fighting me? Oh come on... you've never been that strong, Janie." He pushed my legs back open, and thrust inside me. I could hear screaming, and what sounded like sirens in the distance. I couldn't get Gabe out of my mind... I didn't even know how badly he was injured. He pumped in and out of me, and grabbed my face. He turned my face so I was only able to look at him. "This is all your fault, bitch. Everything you've gotten. I'll always be looking for you." He thrust harder, and I moaned in pain. I could hear the guys outside the door, sobbing and yelling for him to stop. Over everything else, Gabe's voice stood out. *His cries were the loudest. Oh, please Michael... stop this!!* "And every time I find you, I'm going to have you just as I want." He continued to ram into me, finally slamming harder, and then finishing off with a loud yell. I knew why he made all the noise... and it was disgusting. *My poor Gabe...*

He sat back away from me, and re-clothed himself. My head hurt, and I was just hoping for the end at this point. I was tired of looking at him, so I turned my head to the side. Greg's desk was pretty clean, his whole room was, really. Tears were flowing out of my eyes, while I lay there waiting for Michael to decide what he was going to do. The sirens were much louder now, and Michael started to panic.

"I can't believe you did this to me." He paced back and forth. "I should've known. They all warned me about you..." he trailed off. I saw something shine under Greg's desk. I cautiously looked at Michael, who was pacing so frantically he was oblivious to me for those minutes. I looked closer, and it was his pistol. *Change of plans, Janie. Change of plans...*

I slowly sat up on the bed, and he turned towards me and aimed.

"Hey, easy..." I put my hands up. "I'm just sitting up. What do you mean, Michael? Who is 'they'? And what did they warn you?" I was genuinely curious about this one. He shook his head, and stood in front of me. He put his gun in his pants, at the small of his back. Reached into his pocket, and pulled out a pocket knife.

"I like this better for you..." He opened the blade. "Maybe carve my name on your pretty tits." The look in his eyes had changed again. *Fuck, this guy isn't right...* Without warning, he made a quick slicing motion at me. I was able to dodge it, but as I rolled off the bed, he swung again and the knife sunk into my rib. It went straight into my lung. I knew it because my breath was suddenly gone, and I had that heavy, burning feeling that was all too familiar to me, again.

I screamed in pain, and lurched off of the knife, and towards Greg's desk. The pain in my side made it impossible to run, so this was my only option. I heard Michael coming up behind me, so I quickly turned and pushed the chair into him. It barely threw him off course though, as he just tossed it out of his track. I reached under the desk, and oddly enough, the pistol was positioned to perfect fit into my palm. In one quick motion, I drew on him, released the safety, and aimed at his face.

What I didn't expect was raising, aiming, and also having a gun in my own face at the same time. Now it was a matter of wills...and he had always underestimated mine. I backed away from him into the corner of Greg's room.

"Stay away from me Michael...don't make me do it." He shook his head at me, and we turned in an awkward circle.

"You don't have the balls to shoot me. But I don't know if I like the idea of seeing you dead. If you're dead, then we can't have fun meetings like these." I cocked the pistol, declaring my readiness to shoot. "Oh, come on...that doesn't scare me." My head had enough of his talking and his words. I could see his mouth moving, but nothing was coming out. I took special notice that in between his yelling spells, the joker grin kept appearing. My head hurt so bad that I could barely see, and my body was throbbing in pain. There were moments of white, and moments of black. There was screaming, and immense pain. There were regrets stated, and my anger peaked one last time. I couldn't take hearing how all of this was my fault, yet again. That's when the gun shot rang out.

*　　*　　*　　*　　*

Simultaneously, the police were being let in the house by the guys, and Gabe was being escorted out. I could hear everything happening, but the door was blocked, and I was so weak. I couldn't see straight anymore, and my head felt

fuzzy. My eyelids slowly closed, and to the floor I
fell...

50

These giant fields with flowers... sunflowers, too. They're so beautiful. Gabe's in the distance, but what's he doing up ahead? I finally catch him, and I'm out of breath. Well, what on Earth?! He's got a little girl...oh, and she's adorable. She's got his smile, and long black hair. The two of them are playing happily, including me in all their activities together. Everything is so peaceful here. Suddenly there's a flash of light, and now we're in a house. It's a pretty house, lots of rooms. The little girl is following Gabe around like she knows him. I'm calling for him, but he's not answering me. Why won't he answer me?

My dream was being interrupted by a noise. An annoying noise that was bothering me. The "beeping" noise was driving me insane, and I couldn't make it stop. My mind was whirling out of control, so I steadied myself to calm it. I had a slight deja-vu moment, and remembered to listen. Once my heart calmed down, I could hear voices. And beeping from all over the place. I heard a voice whispering in the hallway, and I tried to focus in on it to see who it was.

"Yes...she's going to pull through. He's doing well, also in ICU... No....not this time. She took care of that." I was lost on the words...*also in ICU*... am I in ICU? I tried so hard to open just one eye, but the strain it put on my head throbbed even harder. My beeping speed up again, as the pain set off my heart rate. I drifted back off to sleep.

After some time, I could feel something touching me. I had hoped it was Gabe, and that thought gave me enough to open my eyes. *Mom. Dad. Greg.* I frowned.

"Where's Gabe?" They all darted around, and exchanged small smiles.

"He's doing okay honey. He's in a room here at the hospital, too." My mom patted my arm. "Don't move around a lot, okay?" I nodded. My head felt like it was splitting down the middle. "Can you talk honey?" She patted my leg. I cleared my throat, and nodded.

"Yeah," I was out of breath though. "Can't breathe though. Hurts." I moved slightly, and winced in pain. I reached out for a hand, and Greg's was there. He smiled at me. "Change of plans," I muttered, and went back to wincing in pain. The doctor came in just then, whizzing on through.

"Ahh, Miss Taylor. We must stop meeting under these circumstances." It was Doctor Bruschi. He patted my arm, and leaned toward my face.

"How's your breathing?" I shook my head, and the tears streaming down my cheeks told him no lies. "You've got a few fractured ribs, and the new stab wound hit the same lung as before. I stitched you up pretty well, so hopefully you'll avoid infection and start to heal. I opted not to do a chest tube because you did so well this past time." He shook his head. "Janie, I'm glad you got a piece this time." He smiled at me. "Okay, the bad news is that your wrist is smashed to pieces. That's where the mass of your pain is starting from. There could be nerve damage. We'll operate in a few hours. We also stitched your head up, and you've got a concussion." He smiled and rubbed my head gently. "All considered, you're again very lucky. We're going to run a load of tests, and get you prepped for surgery." I nodded, and wrinkled my head. "Questions, Janie?" He waited.

"Where's Gabe? What happened?" He put his face down, and looked up smiling.

"He's doing just fine. Bullet was through and through, did muscle and serious deep tissue damage. He's sore, but he's okay." I nodded, and smiled. I had so many thoughts going through my head, and I was trying hard to remember everything that had happened. Everything was so fuzzy. The nurse appeared and took some blood. The doctor turned to me before he left.

"I'll be here tonight; we need to keep your pain managed. I'll get your meds now, but please speak up if you're sore." He nodded, and left. Greg squeezed my hand.

"How you doing, trooper?" He smiled down at me. "You are tough as nails; you know that? Gabe was right..." He nodded. "He sends his love." He bent down, and kissed my cheek. I blushed.

"Thanks, Greg." I didn't want to bullshit anymore. "Is everyone okay?" I was worried sick.

"Yes, for the most part. You and Gabe seem to have gotten the worst of it, and Michael's not so great. But he's alive. You did good." I wrinkled my forehead. *What did I do so well? The Doctor, now Greg...* "Aaron and I are going to go home and get the house fixed, and put back together. We should be done before you're sprung from here. I'll come back by tomorrow to visit, okay?" He smiled, and patted my shoulder. He shook my Dad's hand, and hugged my Mom. He disappeared, and my mom was back at my side, instantly brushing the hair off of my forehead.

"Oh honey, this is just absolutely insane." I frowned, and nodded. "At least he'll be staying in jail now, no question there." *Really??* I missed that part of the news. Somehow I felt like I was missing all sorts of bits and pieces. I sighed. "I spoke to the nurses, and once you're done with the wrist surgery, they're going to let you and Gabe room together." I couldn't hold back the smile on that one. "Even though you're bruised and beaten, you're so beautiful, honey." She rubbed my cheek, and I smiled. "You're even glowing a bit, I think..." she giggled. My Dad stepped up to the side of the bed.

"Hey Janes, I don't want to interrupt, but the Detectives are here for your statement, if you're up to it." I nodded. "I'll let them in then." He turned, and opened the door. Thankfully, it was Detective Knox, and Special Agent Maddox again. They smiled pitifully.

"Hello Miss Taylor, here we are again it seems." the Detective started. "We'll need a statement the same as before, and we'll tape it just the same." She held up the same black recorder. The special investigator spoke up.

"But before we get started, here's the updates. Michael Comaro is in serious condition with a bowel perforation, and tissue damage from the gunshot wounds. He'll make it, I'm sure. And face trial soon after." She sat at the foot of my bed. "The good news is, Miss Taylor, that with all of this evidence, and now this latest issue...your testimony will most likely not be needed, and he will most like plead out." I nodded. The Detective nodded.

"Ok Janie, are you ready? I need you to start at the beginning and give as much detail as you can." I nodded, and cleared my throat. I closed my eyes, and it was as if I was reliving each moment as they happened.

"I had woken up suddenly, and didn't feel right. I got up to go to the bathroom, and that's when the alarms went off. I finished peeing, and headed to the living room. That was our plan, we all met in the living room if that happened." I wrinkled my forehead. "I remember walking out into the living room, and seeing the broken window. The guys looked around, found a brick...and then he had me. He came up behind me while I was at the bar, and put the gun to my head." I stopped for a moment to get my thoughts straight, and saw my parents shaking their heads. I felt so bad for dragging everyone through all of this.

"He forced us all into the living room, and onto the couches. He stood me up, and said he wanted to see what he had done before. He ripped my shirt down, and exposed my chest and scars." I protectively covered my chest with my good arm, and kept on. "I don't remember what set me off, but I was screaming at him then. Pushing myself on the barrel of the gun. Telling him to do it already. That's when he hit me on the head with the end of the gun." I reached up to my head, and it felt like it was the same spot that the last wound had been in. I shook my head. The Detective broke in.

"That's when Gabe began applying pressure to your head to stop the bleeding?" I nodded. "That corroborates his story, as well. He was covered in your blood, as well as his own." I nodded again. "Ok, Janie... Need a break?" I shook my head, and pressed on.

"He got me up again, and began to pull me into the back bedroom, which was Greg's. There were all sorts of commotion, and I was hanging onto the door frame. Screaming and pleading for him to stop, and then Gabe started to yell, and came at us. The gun shot was in my ear, and I turned to see Gabe falling to the floor..." my breath hitched, and tears stung my eyes. "I didn't know if he was okay, or what...and my grip was slipping on the doorway. Michael wanted me badly, and he was pulling hard. I told Greg to 'change the plans,' and I fell back into the room with Michael."

"He quickly locked the door, and barricaded it with a large chair so it couldn't be opened. I was on the floor, and he threw me on the bed. There was a moment when he had me pinned to the bed getting ready to rape me that I decided to hit him upside his head with my cast. I scratched his cheek, and he went off in a rage. Punching and hitting me everywhere. Guess I did more damage..." I held up my now re-broken wrist. "I need some water, a break, please." I reached for my cup, and took a big drink. I just needed a brief pause. One little break to breathe. I nodded at the Detective.

"While he held me down, and thrust into me, he told me that he'd always find me, and always do that to me. That I was his to do with what he saw fit. Once he had finished, he sat away from me. Suddenly he pulled the knife, and started swinging.. I dodged away from it a few times, and didn't quite make it out of the way on his last swing. That's when I found Greg's gun. I waited for the right time, and made a move to get the gun. When I pulled it on him, we ended up it an awkward circle with guns aimed at each other." I sighed heavily. Things were slowly seeping back into my memory, and the yelling and screaming was the first thing.

"We were screaming and yelling at each other. He kept blaming me for ruining his life, and I kept insisting he was insane. Then his face changed, and he told me he was going to carve his name on my chest. He started to tell me how he would kill my loved ones, starting with Gabe. He took a step, and I shot." I turned my head, and cried. "I thought he was going to kill me. So I shot again. I watched him fall, but I was losing so much blood, I was in and out of consciousness from then on." I shook my head, and the Detective patted my shoulder.

"It's okay Janie, you did what you had to do. No one will blame you for that. Do you remember anything after that?" I shook my head. "You only remember waking up here then?" I nodded.

"Yes, I could hear everyone before I officially woke up again. But no, I don't remember that gap in time." I wrinkled my forehead, and sighed.

"End of recorded interview with Janie Taylor. Detective Knox and SI Maddox. Stop." She stopped the tape roll, and collected her paperwork. She came back to my bedside, and put her hand on my own. "Janie, you've been so brave. I'm proud of you. Just keep your head up, and I'll try to keep as much of this off of you as I can." She squeezed my hand, and I smiled. My Mom approached her.

"Detective?" she smiled at her.

"Yes, Mrs. Taylor?" she waited.

"What will happen now? How does this work?" The Detective nodded.

"Well, there is so much overwhelming evidence in this case against Mr. Comaro, that I doubt it will ever see a trial. Most likely the lawyers will meet with the Prosecutor, who will make an appropriate offer. They will most likely accept it, and Janie will not have to testify. Hopefully nothing will be made public with this route, either. The Comaro's seem like logical people, and they don't want this in the media, either." She smiled, and handed my Mom a card. "Any questions, just call." Both women smiled, collected their things, and headed out the door.

I shifted again, not thinking about how much pain that set off. I rolled back the opposite way reeling from the massive amounts of pain. My Mom tried comforting me the best she could, calming me any way she could find. Nothing was easing the pain, so my Dad scurried out to get the Doctor. He was back instantaneously with a shot of pain meds, straight into my IV line. It burned for a second, and then my whole body was warm, and numb. He was mumbling things as he checked my vitals.

"We're re-testing some of the blood work to be sure of some things, and then we'll proceed with your wrist. I'll keep you informed, it shouldn't be much longer." He turned to walk away, and then paused. "Mr. Lazarus would like to come join you now. Do you mind sharing a room with him?" I smiled happily, and in my drugged state. *Don't drool girl, hold yourself together... But why do they need to re-do my blood work? What's going on?* "I'll send him in shortly, then maybe you two can get some dinner." He smiled, and left.

It seemed like a million years later, and time was standing still. Each second ticked louder, and longer than the one before. Finally, the hospital bed appears, and was rolled in. But it was empty, and I frowned. I closed my eyes to try and keep the tears in, but they were coming out anyway. I felt a finger rub the tear off my cheek, and tuck my hair behind my ear. The hand lingered around my chin just a little too long to be my mom... I grabbed the hand, and opened my eyes. *Gabe!*

51

I checked him out from a laying position, and he didn't look terrible. His shoulder was bandaged up, and looked unmovable. He was smiling, and looked to have way more color than I did. I nuzzled his hand next to my cheek. My parents approached us both.

"Gabe, we're so glad you're alright." She patted his good shoulder. My Dad nodded in agreement.

"We're so lucky she had you guys to stay with, and keep her safe. If you hadn't been there, I'm afraid to think of what would have happened." Gabe nodded at them.

"I told you both I'd protect her...and I feel a little off kilter that I didn't do that properly." He paused. "I absolutely adore, and love your daughter... and I really hope this is the last time that we have to face anything quite like this together." He smiled at both of them, and they each took turns hugging him gently. I smiled at their love. I squeezed his hand, and he turned back to me.

"Love you guys..." my eye lids were getting heavy. My words trailed off and silenced. Sleep over came me once again.

*   *   *   *   *

I woke up later that night, and Gabe was in the hospital bed next to me. My wrist still throbbed, and my pain meds seemed to be wearing off. I didn't want to wake Gabe up, so I quietly pushed my nurse button, and paged my nurse. She came in right away, and smiled to see I was awake.

"Hello, Honey. I'm Laura. Your night nurse. Good to meet you, finally!" She checked my vitals. "How're you feeling?" I scowled.

"Terrible, pain meds are wearing off. My wrist is killing me." She nodded, and took note.

"The doctor had to take a different route with your wrist, he's going to talk to you about that in the morning." I felt myself start to panic, and the nurse quickly noticed. "Oh, it's nothing life threatening honey, I promise." She smiled, and refilled my ice water. "I'll get you some pain meds, these will be pill form, ok?" I nodded. *Anything please! I'm so sore.* She brought them right back, and I swallowed them right down. I tried to relax and watch tv as the nurse checked Gabe's vitals, too.

"How's he doing?" I whispered to her over him. She raised her hand with the thumbs up sign. I smiled, and mouthed "thank you" back to her. She winked at me. I turned it on the only music station the hospital had on television. They played old songs, and now it was, *the Freshmen.* Such a great song, and I sang quietly to myself. *For the life of me, I cannot remember... What made us think that we were wise and we'd never compromise... For the life of me, I cannot believe we'd ever die for these sins... We were merely freshmen...* My eyes drifted back closed again...

*   *   *   *   *

The sounds of the hustle and bustle of the hospital woke me up early. I turned over in my bed, to find that Gabe was awake, and staring at me from his bed.

"Good morning, sweet cheeks." he said and smiled. I smiled back at him.

"We need a vacation." I smiled.

"How are you feeling, baby?" I just groaned at him. The pain was horrible, and relentless. "I'm sorry, love. I should be cleared today, so I'll be able to help you then." He smiled at me.

"You're healing, too, you can't take care of us both." There was an awkward silence, unusual for us.

"Gabe?" I asked quietly.

"Yeah baby?" he was hesitant.

"Do you still love me?" The tears sprung to my eyes faster than ever, and I covered my face with my good hand. His voice cracked on the other side of the room.

"Oh my God, baby..." he sighed. "Look at me Janie. Please stop crying. I absolutely love you. I'd never let some lunatic change that." Everything was just so jumbled inside me. He could tell what I needed, and he slowly sat up. He winced a little once he was up, and adjusted how he carried his weight. He stood, leaning on all the furniture on the way over to my bed. He sat heavily down onto my bed, and delicately laid down with me. He kissed the side of my face, and nuzzled my neck. "You and me, baby." I smiled while the tears flowed.

We cuddled for about a half hour, until the doctor came in with the nurse. He laughed when he saw Gabe had bed swapped. "Oh you two, maybe we need a wall divider?" We all giggled. "Ok, we need to talk." Gabe shifted, and sat up at the end of my bed. "I'm glad it's just the two of you, for now." He smiled. "I've got some news for you… not sure how you'll take it. The reason we didn't send you to surgery last night as we had hoped is that… we're going to have to do your surgery differently. You can't be put under in your condition." He smiled more.

"My condition? What the hell does that mean, doc?" I was getting impatient with his word circles. I looked at Gabe, and his arms were crossed over his chest. The doctor laughed.

"Oh, I'm sorry. Ok, look… you're pregnant." The words burned into my mind. *Pregnant?* Oh shit. My mouth just hung open. I had no words for this. I slowly turned my head over to Gabe, who had a blank expression on his face. The room was silent, and I scratched my head. "I'm sorry for the shock. I'll leave you to it for a bit. We're going to do surgery around 11, with a heavy local anesthetic so we don't have to put you under. Everything else is good to go. Your pain meds are all safe for the baby. You're very early in pregnancy, about 5 or 6 weeks." He smiled, and headed out the door. I was just trying to focus on breathing. Suddenly everything seemed extra difficult.

"A baby? Janie?" I slowly turned my head and looked at him. I thought I was seeing things. *Is that… a smile?!?!* I nodded. "Well, not exactly to plan, but... I'm good with it." His eyes got brighter, and slowly scanned down to my waist. He rested his hand over my belly, and laid it down. *Oh my God...*

My head was spinning with thoughts. *5 or 6 weeks then?* I covered my face with my hands, but was too numb to cry. Peeking out from under my arm at Gabe, who was still enthralled with my belly, my breath hitched. My throat felt tight suddenly, and it was hard to swallow. *What if it's Michaels?* I couldn't push the thought out of my head. It was a real possibility. *A cruel possibility.* But real, nonetheless.

"Gabe," I was out of breath, and my forehead was wrinkled in deep thought. "Is this really what you want? Me, AND a baby?" I was dead serious, no joking here. "Because if it's not, I understand. I won't take anything personally. I mean, this is a lot. And all at once. Who plans for this to happen so quickly?" I stopped, and waited. He smiled, and shook his head. He smiled, and scooted closer to me.

"Janie, when I first met you, I immediately wanted to know you more. Before we were," he paused, and smiled wider. "Really intimate with each there, I already knew you were in a terrible situation. Even that didn't change the way you made me feel. The way you still make me feel." He scratched the back of his head, and went on. "The thing is, I can see past this whole situation you're in, no..." he shook his head. "We're in...to the real you. And you're wonderful, amazing, smart, and beautiful. I know we don't know everything about each other yet, as it's only been a few months of being this serious. But I do love you...everything about you. And I'd love to keep this going....and now," he reached down for my belly, and his finger sprawled out across it. "This is fate. And I already know what you're thinking, and let me tell you... this baby is mine. I can feel it, and I know you'll be more than confident with that, too, once you see the ultrasound, and get your dates." He nudged my shoulder, and grinned. *How can I not love this man?*

He was right, if I wasn't worried that this baby was a product of rape, and a hateful relationship, I would've been instantly in love with the idea like he was. I sighed, and tried to relax.

"It's okay love. We'll do this together, too. We've already got a house, cars, jobs... each other. So, just relax." He reclined in the bed with me, and rested his arm on his stomach. My arm resumed the spot across my face, and I groaned.

"Great," I said aloud, with about as much excitement as I could muster. I lifted my arm enough so that I could see him, and added, "guess we'll have to tell my parents soon." He nodded.

"I think they'll be happily surprised. You'll see." He leaned into me, and closed his eyes. His nose was in the crook of my neck, and he was inhaling me again. I couldn't help the small smile that escaped my lips. *There's absolutely no way I can sleep at the moment... I hurt, I'm losing my mind, and I'm...pregnant.* I shook my head in disbelief. *How do you always manage to get yourself in these situations, Janie!*

52

It was around 11:30, almost lunch time, when I heard my parent's voices coming down the hall. My head darted over at Gabe, and he smiled very ornery at me. The doctor had been in, and told me I'd be going in for surgery for my wrist at 1. Around the corner of the door came flowers, then balloons, then my mom...who was giggling.

"Hello you two!! Brought you some things...to get better with!!" she giggled more. She seemed extra happy today, and I couldn't believe I'd have to ruin her day in mere moments. I started to breathe faster. She came over to my bed, and kissed my forehead. "Hi, honey...how are you doing?" She smiled, then sat on my bed. "Are they fixing your wrist today?"

"Yes," I paused. "The wrist will be fixed at 1, they say. I hope it's close to it, because the pain is ridiculous. Doctor said there may be nerve damage." I shrugged. She scrunched her face at me.

"That stinks. Will they have to put pins in? How long will you be out?" She was full of questions today. I shook my head.

"No pins, not being put under." Now her face was confused, and I caught Gabe smiling and nodding at me out of the corner of my eye. I looked back at my mom, who was now impatiently waiting for the truth. *There is seriously no easy way to say this...* "Looks like I'm pregnant." I braced myself, and waited for her to do... something. Instead, she just stood there, shocked. Then she smiled. *Stunned, maybe?* I could see the hundreds of questions scrolling behind her eye lids. "We'll have our first ultrasound this afternoon to determine the date of conception." I nodded at her, hoping she would read between all the lines I had just provided. She smiled, and turned to Gabe.

"And how are you doing with this news, Gabriel?" Her arms were now crossed over her chest, and she meant business. He turned towards her, and smiled huge.

"I think I'm more excited than Janie is..." he blushed. My mom smiled bigger at him, and reached for him. She hugged him tightly for a moment, and tuned back to me...*is she beaming?*

"Is this what you want Janie? Have you had much time to think things out?" I shrugged. I wasn't sure how to answer that without being selfish, or mean. *Or paranoid.*

"It hasn't sunk in yet. I'm not opposed to the idea at all..." I put my head down. "There's just too many what if's right now for me to be absolutely thrilled." I shrugged again.

"That's understandable honey." My mom smiled at me. "There's so much going on in your life, and until Michael's convicted..." she sighed heavily. "I understand, and I'll do whatever I can to support you." She picked up her cell, and headed for the door. "Oh, am I allowed to tell your Dad about this news?" She beamed. I nodded.

"Yes, absolutely. I wouldn't want him to be left out." Just then the doctor appeared, and smiled at all of us.

"You ready to head back, Janie?" I nodded. He turned to Gabe. "She'll be back there about two hours. I'll have the nurses update you, and did I see Mrs. Taylor?" I nodded again. "Ok, Gabe, your nurse will be bringing in your discharge papers soon, but you know you're more than welcome to stay in here with Janie, until she's discharged as well. She'll probably be in until tomorrow evening, assuming all goes well with surgery. We'll aim for an ultrasound about 4pm today then. I'll be sure to have Mr. Lazarus paged so he doesn't miss baby's first picture. All sound good?" He smiled, and looked us both over. His eyes stopped on me.

"I guess so," I smiled. Gabe stepped over, and kissed me on the lips. He brushed my hair out of my face, and rubbed my cheek.

"It's okay babe. I'll be here when you're all done." As they wheeled my bed away, he whispered, "I love you." That made my nervous heart, smile.

*   *   *   *   *

After surgery, I sat in recovery. My arm was completely wrapped up, but not yet cast. It was immobilized by a brace system of some sort. But thankfully, the drugs were good, and the pain was less than before. I was alone in a small cubical, hooked up to all sorts of beeping machines. I couldn't help but go back through the past weeks' developments, time by time, event by event, in my already stressed out head. Each time I found myself wondering what I ever did to cause someone I loved to hurt me like he did. I never found an answer any time that question came up. *It was never my fault.* I think it was finally starting to sink in. *Then why didn't I see it before it was too late? Before I was in too deep?* With each unanswered question, came another even harder one to answer. Some I couldn't answer, and I knew I've have to learn to live with that.

I rubbed my abdomen, and hoped on everything I knew that Gabe and I would be connected forever with this baby. According to the Detective, with all of the evidence they had, proving guilt was no longer the issue. Sentencing was now at hand, and this made me rest a bit more easily. I looked through the window, outside the surgical recovery area, and Gabe waved through the window.

He was perfect, and so supportive. At this point, I'd do anything to keep him in my life, and the best part is, I don't think I'll have to try very hard to accomplish that. And now the baby. My drugged smile spread across my face slowly, but then wouldn't go away. It was time to move on, and put the past behind us. I could feel it now, and it was calming my soul. I turned my head back to Gabe, and motioned him to come in with me. The nurse followed him in, pushing a large machine.

"Perfect timing, guys. I'm here to do the ultrasound." She was a happy, smiley little thing. "This will be a trans-vaginal ultrasound; meaning, we'll put this inside you like a vibrator." She held up the probe. "Then it takes all the pictures I'll need to get you a date, and you can see your little peanut." She smiled again. *Seemed easy enough, right?* "Just let your knees fall to the sides, and I'll do the rest." I was holding my breath as she pulled the condom over the probe, and slid it into me slowly. *Oh, what an awkward feeling this was...* She turned it around, and on her screen, it looked like a black circle. *With some whit noise...* I checked Gabe's face, and he was all smiles. He grabbed my hand, and squeezed it.

"Ok, here's the baby." She clicked on the picture, and added numbers, codes, and other things. *It's so tiny.* "Everything looks good, but I think doc was definitely off on your dates for you." My heart sank. She finished taking pictures of everything needed for the dates, and printed us a few to keep. My hands were starting to sweat, and Gabe's were, too. "Doc will be in here in a second to go over these, and your surgery with you." She smiled, and disappeared with her big machine.

A moment later, the Doctor appeared. "Hey guys, so, the surgery went great. We'll cast you up here in a few, and you'll have your cast for a few weeks, at least. It'll be similar to the one before, movement-wise. I'll send you home with pain pills again, and you can take them as needed." He paused, and flipped through my chart. "As for the baby...you're about four weeks along. Just freshly pregnant. So, I was off a little on my first estimates, and would put conception about 5 weeks ago. Baby looks great, all normal, and good." He smiled. "Tomorrow we'll discharge you, Janie. Get some rest, and Gabe's welcome to stay." He smiled, and patted both of our shoulders.

The moment he was out of the room, my head was remembering, and counting dates. I could tell that Gabe was doing the same thing. Then it hit me. *Is that possible?!*

"I think I know when it was...or at least the week." I smiled at him, and blushed. He smiled very big.

"When?" his thumb softly brushed over my fingers.

"The first night I spent with you at your place. We were together quite a bit that week, and the weeks after." I couldn't hold back my smile. He wrapped me up with his good arm, and kissed me deeply.

53

Roughly four months later, I was just returning home from the doctor getting my last cast removed. My hands were both free again, and I couldn't stop touching them. I pulled into our driveway to find my parents car was already parked there. Gabe was home from work today, and I was happy to see all of my people. I parked, and slowly got out of the car. My mom rushed over, still beaming, and rubbed my now very visible belly.

"Ohh honey! Look at you! You're absolutely glowing!" She hugged me. "And the casts are finally gone! How are you feeling?" Now Gabe had joined me, and wrapped his arms around me. And my Dad had stepped next to my Mom.

"I'm doing very well." I smiled at Gabe. "And feeling pretty good. Finally have some energy again, and we're getting out more and more." I smiled, and patted my belly.

"Janie," Gabe started, and I turned to him. "Your parents came out here today because Detective Knox and the Prosecutor will be here soon to tell you what's come of the case." I grabbed my chest, and lost my breath. Their hands were all on me in an instant, and I motioned to them that I was alright.

"Well," I sighed. "I guess it's time to get this over with then, right?" We all nodded together. My brain whirred. *I hope he's away forever.* My hands protectively covered my growing baby. *No way he's coming anywhere near you.*

"But, while we wait, we brought the baby some presents!!" She turned me around to the picnic table, and it was covered with gifts. I skipped over happily. I started unwrapping, and there was a bassinet, toys, clothes, a bathtub, and bottles. I smiled at her, and tears filled my eyes. I hugged them both. "It's just to get you started, so you'll have at least the minimums. Once it's here, I can't wait to spoil the pants off of this baby!" She laughed loudly, and a car turned into the drive. The car pulled closely to us, and through the windshield I could see Detective Knox smiling. They approached slowly.

"Hello everyone, Miss Taylor." She nodded at me. "This is Mr. Kent, and he is the Assistant Prosecutor. We wanted to update you on the case with Michael Comaro, and the deal that has been offered, and taken by his lawyers." She stopped, and turned towards the Prosecutor.

"Hello, Miss Taylor. I wanted to personally tell you that Mr. Comaro will be serving 35 years in prison, with no chance of parole. We appreciate you and your family's cooperation during this hard time, and wish to assure you that we are here for you in the future." He reached out, and shook my hand. I half smiled, but had no words. Detective Knox appeared in front of me, and reached to embrace me.

"You're strong honey. You're going to be a great mother." She pulled back, and smiled. "If any of you ever need anything at all, you call me. Use my cell number, please. Your restraining order stands, and will become effective again when he is out of prison in 35 years." She turned to walk away, and waved as she got into her car.

I looked at Gabe as her car pulled away, and he wrapped his arms around me. He whispered in my ear, "Now our forever starts. Relax, baby...now it's really just us." I was smiling, and tears were pouring out of my eyes. My parents were hugging each other, and us. The car disappeared, and the giant boulder that had ridden on my shoulders for the past year was suddenly gone.

My parents helped us move the gifts into the baby's room that Aaron had recently vacated. We missed him, but he was in love, and with his lady friend now. Uncle Greg was very excited for the changes coming to our household, and was helping us get ready for the baby by painting the nursery s beautiful, bright yellow color. *Soon to be the happiest room in the house...*

"Thank you, Sam, and Paul." Gabe hugged them both as they said their goodbyes.

"We'll visit again soon, honey! We love all of you!!" they yelled as they waved and pulled away. Just then, there were hands around my waist, and a hot breath ending in my ear. Then the hands lowered, and circled my swollen belly. His warm arms pulled me into his full body embrace, and I instantly melted.

"Janie," his voice was rough, and ready. "Now it's just us. Really, just us." He spun me around so I was facing him. "No more intrusions, no more lunatics. Me. And You." He looked down at my belly, and smiled big as I'd ever seen him grin. "Please, let me feel you... I really want to." His hands went north, and squeezed both of my engorged breasts. I was heating up pretty quickly with these pregnancy hormones. My hips started to wiggle into him.

"MmMmmm..." was all I could manage to get out. His mouth was over mine, hungrier and hotter than ever before. He tasted sweet, as always, like candy. His hands were eager, too, kneading my skin wherever they touched. He took my hand, and lead me into the house, back to our bedroom. He had already spun me around, and had begun to unbutton my pants. I fell back onto the bed, and he slid them off for me. He stripped off his shirt, and dropped his pants, too. *He is delicious. I am so in love with this man.* He slowly stalked up my body, kissing every inch on the way up. Stopping extra to put his ear on my belly, and whisper words of love to the baby, too. He continued up my sternum, and stopped in between my larger than normal breasts. He licked and nibbled from my breast, to my neck, to my ear… goosebumps slammed my entire body.

"I love this pregnant you…" he sucked and bit my neck more. He lowered his head, and sucked at my nipples. His teeth gently nibbled them, and I instantly fell over the edge. My body was shaking, and loving the extra nipple attention it was getting.

"MMMmmm…Gabe…." I moaned. "I love you, too…" and his mouth engulfed mine again, and this time, he dipped himself inside of me. He pulled out quickly, and flipped me over. As he sunk inside me from behind, he gripped my hips firmly. He drove into me over and over again, until my body constantly clenched on him, and drenched him with everything I had to give. His rhythm changed, and his breath hitched. His fingers dug into my flesh, and he pushed deeper, and deeper into my womb. I felt his release, and his head fell onto my chest.

We both lay together, catching out breath. *How lucky am I?* Caressing his head with my fingers, we lay there completely sated with each other. *In the end of all of this, your dreams seem to be coming true, Janie.* Gabe rolled over, and kissed me gently.

"Baby, I'm so glad we've got eternity to keep that up." He laughed loudly, and pulled me into a passionate kiss. I laughed with him, and realized he was right-- we did have forever. And neither one of us could wait to get it started. I got up, and headed for the bathroom.

There I was, smiling in the mirror. I didn't have bags under my eyes. No bruises on my body. And I was growing a perfect little life inside me. My future is now brighter than ever, and I can't stop smiling. *Oh girl, I see that ornery smile in the mirror... I know what it means. The future's an open book, Janie...*

The Probed Saga

Phoenix Rising

Phoenix on Fire

Phoenix Reclaimed

Facebook

https://www.facebook.com/skyefalcon

http://skyefalcon.in

www.ingramcontent.com/pod-product-compliance
Lightning Source LLC
Chambersburg PA
CBHW051526250626
47156CB00001B/245